THANK YOU,
NEXT

THANK YOU,
NEXT

ANDIE J. CHRISTOPHER

JOVE
New York

A JOVE BOOK
Published by Berkley
An imprint of Penguin Random House LLC
penguinrandomhouse.com

Library of Congress Cataloging-in-Publication Data

Names: Christopher, Andie J., author.
Title: Thank you, next / Andie J. Christopher.
Description: First Edition. | New York: Jove, 2022.
Identifiers: LCCN 2022001758 (print) | LCCN 2022001759 (ebook) |
ISBN 9780593200063 (trade paperback) | ISBN 9780593200070 (ebook)
Subjects: LCGFT: Novels. Classification: LCC PS3603.H7628 T48 2022 (print) |
LCC PS3603.H7628 (ebook) | DDC 813/.6—dc23
LC record available at https://lccn.loc.gov/2022001758
LC ebook record available at https://lccn.loc.gov/2022001759

First Edition: June 2022

Printed in the United States of America
1 3 5 7 9 10 8 6 4 2

Book design by Daniel Brount

To my grandmother, Lorez Alexandria

ONE

PEOPLE NEVER THINK ABOUT WHERE DIVORCE ATTOR-
neys come from. How they are made. In Alex's mind, she
was sort of like a superhero who showed up to save her clients'
assets and, on very rare occasions, their dignity. But no one ever
thinks about how a person decides to make their life's work dis-
mantling other people's marriages.

Alex Turner's origin story was what one might have expected
if one pondered how divorce attorneys came to be, before actually
needing one. She came from a broken home and had a divorce-
happy grandmother, which caused her to grow up too fast. Because all the adults around her were too chaotic, Alex became
really good at putting her emotions on a shelf to deal with
later—or never.

Not feeling anything—and suppressing any stray emotions—
came in handy when she was dealing with philanderers, fraud-

sters, and people who just couldn't stand the sight of each other for another moment. She got paid the big bucks because she could keep her head on straight when everyone around her was losing their shit.

The fact that she was so good at her job often gave people the impression that she was just as cold in everyday life. Just because she was a killer in the courtroom, she'd had more than one guy on a date think she could take harsh criticism that she could not—in fact—take.

Alex was usually neutral about her clients' soon-to-be-former spouses. However, she'd made an exception for Rogan Chase—a comic turned podcaster who espoused specious theories around everything from child-rearing to whether handwashing prevents infectious disease.

Chase had filed for divorce when his wife didn't lose every last ounce of baby weight within three months of giving birth, and he hadn't even told her in a private conversation. Instead, he'd announced it on his podcast. He'd started a hashtag and gotten his wife doxxed, and Samantha had fled to her mother's house.

Unfortunately for Chase, Alex had made some modifications to the prenuptial agreement proposed by his attorney before the wedding—modifications that Chase hadn't thought anything of at the time. She'd added a clause that stipulated that Samantha would receive a substantial payout every time Chase discussed his and Samantha's relationship on-air.

Chase's red face and ample spittle as he hurled insults at his ex-wife while he signed over fifty percent of his assets, including an ongoing share of the income he derived from use of his name and image, warmed Alex's cold heart just a little bit.

In the midst of it all, Samantha leaned over and whispered, "I kind of wish my future income didn't depend on him continuing to act like this."

Alex didn't allow her face to change as she said, "He really should read what he's signing."

Samantha choked on a laugh, and that set off Chase even more. To Alex's surprise, one look from Chase's lawyer got him to choke on whatever shitty thing he'd been about to say until he and Samantha had both signed the settlement agreement.

Alex's spine stiffened when Samantha and Chase's lawyer left the conference room, because Alex saw the way he licked his lips at her. She leveled her hardest stare at him and said one word, "No."

"Well, I was going to ask you for a drink now that my divorce is final . . ."

"And you think that makes you some sort of prize?"

"I still have a lot of money."

Alex snorted. "Like that's a recommendation."

"Not surprised you're still single. If you're not careful, you'll end up all alone with a bunch of cats for company."

"Honestly, I'd rather have a whole *Grey Gardens* thing going than end up with someone like you."

"You have a bad attitude."

"No, sir. You're the one with a bad attitude. You think it's still 1974, when a woman couldn't even have a credit card in her own name, and that someone should see that you have money and fall all over your dick. I'm sure you'll find a woman who mistakenly thinks that slobbing your knob is easier than making her own way in the world, but she'll wise up, too."

"You think you know me—"

"Do yourself a favor and shut up before I encourage your wife to have second thoughts about leaving you someplace to live that isn't a refrigerator box on Skid Row." Chase closed his mouth with an audible snap. "I may not have spent much time with you, but I know you. You're nothing but a racist, misogynist, fatphobic worm looking for a new warm, wet hole to burrow into." And he hadn't even put up a fight when his wife had asked for sole custody. That truly made him irredeemable.

Chase looked her up and down. "Now, I'm hitting on you, so I can't be racist."

Alex rolled her eyes so hard that she thought she pulled something. "Oh, so you've backed down from your whole 'I don't see color, BUT' schtick. But let me spare you. My grandmother was the most famous Black woman in the world in the 1970s and 1980s. She was basically Rihanna, Beyoncé, and Cardi B combined. The first thing she taught me about being a woman of color—particularly a Black woman—is that people who don't see color don't see humanity. You don't see the humanity of any woman, especially not your wife, and I have a good feeling that it would be ten times worse for a Black or Brown woman who you somehow hoodwinked into fucking you."

"You bitter little bitch."

Alex clapped her hands together and laughed ruefully. "There it is."

"There what is? How the fuck did you get through law school? You talk in circles."

"You asked me out and then called me a bitch as soon as I

challenged you. Because I see right through you. You're my bread and butter and the reason I drive a Maserati."

Alex turned to leave, more than done with this ghoul. As the door to the conference room closed behind her, she heard him muttering, "Stuck-up cu—"

A lex was still shaken by her encounter with Chase when she got home from work that night. The only good things about the day were that it was Friday, her DVR was chock-full of her favorite shows, and she'd remembered to put a bottle of rosé into the fridge before heading to the office.

Unfortunately, Chase wasn't the first former spouse who'd hit on her before the ink on his divorce decree was dry. In fact, her clients' former spouses were more likely than a barista or a bartender to hit on her these days. The flirtation from associates at Trader Joe's hawking samples felt like it came from a purer place than when a man who had recently blown up his marriage—likely through some real douchebag behavior—decided that she'd be a good next victim.

On days like today, Alex didn't understand why anyone would get married in the first place. It was all well and good to want companionship, help with household expenses, and someone to have sex with on speed dial, but making it legal seemed unwise for most people.

In Alex's professional and familial experience, getting married was like playing the lottery. Sure, you had all these hopes and dreams about what you might do with the jackpot before the numbers were pulled. But very few people actually won and got to live out those dreams. For most, it was a waste of resources that could be better put to use elsewhere.

And on days like today, she especially didn't understand why some other women were so eager to be married. It ended so badly so often, and even her friends in good marriages sounded as though they were suffering from a very particular form of Stockholm syndrome. If Alex had a dollar for every time one of her married friends started a sentence with "I love my husband, but" and then recounted him doing something truly horrific, she could retire. Even though she'd dated a few guys whom she could have seen herself married to, she had never understood why married men were never expected to make sacrifices, other than the opportunity to sleep with other women without hiding it. And, considering the size of her client base, many of them couldn't even manage to do that.

Somewhere along the line, Alex had decided that marriage wasn't something she wanted. The grind of her job and the weight of her family history made her feel like she was uniquely fucked when it came to romantic relationships. There were men in her dating history whom she'd thought she'd been in love with, whom she'd pictured spending her life with, but none of those relationships had worked out. Now she made it explicit from the beginning that she only wanted to be in a relationship for as long as it was fun for everyone involved.

Alex's negative view of marriage could not diminish her love of reality television shows about the institution—like *Say Yes to the Dress*. She also loved the *Real Housewives*, but that was essentially client development work. But watching a show where too-young women were emotionally abused by their mothers and future mothers-in-law while they tried on dresses that cost more than a used Toyota Corolla and made them look like cupcakes was more relaxing than candlelight yoga.

Even though she couldn't envision getting married—ever—she did enjoy critiquing the truly audacious choices made on the show. It would be bad for her reputation if people knew that she had a secret wedding dress Pinterest board. No one wanted to hire a divorce attorney with a romantic streak, so Alex kept her love for the show a secret. But truthfully, it was one of the few things that made her feel better about her own romantic track record. Even though no one had ever asked her to marry them, at least she didn't have anything with a sweetheart neckline or a see-through panel around her midriff in her history.

So yeah. She loved weddings, specifically wedding dresses. But she had serious questions about them—and marriage in general.

The one thing that truly bothered her on the show was how they never explained how one went to the bathroom in one of those things. What if they were sewn into the dress? Were they expected to hold it until they could take the dress off and perform their wifely duties for the first time? Alex found it fascinating and symbolic of the fact that—unless they won the lottery—wives weren't expected to be human beings. One of her clients had told her that she'd never taken a dump in the same bathroom her husband used after he commented on her stinking up the bathroom on their third date. Before they'd bought a house with more than one bathroom, she'd waited until she got to the Starbucks to go every morning. For ten years.

As Alex sat down with her Big Gulp–sized glass of rosé, she was prepared to watch a twenty-one-year-old who thought a thirty-five-year-old who didn't have bed frame was her soul mate. What she was not prepared for was to see a woman who looked eerily like Alex waxing poetic about Alex's most recent ex-boyfriend.

She'd met Jason speaking on a Black Law Students Association panel at UCLA Law School, featuring four Black law partners under forty. When she'd walked in and seen all six foot four of Jason, she'd been glad she hadn't found an excuse to cancel her appearance. It wasn't that she hated giving back, but she always felt exhausted after socializing with new people. She'd planned to sneak out in the first ten minutes of the happy hour after the panel when Jason brought her over a glass of boxed wine. He'd smiled at her, and the rest of the room had fallen away. They'd talked for the whole cocktail hour and then he'd taken her out to dinner. It had been so long since she'd liked someone that she'd been a little helpless to resist him at first.

Of course that had changed later on, but she'd been intoxicated with Jason that first night.

Seeing Jason on a show about weddings was doubly shocking because Jason had told Alex in no uncertain terms—multiple times during the months they'd dated—that he didn't believe in marriage. That was why Alex had started dating him in the first place. She would never have to wonder whether she'd won the lottery or thrown away her time and money for a dream that only came true for one in a hundred million. There was no danger that she'd end up hog-tied in a Pnina Tornai dress, later trying to furtively poop in the locker room before her third SoulCycle class of

8

the day because a man who hadn't pushed a watermelon out of his vagina thought she was too fat a month after doing so.

She'd thought they were on the same page.

But Jason had apparently lied to her about his aversion to marriage. As Alex watched the photo montage of his relationship history with this other woman, she started to feel sick. At some point, she put down her wine and leaned toward the television. She clasped her hands together so hard that the joints in her knuckles ached. It was better than what she really wanted to do—throw something at the TV.

She didn't even know why. They'd had a nice few months together, but she hadn't been in love with Jason. They were compatible—in bed and out—but she hadn't thought about him when he wasn't around. Her feelings for Jason were warm and pleasant, but there hadn't been any passion between them. They'd parted ways amicably, and she'd thought they would both sail off into another chapter of serial monogamy.

Still, she seethed as she watched this woman pick out a dress to marry a man who'd apparently changed his life plans in the nine months since he'd dumped Alex. She didn't know why, but thinking about him moving on with this woman formed a sinkhole in her chest. Instead of doing anything about it, like changing the channel, Alex sipped her pink wine and really looked at the woman who was going to marry Jason—her handsome, financially stable, erudite ex-boyfriend who'd told her that he'd rather put his balls in a panini press every morning than spend the rest of his life with one person.

And as the woman on the screen picked out a dress that was so simple and classic that it made Alex's chest ache, she realized that Jason had only had an aversion to marriage because he couldn't countenance the prospect of marriage with *Alex*.

After the episode ended on a frame of Jason's fiancée crying as her mother gave her a blank check to purchase the dress she chose, Alex turned the sound down and opened up the Facebook app on her phone. She usually stayed off it because it was for boomers and conspiracy theorists, but she hadn't given up her account because her sister occasionally posted pictures of her nieces on there. They lived a thousand miles away, and she missed them. Hanging out with them on Christmas gave her a vague understanding of why her sister had volunteered to have her vagina ripped open in order to bring them into the world. But she wasn't descending into the bowels of social media at ten o'clock on a Friday night to admire the fruits of her sister's loins.

She was on a mission, a journey, and a quest.

Alex had never looked up her exes before. In her mind, that was for girls who didn't have anything going on in their own lives. Her mother, an anthropology professor, would find it fascinating and might even write a whole book about how the American patriarchy twisted young women's minds. She would then send it to Alex's sister, who wouldn't read it, and then they would have something to fight about over the traditional Thanksgiving dinner that Alex's sister insisted they all attend.

It would be a refreshing change of topic from the ethnographic presentation about stolen Native lands that Alex's mother usually insisted on as a condition of her attendance.

Jason still had a Facebook profile. Sure, he'd stopped posting on it almost a decade ago, but his new fiancée—that felt so strange to say, even in her head—tagged him in a lot of posts. Alex didn't know how long she got lost in photos of Jason smiling at parties and dinners. He'd never even wanted to go to parties with Alex. At first, Alex had thought he'd been trying to keep their relationship a secret—as though he was embarrassed by her—but he'd explained that he was just sort of a homebody. Alex couldn't help but wonder if that was a bold-faced lie.

One thing that Alex knew was absolutely true for her was that she didn't want to get married. Given her family history and the carnage she saw in her professional life, she knew that she wasn't cut out to do the hard work that it seemed to take to make a marriage work. Over the years, she'd dated a few men she'd thought she could make things work with, but that was a long time ago.

By the time she'd met Jason, she'd been so certain that marriage wasn't in her future, she'd stopped hoping to be chosen. She'd stopped dreaming about a future beyond a few weeks or months with any of her romantic interests.

She loved her nieces but wasn't interested in becoming a mother. She might have been a good parent if held to mid-1970s standards—when benign neglect was acceptable. But she'd seen too many contentious custody battles where an extra thirty minutes of screen time was a major issue to take the risk. Even though she'd likely be able to afford help.

Not wanting children made it easier to not want marriage. For most people, it was a package deal. Casual acquaintances often expressed horror when she said that she didn't want children. Even her sister acted like wanting to sleep in on the weekends and pee alone made her the witch from "Hansel and Gretel." Most people got so stuck on the no-kid thing that they let the no-marriage thing slide.

Alex had truly thought she was over the fact that a happy, long-term partnership wasn't going to happen for her. Her family history was riddled with misbegotten matches, and her job had made her jaded. And she'd never met anyone who'd made her question that for long enough to make a difference. She closed the Facebook app and flipped through the contacts on her phone, not quite sure what she was searching for. Before she could stop herself, Alex was methodically clicking through all the profiles of every person she'd dated who had a Facebook or Instagram account. To her horrified fascination, she discovered that all of them were now happily married or partnered. What fascinated and horrified her was that they all seemed to have partnered off right after breaking things off with Alex.

Somewhere in the back of her mind, her mother's words about correlation and causation rang, but Alex wasn't a scientist. She was a lawyer. Where Alex saw patterns, she logically concluded that the common denominator among all her exes pairing up at least semipermanently after breaking things off with her wasn't that all these people were opposed to commitment and partnership. They were just opposed to it with her.

That made Alex sit back and try to take a drink out of her now empty wineglass. She wanted to call someone. Her sister would be busy with her small children, and her more conventional sibling would not have time for any theories about why Alex apparently made her romantic partners want to marry other people.

And she wouldn't call her mother, either. Dr. Maureen Finnegan-Turner wouldn't have any soothing words or any insight into why Alex's discovery made her feel a little empty inside. Her mother would have a reading list and possibly some suggestions for new psychiatrists.

No, the only person Alex could call right now was her grandmother and namesake. In addition to being one of the most famous Black women on the planet, Lexi Turner was the only person who could make sense of why Alex felt so shitty about this. She'd call her in the Uber to let her know she was on her way.

TWO

ALEX DIDN'T ASK LEXI WHY HER PERSONAL TAROT CARD reader happened to be at her house when Alex pulled up in an Uber less than an hour later. Lexi Turner was a jazz legend, a noted actress, and a renowned eccentric. You simply did not ask questions like "Grandma, why is your boyfriend in a large cage in the pool house?" when you were dealing with the great Lexi Turner. Unless you wanted her to tell you about how she'd been into BDSM when the woman who wrote *Fifty Shades of Grey* was still in diapers.

Lexi was wearing a sequined caftan and a matching head-wrap. Her face was fully made up, and she had arranged herself on a purple velvet chaise as though at any moment someone was going to appear from the kitchens at the back of the house to feed her grapes and fan her. Other than the fact that Lexi was about a half foot shorter and could likely balance a platter on her ample bosom, looking at her grandmother was sort of like looking into her future. Lexi and Alex shared the same eyes and the same face shape. Lexi's skin was a few shades darker than Alex's, but there was no doubt that they were related.

Given that Lexi had an aesthetician on call, her grandmother had more than once been mistaken for her mother.

"Darling." Lexi's voice projected across the great room of her Baldwin Hills mansion, bouncing off the rococo-by-way-of-art deco columns to the foyer. "What's got you so upset? Whatever it is could probably be cured more effectively by a new lover than a late-night visit to an old woman." Lexi looked her up and down and narrowed her shrewd gaze. "At least you don't go to bed at eight o'clock like your normie sister."

Lexi tried to keep up on teen slang, but she was usually about a decade behind. "It's a Friday."

Lexi raised a hand and summoned her into the great room. That's when Alex noticed the blond white woman sitting across from her grandmother. "Alex, this is Star Sign."

Alex didn't balk anymore at the LA woo-woo parade in and out of her grandmother's house. Sometimes she got lucky and the energy worker that her grandmother was working with was just a Goopy massage therapist. Sometimes she was not lucky and ended up having to use a package of sessions with her grand-mother's new shaman friend who spread a substance that smelled remarkably like manure all over her body before chanting off-key in a spectacle of cultural appropriation that was uncomfortable for everyone involved.

"What is Star Sign doing here on a Friday night?" Alex nar-rowed her eyes at the woman. Lexi was a kind and open soul who happened to have made a lot of money touring and selling jazz records over the past forty years. Although she'd had some down times during the eighties and nineties, a few of her songs had become hits again after she did a duets album with a wildly famous pop star. Lexi's financial security and her openness made her vulnerable. Since Alex's father had died—although he likely would have been at Lexi's door with his hand out—Alex felt as though it was her responsibility to protect Lexi.

"I called her after you said you were coming over," Lexi said, as though that explained why a practical stranger was here to greet her. "Your chakras seemed out of order, and I thought she could help."

"My chakras are fine." Alex didn't have a spiritual problem. She was just thrown by the fact that her ex had found someone to marry before she'd even gotten it together to go on a single date after their breakup. "I was just upset."

Lexi stood up and crossed the room in her usual elegant float. Alex had met a lot of famous people because of her grandmother. LA was a small town, and it got smaller when you were related to a legend. Some of those famous people had stage presence but seemed to fade into the background when the stage lights weren't on. Others, like Lexi, couldn't or wouldn't turn it off. All the light in every room seemed to fall on Lexi's face wherever she went.

Her grandmother led her to one of the couches and touched her shoulder until she sat down. Then Lexi pointed her long fingernail to a steaming cup of tea. "Drink that."

"What is it?" After accidentally ingesting magic mushrooms from the manure shaman, Alex didn't drink or eat anything at her grandmother's house without ascertaining its origins.

"It's wild sweet orange tea, with a little bit of bourbon." Lexi rolled her eyes. "One bad trip, and it's like you don't trust me anymore."

"I ran around in my underwear at a party you were throwing." Alex was still mortified thinking about it. "And I was a teen."

"It was the most interesting thing that happened that night."

Alex nearly choked on her drink. After the mushroom trip and the underwear incident, another interesting thing had happened that night. Alex's face heated thinking about it, but Lexi didn't know—could never know.

"You still haven't explained what Star Sign is doing here." Alex turned to the woman, who gave her a broad, seemingly genuine smile. "I don't need my chakras aligned, and I imagine your nights and weekends rate is quite high—"

"Oh, I'm here on my own time."

Alex raised her eyebrows, ready to toss this woman out on her ear.

"I invited her over, Alex. Don't get your panties bunched. Although maybe bunched is what you need. Bunched on the floor after some hot guy has ripped them off—"

"Shhhhhh!" Alex wanted to find a piece of furniture to crawl under. It wasn't necessarily embarrassing to have a grandmother who had a legendary number of famous lovers because she'd moved to Los Angeles in 1970, when quaaludes and cocaine had loosened the already loose morals of hot young famous people. But it made Alex feel like a total square. And it didn't help that she was already feeling something she couldn't yet name about the fact that she seemed to be all her exes' final stop before happily ever after.

"I'm just saying that you need to loosen up. You haven't gotten any since you and that incredibly hot man broke up." Lexi and all Alex's friends had agreed that Jason was the hottest guy she'd ever dated. And it had bewildered Lexi when Alex and Jason called it quits—she simply didn't understand why Alex would let someone that good-looking slip away.

Although Lexi was a pro at offering emotional support, she sometimes lacked understanding of the dating problems of mere mortals. Lexi had never been dumped. Eight husbands, and she had always been the one doing the dumping. Once, Alex had asked whether Lexi had preprinted prenuptial agreement forms at the ready in case she got in the mood to get married on whim.

"I really thought you should have married that man." Lexi wasn't going to let this one go.

"I hear you, Grams. He is very hot." That wasn't a lie. To make matters worse, she'd finally felt like she had a real partnership on her terms with Jason. They were both focused on their careers and didn't feel like they needed to get married to be secure. They'd had an understanding, or so she thought. "I thought that I'd finally met my match."

"I don't know why you're so afraid of getting married," Lexi said, as she moved to mix another drink. "It's not a big deal."

"It's just not something I feel like I need." What Alex left out was that she felt like needing it was somehow wrong. Her parents' marriage had been more like a business partnership, and their split hadn't been particularly acrimonious.

Both of them were professors and found dramatic displays of emotions gauche. Alex and her sister had come home from school one January afternoon to find that their father no longer lived with them. He'd moved out of their Minneapolis craftsman, and their mother had announced that he had taken a teaching job at USC.

He was so far away that they didn't spend nights and weekends with him. They didn't see him again until the summer, when their mother had a monthlong research trip and dropped Alex and her sister off at Lexi's house.

And even then, they hadn't seen their father much. He didn't really have any interest in entertaining little girls when there were papers to publish and panels to speak on. Alex and her sister were only trotted out when he needed to put forth a family-friendly image. Alex's sister thought she was being uncharitable and that she should give their father more credit. But the man had pawned them off on Lexi every chance he could.

And it wasn't all bad. Lexi was the coolest grandmother on the planet and always made time to hang out with her granddaughters—even taking them with her to tour in Japan once. True, she didn't bake cookies and make tea that didn't contain booze or drugs, but she called over her personal tarot card reader and mixed a mean martini when Alex was in a crisis.

Lexi handed Alex a martini with a flourish and sat back down, carefully arranging the folds of her caftan. "Take a sip and try to clear your mind."

Alex tried not to laugh because one martini after her huge wine and the bourbon tea, and her mind would be nothing but muddy. She took a sip and thought that maybe it was strong enough that she'd fall through the floor and into a wonderland.

"My mind is clear, Grams." And that was true. She knew because of one stupid television show and some Internet sleuthing turned doomscrolling that she was the last stop before matrimony or serious commitment for almost every person she'd kissed since starting college. It couldn't be any clearer. There was something about her that made people never want to date a new person again.

Honestly, she should put out a shingle for people wanting to lock down their person—break up with them, let them date her for a few weeks, and then swoop back in. They'd be ready to lock it down then.

Lost in her own thoughts, she flinched when Star Sign said, "I need you to touch the cards with intention." Alex's eyes were closed so the woman couldn't see her rolling them before doing as instructed.

Alex tried to keep a straight face as she listened to the cards shuffling and being placed on the giant mahogany coffee table between the three women.

"Open your eyes," Star Sign said. She'd placed six cards in two rows of three. "The top row represents your mind, body, and spirit. And the bottom represents your past, present, and future."

Then Star Sign went through the top three. Her mind, body, and spirit were apparently all fucked up and she needed to tend to all three like a garden and be willing to call in others for help.

Fat chance of that happening. She'd never been able to rely on anyone for anything concrete and practical, because—until her sister had become a grown-up—she was the only practical person in her family. Growing up, she'd been the one making grocery lists and cleaning up the house on Saturday mornings because her sister was too little and her mom was too busy building her academic career.

And Lexi wouldn't know practical if it died in her bed after hours of lovemaking. Alex had had to explain—more than once—why chocolate cake was not an appropriate breakfast for children. As a child.

It was no wonder their father had turned out to be such a self-indulgent narcissist. No one had ever told him no. She never talked about that with Lexi because her father had died before he'd taken the time to grow up. A fifty-year-old man who didn't have the common sense to not sleep with his grad students also unfortunately did not have the common sense to make regular doctor's appointments and manage his health well enough to live longer than fifty.

Alex's thoughts had turned bitter, and she'd tuned Star Sign out until she flipped the Prince of Wands as the past card. And when she'd described this figure—essentially a self-centered egotistical flash in the pan—only one person came to mind.

Will Harkness. Her teenage dream and nightmare all in one package. If Orlando Bloom hadn't gotten there first, Will Harkness would have been the agent of her sexual awakening. When they were both seventeen, he'd given her a swerve so hard that she'd gotten whiplash, and Alex wondered whether some of her problems with romantic relationships were born the night he'd rejected her.

Over the past few years, she'd done her best to forget all about the time she'd had a crush on Will Harkness, because he'd been married. And now that he was divorced, she'd kept up her efforts to think of him as a brother. Or a Ken doll.

Lexi looked at her knowingly when Star Sign flipped that card. Lexi knew Will quite well. When they'd met, she'd been dating his father.

"He's in the past section, Grams." Alex knew that she and Lexi had cut Star Sign out of her own reading. But she and Lexi had discussed the whole "Alex and Will thing" ad nauseum. "And he's a fuckboy without staying power. According to the cards. That doesn't sound like Will."

"It really could be anyone who ignites the passions. It doesn't mean that he ignites passions all over town," Lexi said, unable to let it go.

Star Sign flipped over the card supposedly representing the present—the Tower. Lexi gasped, and this time Alex failed to keep her eye roll under wraps. "They are pieces of paper."

"This card represents a great unraveling of everything you thought you'd ever known, Alex. Please take it seriously." Alex looked into Star Sign's earnest face and didn't start laughing uncontrollably, the way she wanted to. Because she saw the other woman's point.

Even though seeing her ex on a stupid show, looking happy with a woman who looked a lot like Alex but with bigger boobs and more time to spend with a curling iron, wasn't great for her ego, it wasn't a great unraveling of everything she'd thought she'd ever known.

"I think what Star Sign is saying is that your whole loner schtick isn't working for you anymore, and you need to unravel and let people in."

They'd had this conversation before, too. Many times. More

than the Will Harkness conversation. More than the conversation about how Alex was too hard on her dad and that it would do her good to forgive him even though he was dead. According to Lexi, Alex's real problem was that she didn't want to truly let anyone in, that she kept her feelings bottled up and never allowed anyone to take care of her.

"I let you in tonight, Lexi." Alex gestured with her half-consumed drink. "I told you something deeply embarrassing that happened, and I came over so you could comfort me." Not that a tarot card reader and copious amounts of varied booze were really constructive, but Alex was not going to say that.

"Here's what I think, Alex—I think that you have to look at why you're embarrassed by that silly, vain, boring man marrying someone who will tolerate his silliness, vanity, and boring anecdotes about football."

Lexi shuddered at the thought of a game with balls that didn't involve having the entire cast of the Chippendales exotic male dance review over to her house circa 1985. She thought sports were provincial, but G-strings and wavy mullets were the height of class.

"Like you said, he is extremely hot." Alex knew it wasn't a great defense.

"Do you still have feelings for him?" Star Sign asked.

Alex wasn't sure if she'd ever had real feelings for him at all. She'd enjoyed his company and having sex with him. He was extremely hot, and that made it a pleasure to show up at parties with him. But thinking of him had never made her heart beat faster. If he wasn't around, she barely thought about him. That was one of the many reasons it had been so great to date him—he was enjoyable without being a distraction. And she'd thought that he'd been satisfied with that.

"Alex doesn't do love, Star Sign. She's very practical and level-headed. Gets it from her dull-as-dirt mother."

"Romantic love is gross, Grams. It makes people dumb."

Lexi rolled her eyes. Alex had certainly missed the drama genes from her grandmother. "That's because you've never let yourself fall in love." If Alex didn't stop this right now, Lexi would float over to the baby grand and break into song.

"Are you really surprised that I've eschewed romance?" Alex didn't mean for her words to sound so sharp, but they did prompt Star Sign to pack up her cards and stand up to leave.

"What about the future?" Lexi asked.

The other woman made a strange face. "Still to be determined."

"But what did the cards say?" Alex genuinely wanted to know, if only so she could mock the whole exercise. Cards did not tell the future. They were pieces of card stock with pictures and words and symbols. Sure, they had meaning for some people. But not Alex. She saw the world as it was and made decisions with cold, hard facts.

Star Sign looked at Alex. "You honestly don't want to know."

And though she didn't believe in woo-woo shit, that made her stomach turn. Part of her wished that she could know the future. If it were predetermined, then she wouldn't have to work so hard trying not to fuck hers up. But she couldn't press the other woman, because she hurried out of the room.

"You really need to learn to have more fun, Alex," Lexi said as she finished her drink. "I was going to have her do a reading on the whole world next."

"I can tell you what's happening in the world. It's going to hell in a handbasket."

Lexi laughed at that. As she finished laughing, it looked as though she was about to say something serious, but whatever sentiment she'd been about to express died on the vine when Will Harkness walked into the room.

THREE

WILL HARKNESS WAS THE LAST PERSON ALEX TURNER wanted to see. Pretty much ever, but especially tonight. Every time she saw him, she had to take a deep breath, mutter "Not today, Satan" three times, and count to ten. He'd pushed her buttons since the day they'd met, with his perfect jaw and permanent smirk.

He was too much. Every time he walked into a room, he sucked up all the air. And it wasn't because he was loud or flashy or needed to fill every moment with conversation. It was definitely the opposite. He'd had this stern quality, ever since Alex had known him, that made people want to please him. The less he said, the more people reacted to him.

In another time, Will Harkness would have been a king or warlord. He conquered everything he set his gaze on. He mastered everything he ever tried. Intellectually, Alex knew he was fallible. But she'd never figured out how.

He bent and gave Lexi a kiss on the cheek. "My sweet boy." Only her grandmother would take a look at this man and call him sweet. He hadn't been sweet when he was a teen and moved in along with his father, Lexi's fifth husband—a British shipping magnate. And he hadn't been sweet when Lexi had thrown over his father for her sixth husband. But not being sweet had nothing to do with Lexi. Her grandmother hadn't cut Will off like she had his father. Will had the infuriating habit of showing up when he was least expected. Or wanted.

"What are you doing here?" Alex was deeply irritated by Will, and she wasn't about to hide it. If she let on for just one moment that she didn't completely hate Will Harkness, he would jump all over it. They had always sparked off each other like flint and steel. It was sort of exhilarating, but she would never let him know that.

Will hadn't even looked at her until she spoke. He treated her like furniture because he knew it annoyed her. But when he did finally clap eyes on her, Alex almost wished he hadn't. He had piercing green eyes that couldn't be described as anything but menacing. They contrasted with the slight tan of his skin courtesy of his Italian mother. And she had the eerie feeling that they saw right through her. "Visiting my stepmother."

"Your ex-stepmother." Alex's words had no bite because he'd called Lexi his stepmother knowing how Alex would respond.

Will had the audacity to grin at her, and Alex could barely keep herself from snarling at him. "What are you doing here?" he asked. "It's Friday night, and I would have thought you'd be off feasting on the heart of whatever loser you were seeing."

His words burned her. She had to keep herself from responding with something that would tell him how much his words affected her. She couldn't afford to let her guard down with any man, and Will Harkness was not any man. When he'd shown up shortly after her fifteenth birthday, he'd been everything she'd ever dreamed of. He was a one-man boy band.

Even now, she could almost smell the Drakkar Noir that he used to wear too much of wafting through the air. Despite herself, she could still look at him and feel seduced by his beautiful features and the easy charm that draped over him and got him anything he wanted.

"She saw the last loser on some show about weddings, and it sent her into a tailspin." Of course Lexi was going to tell Will everything. As much as Alex usually appreciated her grandmother's honesty, she wished it wasn't quite so indiscriminate.

Alex turned to Lexi. "Can't we talk about something more fun?" She looked over at Will and tried to find something about his appearance that Lexi would object to. "Like how Will should shave his beard?"

Will grunted, and Alex wished he hadn't. When he did things like grunt and lean in doorways, it made her forget how much she hated him, and that was the last thing she could afford to do under her current circumstances. Despite her silly feelings about Jason being on some dumb show about wedding dresses, the events of the evening had put her on edge.

"Aw, you let one frog escape and he turned into a prince for someone else?" Will's words were laced with derision, and it made

Alex want to slap him. It was fine that he'd rejected her on her birthday—it would be very immature to still be punishing him for that now—but it was not fine that he still teased her like this.

One would have thought that Alex would be accustomed to Will's teasing, given that he'd been doing it for half her life. But it was like an irritant that kept coming up. He was like eczema in human form.

"We're not going to talk about this." Maybe if Alex was declarative enough about it, both Lexi and Will would let it drop. "And you still haven't said what you're doing here."

That's when Will held up a paper bag. That's also when Alex noticed that the enticing smell that had entered the room with him was actually food. Will was doing one of the only things riskier in Alex's mind than getting married—opening a new restaurant. She hated him but was willing to admit that his food was very good. It was so good that she might stick around to see if he'd brought enough for her to eat. She'd lost interest in dinner during her mini existential crisis, and now the sounds coming from her stomach were menacing.

Lexi clapped her hands together. "You brought me dinner, like I asked."

"You didn't tell me he was coming over." If Alex knew that Will was coming by, outside of a large party where she could effectively dodge him, she was always sure to make herself scarce.

And the look on Lexi's face told Alex that she knew that Alex made a habit of avoiding Will, and that's why she hadn't said anything about Will stopping by with her dinner. But Lexi didn't feel guilty about it. She couldn't have planned for Alex to stop by, but it played into her hands. Lexi had been trying to throw Will and

Alex together for ages. First, she had the excuse that they were the same age and should be friends. Then, somewhere along the line, she'd gotten the idea in her head that they should date each other. And nothing that Will or Alex did or said would dissuade her.

Lexi would never accept the fact that they did not belong together—not in the romantic sense, not as friends, not as anything but acquaintances who needled each other.

Will looked at her, and she didn't see the usual derision or scorn there. "There's enough for you."

He was just earnest enough that she'd look like a bitch for walking out in a huff, and he was a really good cook. "I suppose I could see what all the fuss is about."

Will had not anticipated seeing Alex Turner tonight, but he should have. Lexi was always trying to get them together. Lexi had the ill-conceived notion that Will and Alex were a perfect match. If he didn't love his former stepmother more than any member of his biological family, it would bother him enough that he wouldn't come around. But Lexi didn't know—couldn't know—why he and Alex hated each other. He'd allow her to maneuver them into the same room if that kept her happy. After all, if she was scheming, that meant that her mind was still sharp.

Yes, he wanted to see Alex because that meant that his stepmom was still mentally all there. Sure. It had nothing to do with the fact that he liked to make Alex shoot darts at him with her gaze.

He made a motion toward the kitchen, and both women moved there, Lexi with a sly smile and a flounce that wouldn't have been out of place on a stage, and Alex with a side-eye that would make another man's dick freeze right off.

Will didn't look at her as he plated up the meal that he'd planned to share with Lexi. He could make it stretch. He opened the fridge to see if there were any leftovers he could use to augment the meal. It was late—almost midnight—but he hadn't eaten since the staff meal at four. Lexi was a night owl, so he knew she'd probably had lunch around the same time.

He'd never thought he'd work harder than when he was coming up through the ranks of a Michelin star kitchen with a tyrant of a boss, but opening his own restaurant was another beast entirely. It wasn't just the long days of recipe testing and assuring investors that he wasn't throwing their money down the drain; it was waking up in the middle of the four hours he was allowed to sleep worrying that he wasn't up for this.

Two years ago, he'd been married and between jobs. Now he was divorced and social media famous because he'd started making Instagram Live videos of the meals he was cooking at home. Some people on the Internet had found his videos and thought he was sexy, and he'd gained so many followers that he now had the opportunity to own a restaurant—his lifelong dream.

But the social media notoriety was a double-edged sword. It meant that his marriage falling apart had been a public thing. He'd never wanted to be divorced at all. The fact that he and his ex were part of a listicle of "Celebrities Whose Marriages Didn't Make It," made it just a little bit more painful. All this opportunity was a good thing, but it didn't make him any less divorced and stressed-out. But taking care of Lexi—at least by feeding her—made him feel better. So he made sure to do that.

And he knew that Alex didn't take care of herself well enough to recall the last time she'd eaten. The woman was infuriating that way. Even as a teen, he'd had to remind her to eat instead of going twelve straight hours studying. Her single-minded determination and focus were probably why she was the best divorce lawyer in town, but they were also why she looked like skin and bones tonight.

Both she and Lexi sat on the other side of the island and watched him. He could feel the pride coming off of Lexi. She was the one who'd guided him to food. When he'd shown up at her house with his father, he hadn't quite known what to expect.

Lexi Turner was a legendary jazz singer and actress. Even though jazz wasn't as popular as it had been during her heyday, he'd heard of her. And he'd been shocked when she'd married his father, a shipping executive with no discernable charm.

Will had been unprepared for Lexi's kindness and warmth. She hadn't gotten irritated when he'd stopped heading to his mother's place on the weekends and stayed at Lexi's. And she hadn't kicked him to the curb the same way she had his father when she'd realized that Michael Harkness was not capable of keeping up with her.

No one could keep up with Lexi, but that didn't keep her from trying to find love over and over again. Even now, he would put good money on her having at least three boyfriends.

Will admired Lexi for that. She failed and tried again, no matter how public and messy her failures were. Will didn't have that in him. He'd tried once, and now he was done. He couldn't afford another failure—literally.

"How is Caleb working out for you?" Alex had told him that she couldn't represent him in his divorce case—something about a conflict of interest because she hated him—so she'd referred him to a colleague. According to her, he was "not as good as me, but very, very good."

Will looked up and saw that her interest was genuine. "Well, April hasn't taken my clothes and shoes." And there weren't any children involved. "I guess I'm doing all right."

"Are you dating anyone new?" That must not be Lexi's first martini if she thought he was going to be dating again. Now. Or ever.

Will didn't want to disappoint her, though. Lexi would expect him to be resilient and at least make the effort to put himself out there. So he just grunted and put her plate in front of her. Branzino in a light lemon butter sauce, over roasted fennel, with microgreens on top.

"So, no?"

He ignored Lexi and poured a glass of the sauvignon blanc he'd found in the fridge for himself. He held up the bottle and looked at Alex. She shrugged and said, "Why not, I'm sleeping in the guest room tonight anyway," so he poured her a glass, too.

They ate in almost silence, punctuated by Lexi's exclamations about how "my boy is so talented" and little sounds that Alex made in lieu of words. He might avoid Alex Turner as though his life depended on it, but her reaction to his food was gratifying on a level he didn't want to think about.

But then he had to go and ruin it. "So which douchebag was on a wedding show?"

"Since when do you keep track of my douchebags?" Alex's voice was strained, like it always was when she was spoiling for a fight. He would give her one if they weren't around Lexi. Lexi hated when they fought, so he tried to limit their skirmishes to when she was not present.

The number of times they'd fought over Saturday morning television as teens—Lexi had never risen before noon—had to be approaching infinity.

"Listen, as long as you weren't somehow fooled into being on a wedding show with him, I wouldn't worry about it." Not that Alex would ever be fooled into getting married, much less appearing on reality television. No one could keep up with Lexi, but she sometimes tried to slow her pace to let someone catch up. Alex left most people coughing on her dust and seemingly felt no remorse about it. "I don't understand why this would even be bothering you. You don't want to get married."

Lexi scoffed. Another great thing about her was that she never believed the worst things people believed about themselves. She wasn't naïve, though. Lexi just knew that the worst thing people believed about themselves wasn't usually the actual worst thing about them. Usually someone's worst quality was something that they weren't even aware of, or even something that was usually a virtue.

As for Alex thinking she wasn't cut out for marriage, that was just smart in Will's book. Will might not be as quick as Alex to write the whole thing off, but he didn't need to try more than once.

"It's not bothering me." Alex's protest sounded weak, and he didn't like that. He started looking in the cupboards for something he could put together for dessert. "It just feels weird. He said he didn't want to get married—ever—either. And now he's marrying someone else."

"Trust me, you dodged a bullet." Will shook his head. "You don't want to get married."

"I don't, but it feels weird that he said that he didn't want to get married—until after we'd broken up. Like, just dating me for fun wasn't enough. I'm essentially like food that leaves guys hungry an hour later. I'm cotton candy."

Will really didn't like to hear that note of vulnerability in Alex's voice. Even though she hated him, they had always held off on killing each other out of a sick sense of mutual respect. After all, she was biologically related to Lexi. If he made Alex cry—she'd never cried as a teenager when he'd pulled idiot pranks on her—then Lexi wouldn't like him anymore. She wouldn't welcome him into her home even though his father was persona non grata.

And he couldn't lose Lexi.

Something about Alex feeling like this douchebag getting married to some person who couldn't measure up to Alex threatened to throw off the balance. Will was the only wounded bird allowed in the house at the moment. "Why would this even bother you? Again, you told him flat out that you didn't want anything serious." And Alex wasn't cotton candy. She was Thanksgiving dinner. But she wasn't for him, and he would never tell her that. She'd never let him forget it.

"Yeah, until three months in, he was part of an extensive roster. He wasn't even the number one draft pick." That really set Will's teeth on edge. It might be really caveman of him, but he had been witness to his father's bad behavior with women and knew that there weren't enough decent ones to fill any roster, but especially Alex's roster. She might be tough, but she deserved to be treated with care. "I just want it to make sense, you know?"

Will shook his head and looked Alex in the eye. He tried not to do that very often because she didn't miss anything with those piercing light brown, almost green eyes. And he'd always had to be careful not to hold her gaze for too long. The first time he'd done that, he'd thought about kissing her. That might be half his lifetime ago, but he'd known then that it would end in tears.

"It only makes sense if he was a wishy-washy douchebag that can't handle a woman who won't just roll over and do what he likes."

Will didn't really know what it would be like to be in a relationship with Alex. He didn't let his mind go there. But he did know that she wasn't a pushover. She had more spine than the hard-ass chefs who used to throw boiling hot pans of sauce around the kitchen if it wasn't seasoned to perfection. She had more spine than his wife's divorce attorney, who had somehow gotten him to give up his golf clubs, which his ex-wife would never use.

Will tried not to think about his ex-wife. Even though they'd worked together for years, they hadn't realized how ill-suited they were until they'd gotten married and actually had to live together. When they were each doing separate jobs at a busy restaurant—she as a master sommelier, he as the chef de cuisine— it felt like it was a perfect match. But once they'd gotten married, they'd realized that they had nothing to talk about beyond their work.

Add that to the fact that she'd wanted to start a family and he'd come to the realization that he didn't want kids at all, and it had become clear that they'd needed to call it. Will felt guilty for hurting her, and April felt like he'd lied to her.

Everything had always been easy with April, until it wasn't.

He felt like an idiot because he'd missed the signs that they weren't well suited. He'd been so focused on making his career a success that he hadn't seen the fork in the road that they'd been headed for since the very beginning of their relationship.

Alex wouldn't have let him go blind like that. She was the kind of woman who demanded attention—she demanded an equal. And unfortunately, he didn't know many men who were up to the job of being that equal.

He only knew that he wasn't going to start dating again, because he would never find anyone like Alex. And if he could never find anyone like Alex, then he might as well not even try.

FOUR

ALEX LOOKED AT THE LIST ON HER YELLOW LEGAL PAD
and hated herself a little for making it. She'd always prided
herself on her ability to walk in and out of her dalliances and
flirtations with grace and ease. No commitments, no rings, no
silver-framed photos on pristine mantels, and absolutely no heart-
break. Just have fun and forget them. She'd even fooled herself
into believing that she'd forgotten some of the names on the
list—names that had popped into her mind much too easily as
soon as she'd put pen to paper.

It didn't bother her that the list was long—a page and half.
After all, she was in her thirties and had a rather voracious ap-
petite for sex and affection. Because she didn't believe that long-
term relationships between human beings were viable now that
people lived past the age of thirty-five, of course the list was going
to be long.

No. She hated herself because making the list had forced her admit to herself that some of these endings had hurt. She hated that she'd fooled herself into believing all the while, telling herself and her partners, that she could keep it light. That weakness made her feel like she was chewing on a piece of glass.

She loved her grandmother—she did. But she was bewildered by her willingness to depend on another person again and again. Alex knew that there were very few people she could depend on, and she could never depend on a person once she'd slept with them.

Even her family, she realized, was dependable in very specific ways. She could depend on Lexi for a dry martini, a shoulder to cry on, and innovative spa treatments. Lexi always had an open door, but there was never any telling what sort of chaos there would be inside that open door. Her mother was dependable for a dry, academic response to any problem, a spotty cell phone connection in whatever part of the world she was currently exploring, and—in Alex's younger years—perfectly adequate financial support. Alex could rely on her sister to judge her as harshly as possible—even more harshly than she judged herself—all the while pretending not to know what their conversations were really about.

And Will was always there to antagonize her. And feed her. The second thing was the one that kept her from launching him into the sun.

But Alex had never truly relied on any of the men on the list in front of her. They had been momentary distractions that some part of her had hoped would turn into something more. Maybe it was the part of her that had always hoped that she'd be spending summer vacation with her father instead of being pawned off on his mother. It was the part of her that she hadn't been able to harden up and cut off from her emotions.

She hated that bit, all the while seeing the necessity of it.

Alex didn't know how long she'd spent staring at that list when her friend and former client walked into her office.

"Don't tell me you've gotten married again and are already contemplating divorce," Alex greeted her. Jane was a powerhouse talent agent who had a roster of clients that would make the guy they based Ari Gold on incandescent with jealousy. Essentially, if you were young, Black, and talented in Hollywood, Jane was the person you wanted representing you.

While Jane might be an excellent judge of talent, she was less discerning romantically. She'd eloped with her now ex-wife to Vegas without a prenup, and Alex had saved her millions of dollars. After that, they'd become friends on the condition that Jane would never, ever do that again. But Jane looked like a slightly older version of Jodie Turner-Smith and had incredible amounts of charm, so Alex wouldn't put it past her.

Jane sat down in the leather chair on the other side of Alex's desk and rolled her eyes. She unbuttoned her tailored Italian blazer and shook out her waist-length dreadlocks. Most people would be intimidated by that. It usually meant that someone's movie wasn't going to get made or that a studio had passed on a pilot that Jane had packaged and someone at that studio was likely going to be fired.

But Alex wasn't. Once you've negotiated over the most intimate details of someone's life, it was hard to be intimidated by them. It was one of the many reasons she hadn't been able to take

Will's case. She didn't want to see inside his marriage, because that would have meant seeing inside his mind.

Part of her wanted to keep the fantasy that Will was just Lexi's stepson, and handling his divorce definitely would have shattered that for her. No one was a good person when they were getting divorced. It brought out all the pettiness, jealousy, and greed inside a person. Alex might resent him for rejecting her when she was teenager, but she didn't need to delve that far inside his life. She'd probably start feeling empathy for him and then have feelings for him, and she was busy enough trying to sort through her unwelcome feelings about Jason getting married.

Jane snapped her out of her wedding-dress-show malaise. "I'm dating a total fuckboy right now."

This was new. Jane usually didn't have the time of day for fuckboys. It might be bad for Alex's business, but she was all right with that if it was good for Jane. "Good for you."

Alex must have sounded distracted, because that made Jane look at the legal pad before Alex had a chance to hide it. Jane was not used to having to compete with anyone or anything for attention, and she didn't like it. "What the fuck is that?"

"Tell me about this fuckboy. Where did you meet them?" Alex made the mistake of trying to slide the list off her desk, and Jane wasn't having any of it. She took the notepad and squinted while examining it. "Do you think it's time for reading glasses?" That question earned Alex a look that would send most people into shock, but Alex was desperate.

She didn't want to have to tell Jane about the dumb show with the dumb guy Alex should definitely not be thinking about anymore. She definitely didn't want to tell Jane that the dumb show with the dumb guy had sent her into a tailspin of research on her own romantic history when she had plenty of real, billable work to do.

"Is this a list of everyone you've fucked?" It was the disgust in Jane's voice that did Alex in.

She slammed her head on her desk before admitting it. She couldn't look Jane in the eye. "Yes."

"Why would you have this? Why would you make this?"

Alex rolled her head to one side and opened one eye. She couldn't take the full force of this lecture. "You don't want to know."

But Jane was on her own track with this now. "Why wouldn't you make a password-protected spreadsheet? Anyone could find this." Jane stood up and started pacing, gesturing with the notepad. "This is not like you. Something happened, didn't it?"

Alex straightened up enough to put her chin on her hands. "Sort of."

"Tell me." If Alex hadn't been raised by her academic mother, she would have spilled her guts right then.

"You really don't want to know."

Jane dropped to her seat and put her face at eye level. Alex winced. "Now I have to know."

"Can we do this someplace else?"

Jane's whole face lit up; she knew that she'd won. She liked nothing better than winning. "I was coming here to bring you to lunch anyway."

Alex leaned over and took her purse out of its locked drawer. Jane stood and they walked out of Alex's office. "You have a password-protected spreadsheet, don't you?"

"Of course I do. I have my assistant update it biweekly."

"Be careful you keep them happy, or they'll publish it as the *Bi Weekly*."

Jane laughed, and Alex was glad. She was probably going to blow a gasket at the dumb wedding-dress-show story, but at least Alex would have gotten one laugh.

Alex was delighted to find that Jane had been planning on taking her out to lunch all along. And, as a bonus, Jane surprised Alex with their friend Lana—Jane's college roommate and an utter delight.

When they arrived at Verdura—the newest vegan hot spot in the city—Alex made a beeline for Lana and hugged the stuffing out of her. Since her friend had decided to leave her psychology practice after having her third kid, it had been difficult to get an audience with her.

After they hugged and squealed, Lana pointed a finger at Jane. "They had better serve alcohol here. I took an Uber, and I have a babysitter for the rest of the day."

Lana looked a bit wild-eyed, and Alex's first guess was that stay-at-home motherhood wasn't totally agreeing with her. Her normal blond, easy-California-girl aura was kind of muddy. Alex had clearly been hanging out with Lexi too much if she was thinking about muddy auras.

It was disconcerting to see the mentally healthiest person she knew off-kilter. While Jane was always a wild card, Lana had always seemed so steady. Alex had always looked at Lana's relationship with Greg and thought she could sign up for something like that if she met someone like Lana's husband—a calm, steady, responsible accountant with an apparently kinky streak in bed.

"I guess I'll tell my clients that their little careers are just going to have to wait." Jane had minions who could handle her clients for the afternoon. She was at the top of the food chain at her agency. The walls shook when she was unhappy. She embodied hashtag boss-babe goals without the hashtag. She just had the sort of presence that dared people to question her. Since Alex knew her so well through their professional relationship, she also knew how much compassion Jane had. She might be responsible for building empires and legacies for her clients, but when her friends were in crisis, empires could wait.

Jane held the philosophy that she was who she was, and that anyone who didn't like it could choke on it. Alex actually shared that philosophy with her friend. Jane would also do anything for her true friends. Alex agreed, so it was good that they'd found each other.

Alex laughed and shook her head. "I guess I'm not going back to the office this afternoon." It was a good thing she didn't have any court appearances and wasn't going to miss any filing deadlines. She sent a quick text to her assistant saying that she'd be out for the rest of the afternoon.

"So, what's up?" Even though Jane would clear her schedule for her friends, she always got straight to the point.

"I just miss you guys," Lana said. "I'm so tired and bored only having people under the age of five to talk to all day."

Alex shuddered. Lana's kids were cute, but they were also mildly terrifying. "I can barely sustain interest in a conversation with an adult man. I would totally flounder with children."

Lana scoffed. "I think you would be great in a relationship, but that would require actually trying."

"That's easy for you to say; you actually won the lottery with Greg." Lana and Greg's relationship was truly the only one that Alex could even imagine aspiring to.

"Not so," Lana said. "Remember when Greg wanted an open relationship?"

Alex nodded. "As I recall, you had a three-month-old."

Lana scrunched her forehead. "And I was so tired I cried at the concept of finally getting my kids to bed and then trolling for tail on Tinder."

"I told you that Tinder was over, and I would set you up on Raya." Jane was always there with the hookup.

"So I could troll for D-list tail?" Lana cringed. "No, thank you."

"You only have to find one." Jane must have found her fuckboy on Raya. He was probably an Australian DJ. "Listen, it is a truth universally acknowledged that the female partner in a heterosexual open marriage is the more desired partner. Most straight women don't want a secondhand dude on layaway from his marriage.

"So, all you had to do is find one guy while he was trying to slide into the DMs of some woman he's never going to get. You'd go out looking fine and let some guy take you out and buy you lobster. Let him eat your clam guilt-free if you want, and when you get home Greg is going to be singing a different tune."

All three women stopped talking when the server approached the table and took their order. Jane ordered a vegan cheese plate for the table and a round of martinis.

"But that's not what I wanted, and it's not really what Greg wanted, either." Lana shook her head. "And it's not the point."

"What is your point?" Alex asked, frustrated with Lana's therapist-speak.

Lana pursed her lips, and Alex imagined that was how she looked when dealing with a particularly recalcitrant analysand. "My point was that Greg isn't perfect, and neither am I." She laughed. "He actually thought he was helping. Turns out that his sleep-deprived brain thought I was ignoring him because I wasn't in love with him anymore, and he thought the only way to keep me was to open up our relationship."

"Shit, that's almost romantic," said Jane.

Alex looked at both her friends as though they were crazy. "Or it's proof that men are impossible to understand, and even the best ones are more trouble than they are worth."

Jane shrugged. "Some of them are okay . . . in small doses."

"The fuckboy is that good?" Come to think of it, Alex had never seen Jane looking so relaxed.

"He's serving his purpose." Jane squinted at Alex. "Now we should talk about what I walked in on in your office."

Jane hadn't forgotten. Of course she hadn't.

"It's nothing—"

At the same time, Jane said, "She was making a list of every person she's fucked."

The restaurant had experienced a little lull in sound at that exact moment, and Alex wanted to crawl under the table and maybe die. It was such an immature thing to do. She might not be apologetic about who she was, where she came from, or what she looked like, but she was definitely embarrassed by this behavior.

And then Lana put her therapist face on. "Oh?"

"I saw Jason on *Say Yes to the Dress* with his new fiancée last night." Now that people were looking at them, Alex figured that it was time to rip off the Band-Aid.

"He's hot, but who's dumb enough to marry that bargain-basement Michael B. Jordan when the real one is just wandering around?" Jane sneered. She'd never liked Jason, and her assessment of him was correct. "Does he even have a job?"

Jane knew that Jason had a job. He was in mergers and acquisitions at one of the most powerful law firms in town.

"And why are we upset about this?" Lana asked. Fuck if Alex knew. "The breakup wasn't dramatic, was it?"

"I told him before we started dating that I didn't do long-term relationships. I see too many of them break up to ever think about putting one of my own together." Alex didn't say the next part. That even the people who seemed to have everything figured out, like Lana and Greg, had a hard time making marriage work. And no one had ever made a case to her explaining why it was worth it to try.

Lana was one of the happier married people she knew, and her husband had suggested they open up their marriage while trying to take care of a newborn. Granted, he'd been incredibly sleep deprived and walked it back once they'd communicated. But it just seemed like so much effort that only bore fruit about half the time.

As far as Alex saw, marriage was a foolish gamble.

"Then why did you make the list?" Lana pressed. She'd clearly decided to hone in on Alex's issues. That was the problem with having a friend who was a therapist—they were too good at compartmentalizing when it was time to focus on another person's problems.

"I don't know."

Jane scoffed. "You know."

Alex was momentarily saved when their cocktails and "cheese" plate arrived. She really didn't know why she'd started listing the people she'd been involved with over the last decade.

"Maybe seeing Jason ready to commit to someone made me feel like . . . I don't know . . . that he agreed too easily to no strings with me. But that he really wanted strings. Just not with me. But I don't want strings. I take care of myself." She'd always had to take care of herself—emotionally at least. Her parents made sure that she was clothed and fed but didn't feel the need to coddle her feelings. And she'd only spent summers with Lexi. She'd always felt seen by Lexi, but she wasn't exactly around for talks about the fact that the boy she liked didn't invite her to the dance. "I shouldn't even have feelings about this. We should be laughing at how bad his fiancée's dress is."

"It would bother me, and my heart is completely dead," Jane said, lifting her drink to her lips. "Thank goodness my coochie didn't suffer the same fate."

"Maybe that's it—I just don't like to lose. And seeing him on TV signals some part of my lizard brain that says, 'Must not lose man.'" Alex knew that dating and relationships weren't a competition unless it was a season of *The Bachelor*.

"The fact that you're thinking about this so much says a lot." Lana took a sip of her drink and a bite of her "cheese."

"You're having therapist thoughts that you're not sharing with me." Alex knew that Lana really tried not to analyze her friends, but she could see that there was something that she wanted to say that she wasn't saying. "Spill it. I'm in crisis, and I promise that I won't be mad."

"I think that you've been cut off from your emotional needs for a long time because your parents weren't great," Lana said. And then she stopped and took another big sip of her drink. Alex braced herself. "And I think that none of the men you've dated have been right for you."

"Well, duh." It had been years since she'd considered a really serious commitment. And the few men she'd considered committing to kind of sucked.

"I think they're exactly like your father." As soon as Lana said that, something clicked into place for Alex. She did tend to date men who were aloof and critical, and a picture of her father was in the dictionary next to both of those words. Every time she'd tried to share news about what she was doing growing up, he'd found a reason to make her wrong or bad. "And you seek those kinds of men out because you're trying to fix it now. But you can't fix it, because he's dead. Part of you knows that, because you're never emotionally attached to these guys."

They were all silent for a long moment. Because Lana was right. And it pissed Alex off because she hadn't known that she was doing something that was so obvious to someone who knew her.

"I used to get emotionally attached." And maybe she'd been on the way to getting attached to Jason, despite her defense mechanism of keeping men at arm's length? "I wish I could talk to these guys and figure out why they married the next person they dated after me. At least the ones who had potential. Like, why am I always a fling?"

"Do you want to be the ring?" That was Jane's question—always going for the bottom line.

"Relationships are bad and gross. Sociologically speaking, the happiest people are single childless women." Alex scrunched up her face. "Sorry."

Lana said, "No, you're right. Marriage is fucked."

Jane took out her phone. "I still think you should get on Raya immediately."

"But I still feel like I should figure out why no one seems to want more with me," Alex said. "Because if I wanted more, I want to know that I could have it."

"You already have a list of guys you've fucked. Maybe you should start there?"

"That's way too many." Alex might not be into the idea of marriage, but she was definitely not opposed to sex.

"Well, how about guys that you've had actual feelings for?" Lana suggested.

That got Alex thinking. There weren't that many guys she gotten super serious with. And the number of guys she might have wanted to get a ring from—back before her defenses had hardened—was even smaller. "That's like five guys."

"Any of them sociopaths?" Jane asked.

"We really should stop labeling run-of-the-mill narcissists as sociopaths," Lana said. It was one of her pet peeves, but the smile on Jane's face said that she had asked for that precise reason.

"Pretty much all of them are the second thing, but I don't think anyone will actually try to murder me."

"I think we should make a short list, find these dummies, and figure out why Alex made them want to get married," Jane said. Always to the point.

"To someone else," Alex added.

Will went to the gym every morning after he visited his kitchen and placed orders with suppliers. It cleared his head and kept his body in good enough condition to work long, grueling hours in the kitchen and to not punch people when his publicist—the one Lexi had made him meet with after his first video went viral—trotted him out to do media hits. It had nothing to do with his image as a *hot chef.*

He felt anything but hot these days. The colossal failure of his marriage had reinforced his belief that only truly disturbed individuals worked in the restaurant industry. It wasn't conducive to a happy marriage or a happy life. But that made him think about Alex and her long-standing philosophy that long-term relationships were destined for failure. Until recently, he hadn't agreed with her. He'd thought he could make the kind of family he'd never had.

He and April had felt like the perfect match. He was an up-and-coming chef, and she was a sommelier with a monthly column in a storied food magazine. Before they'd worked together, they'd met on a podcast, for fuck's sake. When she'd offered to go over his wine list and "punch it up a bit," with a sly wink and a hand on his thigh, he'd known that the chemistry between them wasn't one-sided.

It had seemed to him at the time that they wanted the same

things. As their relationship had developed, it had seemed natural and easy. They'd never fought.

Will grunted trying to deadlift 375 pounds, his personal best. Sometimes it was good to struggle. But not right now, when he was struggling to figure out where he'd gone wrong.

Overall, he'd landed on his feet. April got to stay at the old restaurant and keep his ownership share, but she wouldn't have anything to do with the place he was opening in a month. And his new restaurant was going to be a huge success, according to the people who handled reservations. Before they'd even previewed the food for critics, no one could get a reservation for six months. His publicist had tried to set up a red carpet for the opening night. Apparently, celebrities wanted to eat his food.

And next month, he'd grudgingly agreed to meet with some television producers who wanted him to be a judge on a cooking show. Making food in his kitchen because he was depressed and he didn't know how to do anything else was one thing. But being on television was a whole other beast. He was grateful that he'd been able to sustain himself through social media during a very dark time in the world, but he didn't like the kind of notoriety it brought. Being sort of related to Lexi just magnified it.

Will was happy that he got to open a restaurant and that people were paying attention, but he also missed just being a guy who cooked.

Even though he was ambivalent about the kind of fame that television would bring, it would keep his name in the news. In the age of celebrity chefs, that was apparently necessary to be a success. Added to the fact that he wasn't a creep or a screamer, he was a hot commodity in the world of food.

Although a lot of people would kill for the opportunities that he now had, he hadn't gotten into the industry to be a celebrity chef. He was an introvert, and he'd always hidden out in the kitchen when his father was throwing parties. There had been less of a chance of walking in on adults doing drugs and/or each other if he'd had his nose firmly stuck in a book.

But one of the chefs catering one of his dad's parties had spotted Will and put him to work. The few hours he'd spent with the exuberant German chef learning to dice, chop, and julienne had changed him. He hadn't even minded scrubbing and drying dishes afterward.

After that, he'd started poring over cookbooks and watching cooking shows. His father didn't notice anything until Will decided to go to culinary school instead of law school after college—even as an eighteen-year-old kid, he knew that skipping undergrad wouldn't be an option for him. His father had expected him to go into the family shipping business like him. Every time Will had tagged along to work with his dad, they'd stopped at the corner office at the other end of the hall from his dad's, and his father would say, "You'll sit there one day."

Will didn't think the guy who used to sit there appreciated it very much.

And the last thing that Will wanted to become was his father. Michael Harkness was somehow both a narcissist and spineless at the same time. Will didn't know how a psychologist would diagnose his father, but it had always seemed to Will that his father was addicted to the feeling of falling in love, but quickly lost interest in the hard work a long-term relationship required of him. Will had thought he could make his relationship with April work because he loved her and was willing to work to keep her happy. But it turned out that nothing Will could do was enough. And it smarted.

Will had always thought that hard work was the cure for everything—in the kitchen and in his love life. But it turned out that luck played a huge role in both. And his luck had taken him in directions that he never could have imagined.

But there was always a piece of him that felt alone. Even in his marriage, he'd felt alone. And when he was playing the role of the hot young chef, he definitely felt alone.

All he wanted to do was feed people, and instead he was playing a part.

A fter working out, he headed to the restaurant and worked all day with his sous chef on finalizing the dinner menu. He wanted to get everything just right so that there would be no question that he was a serious chef rather than a social media flash in the pan.

He tended to get lost in his work, and time passed without him noticing. "Do you think it might be time to call it a night?" Will's chef de cuisine, Charlee, called from across the kitchen, which was empty except for the two of them. Earlier in the evening, they'd had a bunch of folks they'd both worked with at other restaurants come in to audition for new jobs.

Will had met Charlee when they'd both been baby chefs at a three-Michelin-star restaurant with a notoriously abusive executive chef. Will had been close to telling the guy off and getting fired when he'd locked eyes with Charlee across the prep table.

They had rolled their eyes and smirked in the very comforting way they had, and the two had been friends ever since.

Even though Charlee was his rock in the kitchen, they didn't have their whole career riding on it. If this restaurant failed, Will might not be able to get a job peeling potatoes in a decent kitchen.

So, when Charlee asked if he was ready to quit for the night, Will hesitated. His ragù wasn't quite perfect. He'd followed all his Italian maternal grandmother's recipes to the letter when writing the menu, but this one wasn't as good as he remembered. And he couldn't stand it.

"Do you think it's the cinnamon?" Will asked.

Charlee pressed their lips into a thin line when he ignored their question about quitting for the night and kept staring into the collection of spices, hoping one of them would be the key to fixing the dish.

"No, I don't think it's fucking cinnamon," Charlee said. "Go home."

He didn't want to go home. It was empty, and he hadn't gotten his cable or Internet hooked up yet. So the only thing to listen to was his thoughts. And that was just about his least favorite activity these days.

Given too much time with his thoughts, he felt like a total failure. And it didn't even make sense. Other than his divorce, he had never been more successful. If he complained about how restless he felt, the guys at the gym would laugh him off or tell him that he just needed to get laid.

Even Charlee might give him that advice. They were firmly in the "Will needs to get some and let his team do their jobs" camp.

The trouble was that he didn't want to get laid. He had the

feeling that it wouldn't make him feel better. He was better off shutting out the world and focusing on work. But until the restaurant opened, he wouldn't get the same feeling of putting his head down in a sweaty kitchen, just trying to stay out of the weeds until the last order was up and the dining room was empty.

He wanted to run a different kind of restaurant than he and Charlee had come up in, but he was starting to realize why the chef they'd worked for had turned into such an asshole. The asshole chef had been going through a divorce, and it had turned him into a real dick.

At the time, Will didn't understand how a breakup could change someone's whole personality. Now he understood.

After his breakup with April, Will was never going to get married ever again. He'd thought he'd feel as though he had roots once he got married, but he felt like he was a plant that had been ripped out of the ground at this point. Moving in with someone was a very distant possibility, but he'd rather be alone with his thoughts than have to share his intimate inner life again anytime soon.

Hell, he'd rather have a prostate exam with a rusty fork than tell another person what he was thinking. And he was getting dangerously close to telling Charlee his thoughts.

"Yeah, let's call it a night."

FIVE

THOUGH ALEX HAD ASSURED HER EX-BOYFRIEND'S ASsistant that she only needed a few minutes of Andrew's time, Misty had cleared Andrew Wilder's afternoon for her. Misty had always had a soft spot for Alex, because while she and Andrew had been dating, he had been less of a screamer. Actually, now that Alex thought about it, her exes' assistants had always been fond of her. Maybe because the guys had directed all their assholery toward Alex during the weeks or months that they'd been dating? That was one thing she could be proud of regarding her relationship history.

Andrew Wilder was a reality television producer whose shows were squarely on the classy side of the spectrum. They'd met at a beach party for a reality television star. Alex hadn't been there to take part in the festivities but had taken advantage of them to gain access to the owner of the home, who'd evaded being served with divorce papers for almost a month. Alex would have normally relied on a process server to do the deed, but three of them hadn't gotten the job done. So Alex had used her association to her grandmother to pose as a grandkid of a celebrity–slash–hanger-on, and that had gotten her in.

As soon as she'd served the papers, the reality star's face had gotten so red that it was almost going purple. They'd picked up an imitation of a very expensive vase and aimed it at Alex's head when Andrew walked in.

He'd had a bone to pick with the reality star, too. They wouldn't sign their new contract. And if they didn't sign their new contract, they wouldn't have been able to afford to pay for their divorce attorney. So Andrew and Alex had tag-teamed them until they put down the vase, accepted the divorce papers, signed their new contract, and promised to seek some counseling for their rage issues.

After that, Andrew and Alex had ended up going to a great little restaurant at the beach and having a couple of drinks. She hadn't hesitated to go back to Andrew's place, also conveniently at the beach. He wasn't trash in bed—he'd clearly read a manual or two on how to operate a clitoris, and he paid attention—so they'd slept together for a few months until . . . Alex didn't really know why things had ended.

And when Andrew saw Alex standing in the threshold of his office, Alex realized that he'd definitely never intended to run into her again. But, like any professional in the entertainment industry, he recovered fairly quickly and put on a brave face.

"To what do I owe this pleasure?" Andrew asked. He really

was very handsome. In addition to being charming in a way that didn't immediately come off as slick. "You're not here to serve me, are you?"

That caught Alex short. They hadn't gotten kinky when they were together, so he could only mean that he thought she might be here in her professional capacity. And the only reason she would be there in her professional capacity was if he was getting a divorce. Her online stalking had revealed that he appeared to be deliriously happily married to an interior designer.

Suddenly, she felt really awkward. She really should have been feeling awkward before she'd showed up at her ex-boyfriend's office to ask why he'd ghosted her. But it had seemed like a decent idea when she was two martinis deep with her friends at lunch. She and Andrew hadn't had an acrimonious breakup—they hadn't really had a breakup at all. He'd stopped calling all the time and so she'd stopped calling. Showing up at his office seemed like a great way to get information.

But now she was standing in his office, planning on asking him why he'd stopped calling, and that felt really weird. And it was even more strange now that he was married.

"I should go—"

Andrew smiled at her, and she felt even more stupid for coming here. He was a nice guy, and he didn't deserve her dumping all her newfound neuroses on his lap. "I mean, you came all the way to Studio City. It must be important." He motioned to the chair in front of him. "If no one's divorcing me, please sit down."

Alex shook her head and took his invitation. "No one's divorcing you."

He wiped his forehead dramatically in a relieved gesture, and

Alex laughed. He was such a nice man, really. So rare in the world of entertainment, and especially reality television.

"It's been a long time, and you're the last person I expected to see in my office." Andrew's words seemed so genuine that Alex had to fight not to slouch in her chair. It was deeply unhinged for her to be asking this perfectly decent man why he'd stopped calling.

"I have a really dumb question for you."

"You're way too smart to have dumb questions." That was only because he didn't know why she was there yet.

Alex was of the mind that it was always better to just be direct. "Listen, why did we break up?"

Andrew's mouth opened and closed several times, but he recovered quickly. He'd dealt with enough bananas folks to have the skills to cover. "Were we ever together?"

Now, that was a real question. And maybe that answered all her questions. Maybe she never got close enough—even with guys who had potential—to classify any of her dalliances as actual relationships. Maybe she was like green juice—she had all the micronutrients required to keep someone's liver humming along, but she lacked the substance to be an actual meal. That would explain Jason's sudden change of heart when it came to his new fiancée.

"I guess I felt like we were a thing. We spent a lot of time together."

When Andrew smiled at her again, there wasn't any heat in it. It was the same smile that he gave to network executives and recalcitrant cast members—only slightly less saccharine than the one he gave to "friends of the show" who overstepped their bounds.

"I shouldn't have come." Alex rose and backed up toward the door.

"No, it's just—" Andrew held up his left hand, twirling his wedding band with his thumb.

Alex's face heated. "I didn't come to start things up again. I just—I feel like this"—she pointed at the ring—"is a thing."

Instead of looking weary of her presence, Andrew looked befuddled. He motioned for her to sit again.

After a split second of hesitation, Alex accepted his invitation. Andrew's assistant appeared with a tray of water and coffee, as if she'd been summoned by magic. Alex guessed that Andrew had a button in his desk, and she was lucky that it wasn't a button that made a hole open up under the feet of unwanted visitors.

"The last I heard you were seeing that venture-capital guy?" Andrew asked as he poured himself a cup of coffee with a heart-stopping amount of heavy cream. While they were dating, he'd explained that it had to do with intermittent fasting, but if fasting involved heavy cream, Alex would be fasting all the time when she ate dessert.

Alex poured her own coffee. "He was in mergers and acquisitions. And we broke up."

"So you came here to find out why I dumped you?" Andrew sat back in his chair. "Because one other guy dumped you?"

"It's more than one other guy, okay?" Alex felt her hackles rising, which was probably a clue as to why she was frequently dumped. She wasn't very agreeable.

"I mean, you've been dating for a long time." Alex gave him a look, and he backtracked. "Not that long, but long enough to know that men are fickle beasts."

"I don't think it's that simple."

"It's also clear that you couldn't be less interested in committing to one person."

That made Alex's heart stop for a second. Alex and Andrew had dated years ago. Early on, when she wasn't quite so negative about her long-term prospects, she'd thought she was open to something serious. And she'd never told Andrew that she wasn't sure that long-term relationships were viable. It tended to be a bummer when she started quoting divorce statistics. She'd learned to keep her mouth shut when people asked why she had never given marriage a try. It didn't make sense to her in the long run. Sort of like an investment that was nearly guaranteed to fail or leave one without a home to live in. Why make that kind of investment when one could make others that might not have as high a yield in happiness but were infinitely less risky?

"I never said I wasn't interested in commitment. I said that I think marriage is foolish." Alex looked down at his ring. "I mean, not your marriage. Your marriage is fine. I'm sure you're very happy and will have decades—centuries—of memories to share."

Andrew's mouth quirked up on one side, and Alex remembered why she'd found him so charming. "You know what your problem is?"

Again, her hackles were raised. It was one of those weird things. When she used to ask her father why she couldn't spend time at his house during her summer visits, he always made it about her having a problem or wanting to pin him down. But Andrew didn't know that, so she couldn't blame him for making this—her showing up at his office to ask why their relationship hadn't worked out when he'd clearly moved on almost immediately—about her. "What's my problem?"

"I never felt like I could make you happy," Andrew said. "You never let me in or let me know how you were feeling."

"That's not true—"

"After sex once you high-fived me and said, 'Good game.'"

That was true. She had done that. But she never knew what to say right after sex. She would have wanted a cuddle but never wanted to seem clingy. She could see how post-sex performance dissection might push a guy away.

"I see your point." Alex smiled and picked up her purse to leave. "That's a good note. Maybe I'll try silence next time."

"Honestly, it would have been charming if I'd thought it was a joke. But I knew then that you were never going to let me in." Andrew looked a little bit sad about it.

"I'm sorry." Alex wasn't quite sure what to say, but that seemed appropriate after walking in here and dredging up ancient history.

Andrew smiled and looked down at a frame on his desk that Alex guessed held a picture of his wife. "It's all right. Things worked out for the best."

"For you." She hadn't meant to say that out loud.

Andrew looked her in the eye and said, "They'll work out for you, too." She didn't know how he could seem so sure of that, but part of her wanted to believe him. Maybe seeing Jason on that show was a wake-up call of some kind. She wasn't sure yet what she was meant to wake up to, but she was starting to think that fucking and running wasn't good for her. She wasn't sure she could hack it at celibacy, so she might actually have to open up.

She opened her mouth to thank Andrew but didn't get the words out.

The door to Andrew's office opened, and the last person she expected to see there walked in.

Immediately, Will Harkness looked at her, and his face screwed up. He crossed his beefy arms across his chest and said, "Alex, what the hell are you doing here?"

Alex could never stop herself from talking back at Will Harkness. It was a disease. So she responded in kind. "I could ask the same thing of you, but you're always devising new ways to ingratiate yourself into my life and annoy me. I presume you had a tail on me and followed me here."

"Why on earth would I do that, when you just show up wherever I happen to be?" He stepped closer to her, much closer than someone who was practically related to her would step. She could smell him. He must have been cooking today because the scents of lemongrass and sage filled her nostrils. Or maybe that was just how he smelled, clean and earthy. It was both intoxicating and infuriating.

"I do not show up wherever you happen to be." And then she realized that she might have to explain what she was doing here, and that would be unacceptable. The last person on earth that she could show any doubt or weakness to couldn't know that she was doubting a whole a lot about herself. He'd made it very clear years ago that he was not attracted to her, and nothing he'd done in the interim indicated that he'd changed his mind.

"Well then, what are you doing here?"

Andrew saved her from answering. "She came here on business."

Will looked at Andrew then. "I'm sorry, man," Will said, reasonably assuming that Alex would only be here on business if Andrew was getting divorced.

"No, this was an information-seeking mission." Alex didn't want to have any rumors starting about Andrew, given that he'd been pretty gracious in not kicking her out once he'd realized why she was here. "For another client."

Will looked puzzled by that explanation, but he just grunted in response. He was the master of the manly grunt, which could mean any number of things coming from him. Back when she'd been a smitten teen, she'd learn to decipher most of his grunts. And even after she'd forced herself not to think about Will as The One, all the various grunts were ingrained too deeply to root out. The one he'd just given her was the "I don't believe you, but I'm letting this go—for now" grunt.

She'd take it.

"What are you doing here?"

And he looked annoyed that he was going to have to come up with a response that was more than a grunt. "I'm supposed to be meeting Andrew about a possible project. And I just saw that your assistant canceled, and she wasn't outside. Sorry for barging in." Will's reason for being there surprised Alex. He seemed ill at ease about his newfound social media fame, and a reality show would bring even more of the same.

Will was so not LA that Alex had often wondered why he stayed here. If she had to picture it, she pictured him in New York. Someplace dirty and loud, where he could disappear. Someplace where the energy would match his shitty personality. He stuck out in Los Angeles like a misanthropic sore thumb.

She patted his arm in a pantomime of the long-standing friendship they allegedly had. "Try to look happier about making money, Will."

He grunted again, and Alex turned to Andrew. "Thanks."

Andrew winked at her. "Anytime."

SIX

WILL DIDN'T LIKE THE WAY THIS FUCKER LOOKED AT Alex. He remembered that they'd dated for about a minute a few years ago, but he'd been willing to put it out of his mind to take this meeting. And he knew he was projecting, but he thought that wink before Alex left crossed a line. It said, "I've seen you naked, and it was pretty fucking great." Will would never be able to look at this guy and not see him looking at Alex like she was his afternoon snack. Even though everyone had told him that Andrew was maybe the only good guy in reality television, Will wasn't sure he could work with him.

But Will got a handle on his irritation when the door finally closed behind Alex. He couldn't manage it when she was sashaying toward the door on the high heels that put her at almost his eye level. He didn't watch her leave, but he knew the cadence and curve of her hips as surely as he knew the timing on poaching the perfect egg. It was in his head as much as anything that he'd gotten screamed at about in his job just out of culinary school.

There was nothing about Alex that he'd ever known that he'd forgotten. And when he'd walked in and seen her talking to that slick—admittedly good-looking—guy, Will hadn't been able to keep himself from seeing red. Andrew had been smiling at her in a way that was too familiar, and Will couldn't help but hate him for that.

After talking to him, Will had confirmed for himself that the guy wouldn't have been good enough for Alex, even if he weren't married. And Will didn't believe Alex's excuse for being there for a second. She was too familiar with this guy for this to have been a simple information-gathering exercise.

Will sat there and tried to hear Andrew out, because he'd promised his publicist that he would. And the money and recognition from going on reality TV could sustain interest in his new restaurant after the hype within the industry died down. Sure, Will hated the idea of becoming a franchise or a personality more than a working chef, but he needed to make a living. And after all this publicity was over, hopefully he could disappear back into the kitchen on the strength of his food. He needed to be thinking about the future, not how he'd started thinking of Alex as his.

Will intended to make it through the whole meeting without asking. But he couldn't even get through a few minutes. He didn't even sit down before he asked, "What was Alex really doing here?"

Will knew that he'd caught the other man off guard, because Andrew actually rocked back on his heels. "How do you know her?"

"She's family." It wasn't technically true, but it was what Will told himself when the overwhelming need to know and protect Alex got the better of him. It was a more acceptable explanation than the real answer—that he couldn't not think about Alex since his divorce. He'd tried for years and years before meeting April, acutely aware of how messy it would be if they finally gave in to the roiling thing that had been between them nearly from the start. He told himself that it was easier for both of them if Alex believed he was totally indifferent to her—if she thought that he saw her as an annoying sort-of relative that he only tolerated so that he could maintain his relationship with Lexi.

Alex could never know that Will cared about her independent of how he cared for Lexi. That would lead them down a one-way street toward disaster. Neither of them could make a relationship with other people work, and neither of their sets of parents had set a good example. According to his ex-wife, they had "matching avoidant attachment styles," whatever that meant. April said it made sense because both of them had essentially raised themselves. Maybe April was right, and the way they were raised was how they'd both ended up alone.

Alex was a threat to everything Will held dear because he didn't feel like himself around her. And he didn't like how she knew how to knock him off-center with just a look or a flick of her hair. He hated how he got indigestion when she rolled her eyes at him. And he was jealous of her relationship with Lexi. Not because he thought Lexi loved her more, but he hated how jealous he was of the way Alex laughed at Lexi's jokes. Will didn't joke. But if he did, he'd want Alex to laugh with him the way she did with other people.

"You like Alex, don't you?" Andrew asked, with his head cocked to the side, like a raptor assessing his prey.

Will had forgotten where he was. He'd let his mind slip over his long history with Alex Turner and had taken his eye off the ball. He'd been so preoccupied with what Alex might be doing hanging out with a random reality television producer on an ordinary Wednesday that he'd forgotten himself.

Will couldn't tell this man about what he truly felt about Lexi. She was a like a piece of him that he'd never been able to hold on to. Every time he finally felt as though he had a handle on her, she slipped away from him. He cared about her, but she always managed to infuriate him. He couldn't have her, but it bothered him that a part of him would always want her. She was sort of like family, but she always boxed him out of really knowing her.

And she could take perfectly good care of herself, even around a douchey reality TV producer who looked at her like she was a black truffle that he wanted to shave a piece off of.

"She's a pain in the ass." That was the best that Will could come up with. The only concise way that he could describe what she meant to him. Alex was a pain, but she was a pain that he wouldn't know that he was alive without.

Luckily, this Andrew douche didn't know all the stuff packed into that one sentence. So he laughed and pointed to a chair in front of him.

Because Will didn't think that the man in front of him had it in him to really get someone like Alex and all that made her, he sat down to hear the guy out.

SEVEN

ALEX DROVE UP TO THE BUILDING THAT WOULD BE-come Will's new restaurant; she didn't know where he lived anymore. She'd never been invited to the house he'd shared with his ex-wife, but she'd had the address for holiday card purposes.

All she knew about his current living situation was that he'd let his ex keep their little Los Feliz bungalow, and Lexi did not approve of Will's bachelor pad. Apparently, he'd reverted to sleeping on a mattress on the floor of a studio apartment. She guessed he was so busy with his new restaurant that he didn't have time to sleep and felt his home was not relevant.

Alex didn't like to think about where Will Harkness slept, because that would lead to her thinking about Will Harkness not wearing clothes. She would then think about whether Will Harkness had gotten more tattoos since she'd seen him at Lexi's last

Labor Day barbecue. The one he'd attended with his ex-wife, who was nothing like Alex, because Alex was the opposite of Will's type. This was a point Will had made very clear when he'd rejected her. Thoughts about Will that led to anything other than what he was cooking for her and Lexi for dinner were entirely fruitless.

He was the most frustrating man she'd ever met, and she couldn't imagine that he had anything nice to say about her. She couldn't get the image of the two of them talking shit about her after she'd left out of her mind.

Not that she'd ever known Will to talk shit about her. He merely looked right through people he didn't like or no longer had use for.

Still, she sat in her car in the rare street parking spot she'd found on Fairfax for way too long. She didn't voluntarily run into Will. She tried to space out their encounters by weeks, if not months. She didn't spend time that she didn't have to spare thinking about seeing Will and Andrew together. She didn't turn their images over in her head, comparing one to the other. She did not think about how real and earthy Will was when compared to Andrew. And she most certainly did not recall that she'd first been attracted to Andrew because he and Will shared a certain shrewdness and way of solving problems and looking at the world that inspired her.

But her curiosity compelled her to figure out what they'd said about her. She would have to be incredibly persistent about getting that information from Will, but he was as prone to glossing over the truth to protect other people's feelings as Andrew was.

Plus, it would be weird if she contacted Andrew again after their last awkward meeting.

She got out of her car and walked around the building that would soon house Will's restaurant. The front door would be locked for a few more weeks, but the back would likely be accessible given the pace of deliveries at this point. It had been a dumb idea to wear heels today, but she hadn't exactly planned on skulking around in alleys when she'd gotten dressed. And she hadn't slept very well the night before, given all the Andrew-and-Will comparison matrices she'd been busy composing in her head. Honestly, she could write a treatise on the topic with how much thought had gone into it.

Predictably, she tripped and fell about twenty steps from the back door to the new restaurant, Solitudine—the Italian word for loneliness. For a few moments, she was frozen in shock, like when a baby fell and didn't know whether to get up and dust themselves off or start screaming for their mother. She felt searing pain from her injury—almost so much she froze. Tears hit her cheeks, and she picked up a grimy hand to wipe them off. And then she dragged a pebble across her face.

"Ouch."

"Are you okay?" Alex's spine stiffened. The last person she wanted to see was standing behind her, watching her sit down in the dirt. And there was a hint of amusement in his voice.

Before she turned, she wiped her face again with her other hand. And then she gathered all the dismissive, haughty energy that she could muster before looking at him. She was glad she did, because he looked good. If she were being honest with herself, she would admit that he always looked good, but she didn't want to be honest with herself at the moment.

He was the perennial enemy. Or actually, more of an irritant that she could never get to go away. Will Harkness was a chronic ailment that made her itch all over.

"I'm fine." She'd meant for the words to sound breezy, but they didn't. And he knew that.

He moved close to her and grabbed her upper arms. He was a lot bigger than her—a lot bigger than he'd been when they'd first met. She felt enveloped by him immediately. He smelled like herbs and expensive soap. When he stood up with her in his arms, the skin on his neck was so close to her lips that she could taste it.

That was why he was so irritating to her. She was so attracted to him that she forgot herself when she got too close. And despite her efforts to avoid him, he always popped up when she least expected it. It was a conundrum. One of the few she couldn't solve.

"Now you have me wondering if you're following me around and why." He still sounded amused, and that made her want to kick him in the balls. The only thing stopping her was that he'd picked her up off the ground and was now ushering her inside the back door to his new restaurant. Hopefully, he already had a first aid kit because she could feel blood running down one of her legs. "These shoes are stupid."

"These shoes are expensive."

"And stupid." He still had ahold of one arm and she had to run on her tiptoes to keep up with him. "You're tall. I don't understand what you have against flat shoes."

She hated when he noticed things about her. It meant that she couldn't keep up the lie that he didn't really see her and that's why he'd been indifferent to her charms all those years ago. "Do you have Band-Aids?"

A muscle in his neck ticked, and the corner of his mouth rose as he gave her a sidelong glance. He grunted, and when they got to the kitchen, he picked her up—like she was nothing, and she was not nothing because she was tall—and placed her on the counter.

Even though he was manhandling her, he was very gentle about it. She couldn't appreciate that. Wouldn't allow herself to appreciate that. But it was hard when she was busy trying not to appreciate the way his ass looked when he bent over to rifle through a cabinet across from where she was sitting. It was difficult not to appreciate how gentle he'd been with her when his white T-shirt, the expensive kind that you bought already looking broken in, stretched across the muscles of his back.

He'd gotten bigger since the divorce, but not in the dad-bod way one might have expected. The same thing happened with some of her clients. They realized that they'd have to go out and date again if they wanted to find someone new to have sex with, so they got trainers, did keto, and lifted heavy things. As though being hard on the outside could stifle any of the vulnerability that getting a divorce had exposed in their bodies.

A lot of the women starved themselves, and Alex had more than once had to have a talk about disordered eating with a client. Divorce was hard enough without being hungry the whole time.

Alex wondered if Will worked out because his failed marriage made him seem soft. Knowing him, he wouldn't have thought about it much. If he'd no longer had his woman in bed with him to occupy his morning—she hated thinking about him with his wife, and she hated that she hated thinking about it—he would use that energy someplace else.

When he straightened and turned back to her, she said, "You look good," before she could stop herself. He kept advancing, and she had to crane her neck up to meet his gaze, which was still amused until he looked down and saw the wicked scrape on her knee. Then he scowled.

Something at her center clenched. She must have flinched and squeezed her legs together because Will put his hand on her thigh.

He'd never done that before. They'd never had the kind of flirty relationship that made a hand on the thigh appropriate—even though that kind of relationship was the only thing that Alex had wanted that first summer. Back then, every single punch on the shoulder had sent her spiraling through fantasies of what it would have been like to press her whole body against Will's.

For more than a decade, she'd ruthlessly cut off thoughts about Will's body. Why couldn't she ignore them now? Maybe it was because he'd made himself truly unavailable by getting married and now he was divorced. And now that she was having a moment of vulnerability, a scintilla of uncharacteristic emotion, she was open to those dangerous, useless feelings again.

"You really did a number on this knee." He crouched down to inspect her injury. Alex tried not to gasp out loud. His motions mimicked one of her favorite fantasies about Will—the one involving him crouching in front of her, spreading her thighs, and eating her out.

The power with which her adolescent crush on Will Harkness still affected her should have shocked her. She'd wanted Will for longer than she'd wanted anything—even though she'd done her best to put her feelings for him out of her mind while he was married. This storm he stirred up inside her wasn't a surprise to her body, even after all this time. He showed a moment of tenderness toward her that wasn't incidental to his love for Lexi and she was ready to fall back with her legs open.

If they didn't have such a complicated history—if she didn't know that opening her legs to Will would definitely lead to her opening her heart to him—she would be even more tempted to make a pass at him. But she knew that he would turn her down. He didn't think of her that way. She was like a sister to him. He'd technically been her step-uncle the last time she'd made a pass.

She'd kissed him, and he'd called her a weird little pervert.

And she was definitely having perverted thoughts about him now, even as he sprayed antiseptic across her knee. It made her flinch, but she was focused on the dark strands of his hair. She wanted to reach down and thread her fingers through it. It looked like it might be damp.

Her face heated with the thought that she was getting turned on when he was doing just a minimal act of kindness.

But it was more than minimal. He could have made her limp into the kitchen under her own power and slid the first aid kit across the counter for her to fend for herself. He didn't have to be on his knees, fixing her up himself.

"Why are you doing this for me?" Usually, he would have been so frustrated by her presence that he'd just let her bandage her knee herself.

It was their pattern.

He looked up at her, and she struggled to breathe. He was so close, and the part of her that was shoving the teenage crush hormones into her body wanted him to say something like "I want you desperately."

But he didn't say anything close to that. "Lexi would murder me if I let you bleed out on my watch."

Alex rolled her eyes, and Will grunted at her. She would not think about how much she'd thought about his different flavors of grunts. And she would not reach out to brush the tips of her fingers through his beard. The beard was making her feral.

At seventeen, he'd had no beard. Just a jaw that would have been at home on a quarterback but instead found itself on a boy who liked to read and cook. Who didn't even check her out in a gross way when she wore a tiny bikini around Lexi's pool.

Maybe Lana was right and she had a truly fucked-up attachment style. That was the only way to explain her reaction to Will today. Or maybe it was because seeing Will next to Andrew had knocked something loose in her.

She'd never let Will meet anyone she'd dated. And maybe that was because she knew that she'd never felt the rush of chemistry with any of them that she'd felt just being around Will. Even the ones she'd really liked and contemplated keeping around for a while.

Obviously, she'd been making good choices. Then.

Now she'd made the very poor choice of coming to see Will. Except, instead of figuring out what Andrew had said about her, she was sitting on a kitchen counter and Will was touching her.

"All done."

Alex looked down and saw that her knee was indeed bandaged. It still throbbed, but that was her own fault for wearing stupid shoes.

"Thank you." Even though Will didn't like her and there was nothing she could do to change that, she was going to remember her manners. Lexi would definitely hear about this, and Alex hated feeling like Will was her favorite, even though he was.

"You're welcome." She expected him to move away from her, but he surprised her and leaned in. His arms caged her on the counter, and she couldn't move. If he leaned in, just a little bit, he could kiss her. She allowed herself to think about him kissing her for the first time in years. A hot flush worked its way through her blood, and she could feel the pulse beating in her neck. "Now, what are you doing here?"

The hostile edge in his voice was like a bucket of cold water. He had to know that he affected her on a physical level. And he was using it to get her goat.

"What did Andrew say about me?"

Will's nostrils flared. "He didn't say anything about you. Because I was there about a possible show, and that isn't any of your business." He sighed and looked to the heavens. "Since when do you care about what your exes say to me about you?"

"Since you're having meetings with them."

A vein in Will's forehead popped out, and Alex tried not to delight in it. After he'd rejected her brutally, she'd started to get her thrills by pissing him off. She was glad that the weird touching thing had stopped and they were back to hating each other.

"You liked that guy." He didn't ask it as a question, but it was a question when Will was anything less than emphatic.

"Why do you care?" Alex was this close to pushing Will away and stomping out. He couldn't both crowd her and treat her indifferently. He didn't get to turn her on, reject her, and then critique her choices.

"I'm seriously thinking about doing a show with him, and I don't want to work with anyone that you're involved with." He made it sound like it would be distasteful if anyone wanted to be involved with her.

"Well, you don't have to worry about that. He's married to someone else." She looked away, and Will sighed.

"Why are sniffing around your married ex?" He moved away from her then and crossed his big arms across his chest. "You're better than that, Alex."

The idea that he thought she was better than that, but still not good enough for him, said a whole lot that she didn't have time to get into. She didn't have the time, in this moment, to think about the fact that it was vitally important that he know that she was very much not involved with a married man.

"I'm not involved with him, and I'm not looking to get involved with him." She cleared her throat and sat up a little straighter. "Married men are a very complicated luxury that I have no time for or interest in."

Will huffed out a breath, and she remembered why it bothered her that he was still hanging around a decade after his dad and Lexi split up. "You're seriously thinking about doing a show with him?"

He looked at her for a long moment. He was sort of like a troll with his secrets. She wondered if she would have to solve some sort of riddle for him to be honest with her. Sometimes waiting him out helped, so she tried that.

This time, it worked. He didn't like it when she stared at him like he was a bug on the sidewalk in the summer sun—with curiosity and dread. "My publicist thinks it would be good for the restaurant. She's gone on and on about the number of places that fail within the first year."

"She's right, and you should listen to her." Alex had concerns about Will putting himself even more in the public eye, however. Given that he wasn't great about letting people into his life in general, he seemed to be the last person who would do a reality television show. She'd been shocked enough when he started posting live videos from his kitchen. "But you realize that you would have to do more than grunt occasionally. It would involve actual talking."

Will looked away from her. "That's why I wasn't going to tell you. You don't get it."

"What don't I get?" Alex hopped off the counter and walked toward Will. "I've known you for longer than anyone else in this town, and I've never known you to be open about your feelings." Except that one time when he'd been a little too open about how he felt about her.

"Why did you have a meeting with Andrew?" He really wasn't going to let this go, was he?

"I was trying to figure out why he dumped me."

EIGHT

WILL JUST STARED AT THE WOMAN IN HIS KITCHEN FOR a long moment. The Alex he knew would never even care why someone as insignificant as a man didn't want to date her. She had more important things to do and think about. She always had.

One of the many things that had bothered him about seeing her sitting in Andrew's office, smiling at him, was that Will couldn't see them together in the first place. He didn't like rolling that idea around in his brain, the idea that that guy had gotten to touch her in a way she would never allow from Will.

It was the only thing that had kept him from indulging his usually deeply buried fantasies about Alex while he'd been tending to her injuries. Alex was usually careful not to be alone with him. Especially after she'd kissed him, and he'd rejected her.

"Why would you be interested in anything that stupid?" As

soon as Will said the words, he knew they were a mistake. Just like the things he'd said at the end of that first summer. He could see the hurt bloom on her like a plant that only unfurled itself at night.

"It's really none of your business." Will thought she meant to sound angry, but the words didn't have heat. They echoed in the empty kitchen.

"I shouldn't have said—"

"There are a lot of things you shouldn't have said." Alex turned from him, and he stopped himself from following her. They didn't have the kind of relationship that would allow him to turn her body into his. They didn't even really have a relationship, except the one that was mediated through Lexi's presence. They were both moons to Lexi's planetary gravity, and it would mean something had gone very wrong if they actually touched. "You know, I've changed my mind. You'd be great on a reality show, because you're so good at saying the thing that makes other people angry."

"You're the only person that I make angry on a regular basis, and I think that's mostly just my face."

She turned and looked over her shoulder at him with a narrowed gaze. "Your face is extremely punchable."

That was more like it. She hadn't seemed like herself for a few minutes there—as though the fall had shaken her normal surly attitude loose. He wasn't sure what to do with a soft, vulnerable Alex. It turned something inside him upside down, and he knew that he wouldn't be able to stifle the urge to protect her if he saw too much of her soft side. And that was aside from the fact that he'd spent fifteen years wanting to see only her soft side. It was never just teenage hormones. Alex was inimitable. There was a fire inside her that drew him in like a beacon. But he knew that he would get burned if he allowed himself to get too close.

Because all men were drawn to Alex. It wasn't just because she was gorgeous. From her crown of glossy waves to the tips of her pointy—treacherous—shoes, she was built perfectly for him. She was tall and curvy, with skin that seemed to glow from within. She hated when people said it—he didn't know why—but she looked like a picture of Lexi in her youth all grown up.

It was almost impossible to meet Alex Turner and not walk away with a huge crush. The first time he'd met her, he'd barely spoken. She'd talked so fast and had so much to say that he was terrified of stumbling over his words. He'd also been a teenage boy, and his mind had wandered to the possibility of her bikini top slipping off. And then, when she'd flitted off to a party with one of her friends, he'd spent hours thinking about how she must have thought that he was an idiot.

The idea that she would wonder why a man had dumped her was stupid. The only reason that a man would dump Alex Turner was that it finally became clear to him that she was way too good for him.

"I can't believe you went out with that guy."

Her eyes flashed with something that looked familiar—anger—and that filled him with satisfaction. Anything that brought the Alex he knew back was worth the price he would pay in her disdain for him.

"Why not?"

Will stopped to think, knowing that it would drive Alex nuts. Instead of answering right away, he walked away from her, toward the walk-in fridge. He knew that he had food that Alex would enjoy in there. And she was a lot less mean to him when she wasn't hungry.

The clip-clop of her heels on the tile floor told him that she followed him. He let her watch him as he picked out four eggs, some herbs, cheese, milk, and some pastry dough that he'd made yesterday. People would try anything if you wrapped it in pastry dough, and he was testing a meat pastie with an Italian twist for the menu.

"I'm not hungry."

He looked at her then. "I heard your stomach growling when I was fixing your knee."

Her fingers twitched. He liked that. It told him that she wasn't as unaffected by him as she tried to appear all the time. He knew what he'd done at the end of that long-ago summer. He'd wounded her pride. All along, he'd known that she wouldn't want to be with him if she really knew him. He was just someone new. A novel toy to play with. Even back then, Alex had known that boys liked her. He hadn't been willing to be discarded, so he'd pushed her away.

And he'd been paying for it ever since. But it was way too late to do anything about it at this point.

"Fine. But I'm not staying long enough for you to make anything."

Will shrugged. "I have to eat before my sous chef gets here, or I'll be too hungry to taste anything objectively."

It was partially true. He'd pushed himself hard during his workout this morning. And it wasn't because he was thinking about Alex and that Andrew guy. He needed protein before getting to work or they'd end up with some truly wild things on the menu.

He found a bowl and cracked some eggs into it, and Alex finally sat down. She was only ever nice to him when he was feeding her. He turned to chopping onions, and he could feel her gaze on his hands. He loved that she was so lusty about food. It was one of the many things he didn't allow himself to think about very often.

Lexi was the only family he acknowledged, and Alex was her most precious thing. If anything happened between them, if Alex got hurt, Lexi would cut him out without a spare thought. And, according to his ex, he couldn't sustain a relationship with anyone because he had the communication skills of a stump.

But sometimes just waiting someone out worked. Like now. Alex wouldn't let a silence go unfilled forever. "Jason getting married has me all fucked up."

"That fucking guy?" Will liked Jason even less than he liked Andrew. There was something smarmy and disingenuous about the guy, and he'd always felt like he'd dated Alex more because of her connection with Lexi than because of any affection for Alex. Lexi was never that keen on Jason, other than saying how attractive he was. But after talking about his appearance, Lexi had sniffed and stabbed at the filet mignon Will had prepared. The emphasis of the stabbing had told him all he'd needed to know about Jason.

"So?" Will didn't understand why she was so upset about this. Alex had also made her feelings on marriage extremely clear. Practically the third thing he'd learned about Alex Turner was that she didn't believe in marriage. It wasn't until later—after meeting her father—that he'd learned why. "You weren't going to marry him."

"He was on *Say Yes to the Dress*."

"What the fuck is *Say Yes to the Dress*?"

Alex slapped the stainless steel worktable. "You've never seen it?"

Will shrugged. He was not a man who looked down on stuff coded as girly or gay. He loved *Real Housewives* and *Drag Race*, partially because Lexi had introduced him to them and partially because they were really fucking entertaining. But a show about saying yes to dresses would never have piqued his interest. He liked nice clothes but wasn't terribly interested in dresses.

"It's about wedding dresses. Jason's fiancée was on there, picking out her wedding dress and talking about how romantic her story with Jason was."

"And this bothers you why?" Alex had never seemed bothered by a breakup before. After all, if relationships were a scam, then why would you be upset if you willingly signed up for a scam, knowing what it was, and it eventually ended?

"I didn't know why it bothered me until I started doing research and realized that it's definitely a pattern that guys seem to get married or get into committed relationships right after we break up."

"You don't want to get married, so I still don't see why this bothers you." The only time they'd ever gotten into a real fight—something that wasn't just them sniping at each other when they were both at Lexi's house—was right before his wedding. Alex had never said anything about him getting married other than a mumbled "Congratulations." He'd found out that she thought he was making a huge mistake when she'd barged into Lexi's kitchen—not knowing he was there—yelling about why people got married when it was logically the dumbest thing they could do with their lives and their money.

Will had never been tempted to shake someone so much.

"Maybe it's because you're not nice to them?"

Alex scowled at him. "What's with men? Expecting women to be nice to them. Women are brought up to expect no one being nice to them—maybe ever."

"That's kind of a generalization, don't you think?"

Then she crossed her arms over her chest and he knew he was about to get the business. He secretly kind of loved the business when it came from Alex. He should probably take a look at that, but he was going to enjoy it first.

"Little girls are taught that little boys are mean to them because they like them—"

"That was never the problem with you and me. I never liked you."

"Shut up." She held up a hand. "You were not a little boy when we met. You were a teen boy. And teen girls are taught that cishet teen boys are the monsters in the bushes, because they are." She paused for a moment. "Present company excluded."

There she was with the thing again, but she was not going to be deterred. "We're not even taught to expect that other girls will be nice to us because we have to be mean to each other to establish supremacy so that the monsters in the bushes will be nice when they're trying to use us to establish supremacy. And we're not even getting to the part where I talk about what little girls who aren't white are taught to expect."

Will didn't know what to say so he made a soft noise in the back of his throat. He hated the idea of anyone being mean to Alex—except for him. And that was always because she said something bitchy or called him dumb for getting married. But he would never put that into actual words. It would shift the dynamic between them irrevocably.

Luckily, Alex didn't seem to notice that he hadn't actually said anything. "It's fine. All of this shit—race, gender, class—all of it is a social construct. We literally made it all up. Of course, it has significance in almost every aspect of our lives. But remembering that it's all just a story that we tell ourselves about who we are is a good way to stay sane."

"Then why do you care if every guy you've ever dated gets serious with someone else after they date you?" The Alex he knew would never have cared about why someone didn't want to be in her life anymore. One of the many things he admired about her was her ability to just move on.

She looked at him, blinking a few times, as though she couldn't believe he'd put together that many words about feelings. "Because it has significance, Will. It's not important, but it also is."

Will turned over that thought in his mind for a few moments. "I have no idea what that means."

But just because he didn't know what it meant, that didn't mean he was going to let her confront all her exes. At least not alone.

NINE

HOW DID YOU GET ALL OF THIS INFORMATION SO FAST?"
Jane had really come through with her research skills. Alex
was now in possession of the addresses, home values, and current
marital status—and a few criminal records—of every person
she'd dated since her sophomore year in college. "I didn't really
need all this information. I'm only going to talk to, like, five of
them."

Jane shrugged. "I'm still dating the fuckboy, so my assistant
had some time on their schedule this week."

"You do realize that this is the stuff that exposés about bad
bosses are made of, right?" Alex knew her friend was ride or die,
but she didn't want to read about how she'd had her assistants
spying on her friends' exes when they should be trying to develop
their careers.

"If I get in trouble, you'll get me out of it. I have faith in you." That made Alex feel good about their friendship.

"You do realize that I can't represent you in a civil suit."

"My assistants don't know that." It was a real sign of Jane's power that she had two assistants—like Miranda Priestly in *The Devil Wears Prada*. "Why do you think I can get away for lunch so often? And no one interrupts us? They just think you're my lawyer and I need to meet with you once a week."

"And the fact that you return to the office two martinis deep?"

"They think that you're giving me bad news."

Jane had gotten away from the office and her very detailed assistant today so that they could track down the first ex on the list. Jane had called her and told her which exes she was willing to visit with her based on neighborhood and traffic patterns. There was no way that Jane was going to get on the 405 to visit any exes who lived in Long Beach or Hermosa Beach, but she hadn't gotten to drive her new car on the PCH. Brody lived in Malibu, so they'd decided to crank up the soundtrack to *The O.C.* and make it a beach day.

On the way, they were picking up Lana, who said that she wouldn't miss this fucking disaster for the world—and had saved a very special edible for the occasion.

Jane pulled up to the Venice bungalow Lana shared with her husband and three kids. Truly a great house that Lana and Greg had painstakingly restored. It would be a real shame if they ever got divorced. Alex would have to take the house away from Greg—a genuinely nice guy. And Alex would lose the one-tenth of one percent of her that still believed in true love.

Lana walked out of her house, looking like she'd just left the set of a Nancy Meyers movie—sort of like a young Meryl Streep with giant tatas and a smile that only legal pot and a reliable nanny could put on a mother's face.

"Your boobs look amazing." Jane never said anything but the truth. "Like we need to get some pictures of them for your future Raya profile."

"One hundred percent," Alex agreed. "Your body is rocking."

Lana got in the back seat of Jane's Audi. Once she closed the door, she sighed. "You two are sure good for the ego of a woman who hasn't gone to the bathroom alone in five years."

Alex winced. Almost everything any person she respected said made parenthood seem mostly horrific. It would also require her making a long-term commitment to a partner. She definitely didn't picture doing parenthood alone, like her mother had. Of course, her mother had had a village of sorts to help—namely, Lexi. But Alex couldn't imagine doing the job of modern parenthood, which seemed to require a lot more than it had in, say, the seventies, all alone.

"We're going to have so much fun today." Jane ignored the comment about going to the bathroom alone. It had sometimes brought up some tension in their friendship that Jane had no interest in the existence of children. According to her, humans were a scourge on the planet, and we would all be better off if we stopped reproducing immediately. She tended to just lightly gloss over any mention of Lana's children.

For the most part, Lana ignored it. But today, she couldn't seem to pull it off. Perhaps it was the marked lack of a car seat or crumbs littering Jane's back seat. "I really need to keep a hand vacuum in my car."

"I like to keep it clean in case I need to get busy in the back seat." Jane said. "I even have a little sex toy go-bag in the trunk."

"I am definitely doing life wrong if I'm tracking down exes instead of improving my life with things like 'sex toy go-bags.'" They were about to go see her ex who taught yoga for a living, and Alex was stressed-out by how many missed opportunities she'd had because she failed to carry a vibrator in her car. She'd probably be a whole lot less stressed-out with that go-bag. Speaking of which, Alex turned to Lana in the back seat. She might have had to pee in front of her children, but she appeared to be pretty calm now. "Do you have any more of that edible?"

Lana rolled her eyes and dug into the front pocket of her purse. She broke off a corner of a brownie and offered it to Alex.

"You remembered that I don't like fruity pot candy. Thanks, Mom!"

Lana smiled a dreamy smile at her. "You know I always take care of my girlies."

Forty minutes of PCH traffic later, Alex was glad that she'd eaten the edible. She couldn't feel anything below her neck, and Jane swearing at all the "fucking idiots trying to get us killed" didn't really bother her at all.

Alex knew she had a glassy look in her eyes like she'd just spent a lot of time in the ashram before they pulled up to the place. It was actually quite beautiful. She'd met Brody when Lexi had talked her into having a yoga retreat at the ashram for her twenty-first birthday. She'd never let it be said that her grandmother was anything but a genius. By paying to rent the ashram for a day, Lexi was prevented from having to supervise the cleanup of any vomit.

However, Alex had been bound and determined to participate in some kind of debauchery that weekend. And she'd noticed Brody right away. Looking at him now, nearly a decade later, she wanted to give her younger self a high five. Brody was long and whipcord lean. He padded across the studio floor with catlike grace.

And then he smiled, and it was no wonder younger Alex had found him incredibly sexy. She suddenly felt strange and out of place wearing a tank and flip-flops and showing up with her two friends—one of them high enough to be totally absorbed in reading the pamphlets in the lobby.

Brody looked at her as though they'd never met. "We don't have another class until three—"

Alex opened her mouth, but Jane interjected. "Actually we're here to see you." She extended her hand. "I'm Jane Lowry."

Brody's entire face changed in that moment. Jane wasn't famous among the general public, but she was definitely a celebrity among denizens of Los Angeles who wanted to be actors. "Oh shit! Did you see my reel? Are you here to offer me rep?"

This wasn't the first time this had happened to Jane in public. She'd had starlets follow her into bathrooms to slip her a flash drive—something she'd assured Alex wasn't a sex thing. Jane didn't miss a beat when she said, "Um, no. I'm actually here with her." Jane pointed at Alex.

Brody turned his attention back to Alex. "Are you an agent, too?"

"No, I'm actually—we—um—sort of dated for a while." Alex didn't have to search for words very often. It was new thing. "Alex Turner."

To Brody's credit, he recovered quickly. "Alex." Brody walked toward her with open arms. "What gives me the pleasure of your company today?"

And then Alex remembered exactly why she'd stopped finding Brody sexy. He had this weird habit of moving around words in sentences that made them sound just a little bit off. She hated that she judged him for that, and they'd broken up because she'd felt bad about judging him.

When he enveloped her in a sweaty, sweaty hug, she remembered another thing—he smelled like patchouli, and Alex hated patchouli. The hug lingered for a really long time, until it got awkward. When Alex tried to pull away, Brody just held her tighter.

So Alex just stood there, being hugged by an aesthetically attractive if sweaty man for what had to be three minutes. She would never get the smell of patchouli out of this top. She'd probably have to burn it.

She was contemplating industrial detergent when Brody finally pulled back. "How long has it been, my lotus flower?"

Gag. Alex wanted to gag. He was still touching her and growing less attractive by the second. Of all the culturally appropriative trash to spew—

"It's been about a decade." Alex stepped back then, firmly into her own space. Who knew that a yoga teacher could harsh her buzz so quickly and effectively? She hoped that Lana had more of that edible for their beach time. "So, I hear you got married."

Brody had looked as though he'd been about to launch into

some wellness influencer diatribe about time and space and quantum mechanics and manifesting, but that caught him short. "Um—"

"Right after we broke up, you got married." It wasn't strictly a question, but Brody had always had the habit of treating all questions as open-ended. Alex sometimes encountered that in depositions, so she'd learned to phrase yes/no questions as though they were declarative statements.

Except that tactic seemed to blow out a few circuits in Brody's brain. "I'm . . . I'm not sure—"

Then Jane cleared her throat. "Brody, we're on our way to the beach, but Alex is having a crisis because all of her exes have a strange habit of committing their lives to someone almost immediately after she breaks up with them. We're trying to figure out if Alex is simply a rehab for broken men or they are so scarred from their time with her that they cling to the next person they meet like a life raft."

Brody's gaze widened, and he leaned back farther out of Alex's space. "That's some wild, cosmic shit."

"I know," Alex said, trying to memorize Jane's concise summary of her personal quest.

"Well, I did get married, like, spiritually, right after we broke up." Brody shook his head. "But I never thought you had anything to do with it before."

"But you can't know that I have nothing to do with it."

Brody held up a hand. "This is a lot, my little half-Nubian queen." Oh God, that was worse than the lotus flower thing. "I think we should meditate on it."

"I have cabana reservations." Jane never sounded whiny, but she kind of sounded whiny.

"Can I take another bite of edible first?" Alex did not want to meditate sober, that was for sure.

"Groovy." Brody took both of their hands and led them to the meditation room. They grabbed Lana along the way. She smiled beatifically.

Yeah, Alex definitely needed more edibles.

Alex was not a woo-woo person. She tolerated a certain level of woo-woo because of Lexi, and she understood why people believed, because her mother studied anthropology with an emphasis on religious practices. But she wasn't a believer.

She still did yoga for exercise, but that was for her lower back and tension headaches—not her spiritual well-being.

Sure enough, Brody's meditation room had all the woo-woo trappings. But since she'd come here looking for answers and not a discourse, she kept her mouth shut.

Jane and Lana told her that they were on the same page without saying a word. But they were good sports about it and sat on the cushions that Brody indicated. Alex sat across from Brody in front of an altar, and he took her hands.

"You said you had questions. We all have questions, Alex. But seeking answers on an earthly plane when the spiritual—the sexual—plane is more likely to have answers is a dangerous game."

"I just want to know why you think we didn't work out." Alex's regret grew every moment that Brody stared at her. When she was twenty-one, it had felt like he was staring into her soul. At this point, it was just uncomfortable.

"Thinking is overrated." Brody's voice was laced with frustration. "That was why we broke up."

"Because I think too much?" Alex fought really hard not to look over at Lana and Jane, whom she could hear fidgeting and trying to contain their laughter.

"No, lotus flower, it's because you believe your thoughts."

"Of course I believe my thoughts. They are rarely wrong." Alex wasn't arrogant enough to believe that she was always right. But she knew for a fact that she could figure out most problems with little help from anyone else. That's how she'd survived her entire life.

"But you act like they're never wrong, and I need to be with someone who is more open to the world's wonders. Being with you made me realize that I was playing small and being held hostage by my own limiting beliefs."

"Wow." Alex wasn't quite sure what else to say. He really made her seem like an obstacle to his personal growth.

"Yeah, like, you were just so locked into how you thought the world worked, and so closed off to any other possibilities, that I just didn't see us going very far. You never let me in."

Well, shit. That would explain why things didn't work out. "You know. This has been incredibly enlightening."

Alex made moves to get up off the cushion and leave, but Brody stopped her. "I think we should sit with this for a while."

Feeling bad for interrupting his day, she felt obligated to sit back down.

———

P lease tell me that he was the only yoga teacher you've ever dated," Jane said as soon as they got into the car.

Lana leaned up between the seats. "Does he always make that really intense eye contact?"

"Yeah, kind of." Alex hadn't really noticed it when they were dating, but he was really intense about being laid-back. And he'd hated how wound up she got about small things, like politics or a rude driver who cut her off. In turn, she'd hated how lackadaisical Brody was about important things, like having a real apartment in his name so he wasn't sleeping on his friends' couches even though he had a pillowcase full of cash or whatever the Venmo equivalent of that was.

But she hadn't noticed the intense eye contact thing as a problem until he'd practically dragged her into the meditation room at the ashram, with her friends tagging along behind, and told her to stare into his eyes for the answers to why they hadn't worked out.

It had taken her about a minute, but she'd given him fifteen. After barging in on him, it seemed more polite than running out on him so she could have a beach day.

"Did he even do it during sex?" Of course that was Jane's question.

Alex thought back to having sex with Brody. That part she'd liked. He certainly hadn't been lackadaisical about finding her clit, although she'd had to sit through a lot of lectures on whatever fake, exploitative form of Tantra he pretended to practice so she could come.

Those lectures came with a lot of eye contact. "Yeah, he would gaze deeply into my eyes while we were fucking."

"I mean, that's when you only let him hit it from behind." That came from Lana, and Jane and Alex just looked at each other in silent delight at Lana's rare sex joke.

"C'mon, I can make a sex joke, too. I'm married, not dead." Lana sat back and buckled her seat belt so that Jane could point the car toward the beach.

Jane peered at Lana through the rearview mirror and gave Alex a worried glance before turning her attention back to the road. The glance said that they were going to be taking an Uber home—one of Jane's assistants would come to collect hers— because there would be a need for many, many margaritas once they got to the beach house Jane's client had loaned them for the day.

TEN

WILL WAS FAIRLY CERTAIN THAT HE SHOULDN'T BE IN-terfering with Alex's quest to find out why she was the secret sauce in getting all her exes married off, but he felt partially responsible. After all, he'd rejected her so harshly and decisively that—along with the benign neglect from her parents and watching Lexi cycle through men like underwear—she'd given up on love.

It was probably a sign that his ego was out of control that he thought he'd had anything to do with Alex's fucked-up-ness. He probably shouldn't be thinking about her fucked-up-ness at all, because he had plenty of his own.

But he still pulled up to Lexi's house planning to tell her about Alex's stupid search for answers. He didn't know why Lexi had kept him as part of her family after cutting his father out, but he was grateful. Will had known that Lexi was way too much woman for his father before they'd gotten married. And he had liked Lexi so much upon meeting her that he'd told her as much before the wedding.

Lexi had winked at him and ruffled his hair, even though Will had been too old to have his hair ruffled. But Lexi had treated him like the boy he still very much was and folded him into her heart—like she did with all her strays.

It was heartening and sometimes frustrating to show up at Lexi's house and find new people there. She was extremely open to new people and new experiences, and Will worried that those new people and new experiences would harm her. Lexi had protected him from his parents when he was young, and he felt responsible for protecting her now, as she grew older.

Too bad Lexi wasn't really amenable to being protected.

When he walked into her living room, she was hanging upside down from pieces of cloth that were tied to the dark wooden beams that crisscrossed her ceiling. Her eyes were closed and somehow her legs were crossed.

She looked much younger than she probably was, and very peaceful even though she could fall on her head and break her neck at any moment. Didn't people's bones get brittle with age?

Will had tried to figure out how old Lexi was at some point, but he was never able to get a definitive answer. Her Wikipedia page wasn't helpful, and no one had ever seen her driver's license. Accounts in the media weren't helpful because different news articles said she was different ages when she'd left Chicago to move to LA, where she'd parlayed her singular jazz voice into movie stardom with a large side of political activism.

Lexi never corrected anyone when they said how old she was.

She'd once told him that it was because she considered herself ageless.

Will thought she was deluding herself and needed to be more careful.

"What are you doing?"

Lexi's eyes snapped open, and she smiled at him. From his angle, it looked like a frown, though. "Aerial yoga. Want to try?"

Will let his scowl speak for itself. He certainly wasn't going to be encouraging Lexi by joining her. "How did you get up there?"

Regardless of her agelessness, Lexi didn't need to be hanging upside down on her own, with no one to rush her to the hospital if she fell. Lexi inclined her head toward the corner of the room, and that was the first time Will noticed the man standing there. He looked to be about thirty-five, so square inside Lexi's dating age range. And he appeared to have come out of central casting for "yoga teacher."

"Can you get her down?" He motioned to the guy.

Lexi winked at him. "I'm more interested in whether he can get me off, but all the blood has rushed to my head." The man rushed over and had her out and upright with a few deft hand movements.

Lexi turned to the teacher and said with a smile that implied that she was in fact dating the man, "See you next week?"

"We'll work on your camel pose and your second chakra then." And then he walked out the back door.

Will shook his head and took a seat on the couch. Lexi drifted over to the wet bar and poured them both large glasses of water from a jug that had lemon slices and green stuff floating around in it.

"Where do you find these guys?" he asked as Lexi handed him a glass.

She just waggled her eyebrows at him, and he figured it was probably better that he didn't know.

"You're so busy with that new restaurant that you never have time to come see me in the middle of the day." She arranged herself on the sofa opposite him. "This must be important."

"It's about Alex—"

"You're finally going to make a move?" Lexi clapped her hands together and was about to launch herself off the couch and into a happy dance if he didn't put the kibosh on this. Although not wanting to harm his relationship with Lexi was one of the main reasons he had turned Alex down flat when they were teenagers, Lexi persisted in the belief that they belonged together. Apparently, according to a fortune-teller she'd gone to see once on a trip to Vegas with an actor whom she'd only described as "not nearly as bad at poker or as good in bed as the tabloids would lead you to believe," Alex and Will were destined to be together.

Perhaps they were destined to orbit around each other and annoy the fuck out of each other, but they were not destined to be a romantic match. Alex was a cold fish, and no one but a saint could stand to live with Will—at least to hear his ex-wife tell it. Even if they did date, they would break up. And Alex would get to keep Lexi, because she was blood.

Lexi was already doing a fist-pumping thing, which looked sort of elegant only because it was Lexi, when he stopped her cold. "No. I'm worried about her."

That made Lexi turn into Alex's grandmother again instead of her matchmaker. Although Lexi had been pretty laissez-faire with curfews and underage drinking under her roof, she did not mess around when it had to do with Alex's safety.

"What did she get herself into this time?" Lexi's question made it sound as though Alex was perpetually getting herself into trouble, when it was truly the woman asking the question who needed to be extricated from sticky situations more often. "She's always doing things the safe way, but it's not the safe way, if you know what I mean?"

"I have no idea what you mean half the time, but she's not doing things the safe way now." And then he told her about Alex's plan to go talk to all her exes about why they'd broken up and why they'd locked down the next person to cross their paths.

"Oh, she's definitely lost it, but I think it's delightful. She's finally doing something that doesn't make sense."

Will fought the urge to stand up and stomp around the living room. His ex had hated when he'd done that in the middle of a fight. He didn't know why, but when he was feeling angry, he needed to move and not stay still and talk.

But he wasn't really angry with Lexi. He was more frustrated that she couldn't see how silly and risky this endeavor was. "What's the point of all this? Alex doesn't want to get married."

He left out the part about how Alex didn't want to get married—in part—because she didn't want to end up getting divorced a bunch of times, like Lexi, but the older woman was shrewd. "I'm picking up what you're throwing down here, but I think it's good that she's doing something illogical."

"How is that a good thing?"

Lexi took a deep breath and looked at her water glass as though she wished it would turn into vodka. "I did the best I could do as a mother, and I failed."

Will opened his mouth to defend her, given that she'd given him at least double the mothering the woman who'd birthed him had, but Lexi put a hand up.

"I failed, and Alex's father was a shitty human being. He could never, ever take responsibility for his actions, and that was my fault. It was the seventies and eighties and we were all trying to instill children with self-esteem instead of telling the truth."

Alex's father hadn't been around much the summer Will had come to Lexi's house. He hadn't asked many questions about the man's whereabouts because it hadn't been any of his business. Later he'd learned that Alex spent her summers with Lexi because her father was too busy to care for her while her mother was doing research abroad. Will could relate. It didn't seem like either of his parents had put much thought into what kind of time and effort it took to raise children before having him. And he'd have been pawned off on relatives, had either of his parents kept in touch with theirs.

He'd always been able to empathize with the lost quality he sometimes sensed about Alex. Because he felt lost, too.

But feeling lost as an adolescent was no excuse for the kind of unhinged mission Alex was on. "What does Alex's father have to do with the fact that Alex is running all over town interrogating her exes?"

"Why are you so upset about what she's doing? It's not as though you're anything but unwilling acquaintances at this point."

Lexi took another sip of water and smiled at him like the cat that caught the canary. "It shouldn't matter to you what Alex does with her time and reputation."

"It's not that I care about what she does. I don't like the producer guy that I found her talking to the other day. I just don't like any of this." He couldn't name why Alex's quest made him so uncomfortable. He didn't want to.

"Jealous?"

Will did stand up then. He wasn't jealous of Andrew What's-His-Name. He ran his hand through his hair. "I'm not jealous of a guy who spends his time exploiting people's weaknesses. There's nothing to be jealous of about that. He pries open their lives and lays them open for people to pick over in public for entertainment. There's nothing to be jealous of about that."

He didn't dare look at Lexi, because he knew she'd have a shrewd look on her face. She knew that Andrew's profession didn't bother Will enough to cause this kind of agitation. There was something about thinking about that guy with Alex that made Will want to punch through a wall.

Lexi knew, but she wasn't going to say it out loud at this point. She'd always known how hard she could push with Will. When Will had come to her house, he'd been a few steps away from becoming a delinquent. He'd barely passed his classes during his sophomore year in high school because he'd rarely gone to class.

When his father had moved them into Lexi's house, Will had been half-feral and so angry that he didn't know what to do with himself. Most of that anger had been pointed inward. And he hadn't known how to handle all the light and color that Lexi brought into his life. But he knew that he didn't want to disappoint the woman who looked at him as though he was something special and precious.

He'd barely left his room the first week he'd been there. After a month, he'd let Lexi buy him some new clothes. By the time they left the store, she'd made him laugh with how people fell all over themselves to help her and her response to the "star-fuckers."

And Alex was part of all that light and color. He'd never known what to do with her. Never met anyone so self-assured at such a young age. He'd both loved and feared her. He didn't know what to do with what he felt when she was around, who lit him up inside when she laughed at something he said without realizing he'd said something funny.

When she'd kissed him—that one time before he'd put a stop to it—his whole world had shifted on its axis.

Just thinking about it now had him touching his lips.

He'd been so lost in thought that he hadn't noticed Lexi moving across the room to stand in front of him. He started when she waved her hand across his face. "She needs to know the answer."

"What answer?" Will sometimes didn't know what Lexi was talking about, but she usually had a point. He just had to wait for the point to come out. Or sometimes he had to tease it out. "The only answer she's going to get is to date better people."

Lexi clapped her hands together and threw her head back. "He finally gets it."

"You know that I'm not better people, don't you?" Will didn't know why Lexi was so interested in beating this particular dead horse, but she didn't know what she was asking for. After how things had gone down with Alex, he wouldn't even merit forgiveness, much less a chance at proving to Alex that love was worth the risk with the right person.

And he believed that, even after his divorce, mostly because of the woman standing in front of him.

"I know you don't think that you and Alex are destined to be together, and she agrees. But you're both very, very wrong." Lexi sounded so certain of this.

"If we were going to get together, it would have happened by now. Alex would have realized that none of those guys she's dated are right for her." Before Lexi could say that he was right for Alex, he said, "And I wouldn't have gotten married to someone else. We've spent enough time together to make things happen if they were going to happen."

Lexi looked at him for a long moment, with a brow as furrowed as it could get with the amount of Botox in it, before asking, "Have you ever had sex with my granddaughter?"

Will rocked back on his heels. "No."

"But you've definitely thought about it." That wasn't a question.

"Why do you care whether I've thought about sex with Alex?" He could barely get "sex" out when talking about doing it with Alex. In a conversation with Lexi. "She discards men after she has sex with them." The way to Alex Turner's heart was not through her vagina.

"But that's because she dates discardable men." Lexi finally backed off, knowing that she'd gotten to him on some level. "Like the producer."

When Will growled despite his best efforts not to, Lexi shrugged. "He's not a bad guy."

Will could admit to himself that his view of Andrew was colored by the fact that he'd dated Alex, but he wouldn't admit it aloud right now. "You need to talk to her." Will knew that Lexi was the only person Alex would listen to. If he told her to cut it out, she would blow him off. She would continue with this cockamamie plan just to spite him.

"If you think she'll listen to the old lady who keeps on getting married, you have another think coming."

"She's so stubborn."

"Comes by it honestly." Will didn't know whether Lexi was referring to herself or Alex's mother. All Alex's foremothers had a stubborn streak a mile long. Lexi put her hand on his chest affectionately. "You have such a big heart, Will. And I know you wouldn't be here if you didn't have feelings for Alex. Why aren't you going after her?"

"I can't lose you." Will had never articulated to Lexi the real reason why he would never cross that line with Alex. "When things don't work out, she'll still have you." And Will wouldn't have anyone.

Lexi put her hand on the side of his face. "You will always have me." Then, she smirked. "Well, not always. I have standing plans to get lucky every Wednesday night, and I'll pass away eventually."

"Don't talk about that, Lexi. It's morbid."

"It's the truth." She waved a hand in his face. "I'm getting better at telling the truth in my old age. At your age, you should at least not be lying to yourself."

"I'm not lying to myself about anything." Will was getting frustrated. "It would never work with me and Alex."

"So you keep saying." Lexi never gave up that easily, so Will girded his loins for more. "But if you two didn't have anything—if you didn't have a thing from when you first met here—you wouldn't care how many of her ex-boyfriends she was talking to."

"I don't care that she's talking to her exes."

"But you do care that they might get to talking, and talking might lead them to remembering that she's very beautiful and brilliant and that her tongue is sharp. Then they'll remember how she runs hot and cold, but how she runs hot in a good way, in certain respects. And maybe Alex will remember that it's sometimes nice to have a man around." Lexi walked over to the bar, heedless that it was noon. "And you'll feel really horrible then, because you will have lost your chance again."

"That's not what this is at all." Will wasn't that stupid. Even if he did have a thing for Alex, which he didn't, Alex would never, ever give him a shot. "It's too late. And I didn't come here for you to lecture me about my nonexistent feelings for Alex. I came here to tell you what she was doing so that you could talk some sense into her."

"I'm not going to talk her out of going on this journey."

"It's not a journey. It's a mental breakdown."

"Hardly. I've been waiting for her to have a mental breakdown for years. She's so wound up and doesn't know how to relax. This is far too reasonable and proactive to be a real mental breakdown."

"So what do I do?"

Lexi shrugged. "Keep tabs on her."

"You think I have time to follow her around?"

"You had time to come here and harangue an old lady about it. Or did you also come to make me lunch?"

Will sighed, knowing that this conversation had done nothing except renew Lexi's hopes that he and Alex would fall into each other's arms.

And then he went to see what Lexi had in her fridge.

ELEVEN

ALEX WAS FRUSTRATED. SHE WAS STARTING TO THINK that her extremely negative view of relationships might actually be a problem. Even though Brody was mostly full of shit, he might have had a point about her needing to look inside herself for answers.

But now her curiosity was piqued, and she wouldn't be able to stop looking at her past in order to divine how she might avoid going wrong in the future.

Today she was talking to Lyle, the dentist she'd dated after rushing Lana's oldest to his office after Lana's youngest had hit her in the face with a baseball bat while Alex was babysitting. It was the last time she'd offered her babysitting services—partially out of guilt and partially because the anxiety of being responsible for a hurt child almost gave her a heart attack.

Alex and Lyle had dated for a month. He was shorter than

Alex, but he had perfect dark, shiny hair and the nicest smile that money could buy. They'd had fun together, and she truly wasn't sure why they'd broken up. Instead of dropping in on him unannounced, she'd made an appointment with him for a cleaning. Asking him for a life update—finding out why he'd married his dental hygienist less than a year after they broke up—wouldn't be hard if it was part of idle chitchat.

She realized her mistake when she saw that the dental hygienist he'd married was still his dental hygienist and would have sharp implements next to her gums.

"Hi, I'm Gina, and I'll be cleaning your teeth today?" The woman standing in front of her was nothing like her—a bleached blonde with subtly fake boobs and a voice that went up at the end of her statement so that it sounded like she was asking a question. If someone had asked Alex to guess the woman's name, she would not have guessed Gina. She would have guessed Karen or Kayleigh or Kylie. Alex would put money on Gina owning a Pomeranian. Guessing from the color of Gina's scrubs, her nails, and her lipstick, Lyle currently had a lot of pink things in his house that he might not have bargained for when he got married.

Gina didn't recognize her name, so Lyle had probably never mentioned her. Alex was disappointed by that, even though they'd only dated for a month. And Lyle had probably never thought about her after they broke up. Alex was likely nothing more than a fond memory—if that. The fact that Lyle was one of the few guys Alex thought could have turned into something more lingered with Alex as Gina carefully and methodically removed plaque from her teeth. She was really quite skilled, and Alex had been a little nervous to go back to the dentist for a cleaning after so long.

"I really think you should get an electric toothbrush," Gina said after Alex spit out the last of the tooth polish. "It will keep your teeth cleaner between appointments."

"I'll do that," Alex said, flashing her a brilliant smile.

Gina returned the smile, and Alex decided that it didn't matter that *she* hadn't mattered enough to Lyle to mention her to his new wife. It was hard to find a hygienist who was both great at her job and didn't make you bleed, and Alex wasn't letting her go.

"I'll just grab the doctor." Gina made for the door. "There are a few spots of concern that I want him to look at."

Alex's stomach fell. She'd planned to come here and ask uncomfortable questions, not have uncomfortable dental work done. The reason she hadn't been to the dentist for a couple of years was that she was afraid of having work done. She didn't like pain—well, no one liked pain, but Alex went to great lengths to avoid it.

Maybe that was why she'd never had a successful relationship. She bailed before anything got too painful. When she thought about it, it didn't actually seem like a terrible strategy. She still got to have sex and have companionship when she wanted it, but she didn't have to deal with the pain that her clients did when things inevitably failed.

And they always failed. Even though Gina was a delightful woman and a great dental hygienist, there would come a day when Lyle looked at her and wouldn't see that. He'd only see someone who caused him pain. Or Gina would look at Lyle that way. And either they were going to be the people who could look at each other and bear the pain, or one of them would be trying to get an appointment with her.

Most people couldn't live with the pain and took the escape hatch of divorce.

Alex was thinking about how that was the ultimate in job security when Lyle walked in. Even though their relationship clearly wasn't significant enough to mention, his face told her that he hadn't forgotten about her completely.

"What are you doing here?" His voice told her that he wasn't happy to see her. In fact, the tone of the question made her question whether the windows were open, because he looked like he might like to throw her out of one.

"Having my teeth cleaned?" For the millionth time since she'd started tracking the movements and marital statuses of her exes, she questioned her own intelligence. Who did something like this? And why was she doing it?

Part of her didn't want to know the answers. She knew that trying to figure out why she was only lovable in small doses and for the short term in a romantic sense was really stupid. She should have taken Lana up on her offer of a referral to a psychologist.

"Did you say anything to her?" Lyle looked over his shoulder to ensure that no one was lingering outside the exam room. Then he closed the door. "You didn't tell her anything about us dating, did you?"

"No." Alex crossed her arms over her chest and tried to look as intimidating as possible while reclined and wearing a bib. "Why would that be such a bad thing?"

Lyle scoffed at her and reclined her seat even more. "Open wide."

Alex didn't follow instructions. She might follow the law, but she didn't always do what she was told. "Why would she care if we dated?"

"Believe me. You wouldn't have wanted her to put sharp implements anywhere near your gums if I'd told her what you did to me."

"What I did to you?" Alex asked, not believing what she was hearing. Lyle's skin had lost all of its already paltry color when she'd walked in. He'd looked as though he'd seen a ghost. Alex had assumed that he would be indifferent or mildly annoyed. "You broke up with me."

Lyle sighed, apparently resigned to giving her more information. "I only broke up with you after you destroyed my confidence completely."

Alex had no idea what he could possibly mean by that, but she opened her mouth in hopes that he would keep talking. Lyle immediately started poking around with his mirror, hitting a sensitive spot in her back molar that made her wince.

"How did I do that?" Alex asked, though it would be a miracle if Lyle understood her.

Since he talked to a lot of people with their mouths agape, he picked it up. "I was really into you, and it was like you could take me or leave me. At first, it made me want to work harder for your attention, but then it became all I could think about. I couldn't eat or sleep. If you texted me back, I was happy. If you were too busy to hang out with, I was dejected. I thought I was losing my mind."

Huh. Alex hadn't thought about his feelings that much—or maybe at all. She had thought it was annoying that he'd wanted to talk all the time. And she'd started ignoring his "good morning" texts. She hated those, because it felt like someone was trying to keep tabs on her.

She hated feeling like she had to check in with someone else. It felt like she was being controlled, and that was the one thing she couldn't tolerate.

When Lyle was done poking around her mouth, she closed it and wiped off the drool. "I'm sorry that I hurt you." Even though she hadn't been able to see a future with Lyle more than she'd been able to see a future with any of her other exes, she didn't like the idea that she'd hurt any of them.

His statements about their relationship also made her remember how she'd started to feel contempt for him before he'd broken things off. At first, it had felt sexy and fun. But as soon as they'd slept together and relieved the sexual tension, it had started to feel like Lyle was clinging.

"You didn't really hurt me long-term, but dating you made me realize that I was only going after women who thought I was trash, and that I deserved better." Lyle looked a little embarrassed to be sharing that with Alex, but she was grateful for it. This was what she'd wanted when setting out on this ridiculous quest.

Maybe she was too independent for a relationship and she needed to be even more up front about it.

"Gina is really great, Lyle."

His face softened. "She really, really is." But then his face changed when he looked back at Alex. "The bad news is that you need a filling, and you flinch enough that I'd like to use some light sedation. Is there someone who can pick you up?"

TWELVE

WILL WAS IRRITATED WITH LIFE BEFORE HE GOT A CALL
from Lexi asking him to pick up Alex from the dentist's
office. He didn't have time to leave the restaurant today. They
were only weeks from opening. But he couldn't say no to Lexi,
especially when she mentioned that the dentist was one of the
exes Alex had tracked down.

It took him about forty-five minutes to get from the restaurant
to the dentist's office. When he entered, the eyes of the woman in
pink scrubs standing behind the receptionist's desk widened. "Are
you here to pick up Alex Turner?"

Will grunted, because apparently Alex owned his time. He
wanted to deny it, but a part of him also didn't. He liked the idea
of Alex needing him, even though she claimed to need no one.

After his conversation with Lexi at her house the other day,
he'd gotten to thinking a lot about how Alex and his ex-wife were

different. At first glance, they were the same. Both of them were independent, badass women who didn't need a man to validate them. Whenever a woman had seemed like she needed him and gotten too clingy, he totally disengaged. He didn't like anyone looking at him like he was their hero. Not when he was a bad bet.

It was better if he was with a woman who could take care of herself.

He'd realized that he had chosen April because she had never seemed very emotionally invested in him. Their relationship had been convenient and definitely fun at first. Their lives meshed, and the relationship felt easy. Before they moved in together, April had never wanted to talk about feelings, and she'd never made him angry. April would have called an Uber in advance to take her home from the dentist instead of expecting him to drop whatever he was doing and pick her up.

Alex would always expect him to run to her rescue, because she wouldn't even think twice about ruining his day. And if he ever made a move on her like Lexi had apparently been waiting on him to do for years, she would most definitely ruin his life.

"Yeah, I guess that's my job today."

The blonde in the pink scrubs raised her eyebrows suggestively and looked him up and down in a way he didn't like. "It's a good thing that you're so strong."

Will had no idea what the woman meant until they entered an exam room to find a snoring, drooling Alex drooped over a dental chair. Her cheeks were puffed up and swollen, and it made her look younger—like the teenager with puppy fat in her cheeks that she'd been when they'd first met.

But she also looked vulnerable, and Will didn't like the idea that Alex was passed out in the office of one of her exes. He probably hadn't done anything untoward—he was a professional—but Alex had terrible taste in men. But he might have been tempted to make the procedure extra painful if he'd had a relationship with Alex. Will could barely keep himself from strangling her half the time, and they'd never even dated.

"What the hell happened to her?" Will hadn't meant the words to come out that harshly. The hygienist, who had introduced herself as Gina on the way back to the exam room, seemed like a nice person. "I mean, is she okay?"

Gina laughed. "She's just a little out of it. The pain was a bit much for her, and she begged to have someone just put her out of her misery. Lyle gave her a sedative before she walked out with half a filling in her molar."

Will wanted to laugh then. He would never let her forget about this. She was so invested in her self-image as a badass that being too much of a baby about pain to get a filling in her tooth was something he could needle her with for years.

He really liked the idea of teasing this woman too much. It made him feel more alive than almost anything but coming up with a new dish did. Instead of examining that thought further, he carefully picked up Alex from the exam chair, pulling her against his chest. He tucked her head inside his biceps so that he wouldn't whack it on the doorjamb.

It was hard to tell himself that she was just an annoyance, a splinter that he couldn't remove so that it had just become a part of him, when she shifted to get more comfortable. When she was in his arms, he didn't want to drop her. He wasn't annoyed that he would spend hours of his day taking care of her instead of working. He didn't want to deny that he was hers.

He ignored the look the hygienist gave him, like he was some sort of hero out of a romance novel instead of someone who couldn't seem to get rid of a splinter.

Alex didn't know where she was when she woke up, and that hadn't happened since college. But, unlike when she was in college, she wasn't sleeping on a mattress on the floor that had at best dirty sheets and at worst just stains.

No. She spread her hand out and felt the touch of linen. And when she took in a deep breath, she knew where she was immediately. The smell of Will's room hadn't changed all that much, in part due to the fact that he'd never tried to avoid actual showers by using Axe body spray as a teen.

No, after his unfortunate Drakkar Noir period, he'd always smelled like lemongrass soap and sage aftershave. His sheets smelled like him, but with the awesome scent of sheets hung out to dry on a clothesline. This was always what she hoped a man's bed smelled like. And she was often disappointed. Some of the men she'd dated—ones in their thirties—thought that it was too girly to care about their surroundings. So, they lived like college boys, on mattresses on the floor, until they got married so that a woman could take care of that.

That thought made her remember that she was in Will's bed, and Will had been married. If she hadn't known that Will had always been fastidious about his room, she would have assumed that April had introduced him to the pleasures of fine home linens and bed frames. But she hated to give April that much credit and was glad she didn't have to.

She didn't want to think about April at all, because she needed to figure out how she came to be in Will's bed. The last thing she remembered was asking Lyle for stronger drugs. And then she'd passed out.

Her mind had raced back to the day she'd gotten her wisdom teeth pulled. She'd freaked out from the moment her dentist had said that an oral surgeon had to do it, but not to worry because she'd be given a light sedative. Alex had always hated blood and pain, but the idea of having surgery done on her mouth with only a light sedative had terrified her more than she could express.

It was the summer before she'd headed off to college, and her mother hadn't been back from her trip to Cambodia yet. Her mother had been working to assist a UN commission, so it wasn't as though Alex could call her back from that to take care of her and her ouchie toothies. And her sister had been on a summer trip to Italy with her crappy boyfriend, who'd later turned into her crappy husband.

So, Alex had taken it upon herself to take a taxi to the dentist and have one of her friends' moms pretend to be her mom in order to pick her up. She'd made sure that she wasn't an inconvenience to anyone else and gotten things done.

Lying there, still groggy from whatever excellent drugs that Lyle had put her out with, Alex was mortified. Because she had certainly been an inconvenience to Will today. And even though they had little in common that wasn't the great Lexi Turner, neither of them liked to rely on other people. It was probably why they'd always repelled each other. Neither of them wanted to seem weak by having needs that they couldn't meet on their own, so they never opened up to each other in a meaningful way.

But still, because neither of them wanted to need the other one, they understood each other. And they knew that beneath the entirely self-sufficient exterior was an endless void of need. Because Alex knew that her mortification at having to rely on Will that afternoon was prompted by the fact that it was a dent in her shield. She didn't know if Will was keeping score—she only knew that she would be keeping score if the positions were reversed—but he'd patched up her scraped knee and picked her up from the dentist. He had two points up on her.

Alex strained her ears to figure out whether she was alone in Will's loft or not. She'd never been there before; she only knew that it was somewhere that had recently seen some development. She would never tell him, but she loved this place and had been happy for him when he'd purchased it after April bought him out of their house. It helped that April hated it—said it was like living in a garage—but it was so totally cool. It was in a building downtown—Alex winced again thinking about how long that drive had to have been even though it was shorter than bringing her back to her house. The building had been a laundry back in the late nineteenth century, so the ceilings were incredibly high and secured by sturdy metal beams that had withstood loads of earthquakes.

The walls were all exposed brick, and she could see to the other end of the space from the bed. The flat was totally filled with light from the huge windows, whose glass had been replaced with energy-efficient glass when they'd renovated the building.

Predictably, Will had upgraded everything in his kitchen, which she could also see from the bed. That made her think of what it would be like if she was with Will and had the right to wake up in his bed. But the apartment was empty, and Will was not poaching an egg for her while shirtless.

It was disturbing how quickly she was slipping away from her previous "Will Harkness is an irredeemable asshole" stance. Maybe because she'd spent so much time thinking about her history with men who wouldn't have picked her up from the dentist while they were dating because she didn't look pretty enough with half her face swollen.

Plus, she was sure that blow jobs were a no-no for at least a few days, and that would have been a dealbreaker for most of her exes. But thinking about that made her think about the fact that she'd never seen Will's dick. And that felt like it was too close to fantasizing about him the same way she had as a teen. There were only bad things on that route, and she would not go there. Having a crush on Will Harkness was like taking the 405 in heavy traffic. It seemed like a good idea before you saw that you were never going to get where you wanted to go, and it would take you years to even get to an exit.

She had to go to the bathroom, so she moved very slowly and gingerly. Her mouth was dry and the right side of her face throbbed every time she moved, so she knew it would be painful to rectify her thirst problem.

Although she knew that Will would never undress her while she was unconscious, she checked to make sure that she hadn't stripped in front of him and blacked it out like a sorority girl right after rush week. That would make this whole scenario even more embarrassing. Like, it would never cross his mind with any woman, but it especially wouldn't cross his mind with her.

She used his bathroom—the only closed space in the loft—and washed her hands. She ignored the urge to riffle through his clothes. He had a large metal file cabinet thing that he used as a dresser and a rack fashioned out of metal pipes. All his clothes were so neat that he'd know if she moved one shirt even a millimeter.

His kitchen was similarly ordered, with a kind of precision one did not usually find in a busy person. Not for the first time, she wondered where his neatness had come from. He had never shared much with her about his mother, and Alex hadn't taken the time to learn much about his dad. Lexi had gone through husbands really quickly in her fifties and sixties. She said that going through menopause had made her tire of their bullshit more easily.

And that made sense. Alex wasn't planning on contacting a couple of ex-boyfriends because she was convinced that she'd only been attracted to them in the first place because she'd been ovulating when they'd met. Once she'd had PMS, they started to get a whole lot more annoying.

Alex poured herself a glass of water from the tap and had to fight not to drop the glass when the liquid hit the back of her mouth. But at that moment, the pain was worth the reward. She would have gritted her teeth to get through it if the thought of gritting her teeth didn't cause a wave of pain all on its own.

She must have had a pained look on her face when Will walked through the door. His brow furrowed and he grunted at her. "What are you doing up?"

"I'm sorry." She knew she sounded pathetic, but she was always pathetic when she was in pain. "I'll get out of here as soon as I can."

Will just grunted at her again and put a grocery bag down on his stainless steel counter.

"Thank you for picking me up. I thought I told them to call Lexi. She could have just sent a car."

"Lexi was on set."

Alex felt stupid again. They both tried to keep up with Lexi's schedule because they lived with the acute knowledge that she was getting older and something might happen to her. It was one of the reasons that Alex had never considered leaving LA after law school. Lexi had been there for her, and she owed it to her grandmother to return the favor. Lexi had so many points for just opening her home to Alex that she knew she would never even the score, but she had to try.

"She could have just sent a car."

"A chauffer never would have hauled your ass up and down stairs." Will put a plastic take-out container in front of her. "Are you hungry?"

"You don't have to feed me." Alex felt like she was truly intruding at this point and made to move around the counter. Will blocked her with his body and they stared each other down for a long moment. Just like when he'd fixed up her knee the other day, there was a moment that felt like it stretched out longer than the few seconds that it had to have been. She felt as though his unfathomably dark eyes were looking straight through her. The urge to touch his face, feel the texture of his beard on her fingers if she couldn't feel it against other parts of her skin, was almost too much for her.

As much as she'd hated needing him to pick her up from the dentist, she hated the needy feeling that he stirred up in her belly even more. The last thing she needed was to feel want when she looked at Will Harkness. The only thing they had in common was Lexi, and that was the only reason he'd hauled her ass up and down stairs after her dentist appointment gone awry. The look in his eyes wasn't anything but frustration that she wasn't bending to his whims and eating his soup like a good girl so he could lord it over her for weeks and weeks.

She'd caught a look at herself in the bathroom mirror before Will had returned with soup and a bad attitude. She knew her hair was sticking up and out of its usual ponytail and she had half of a Hapsburg jaw from the swelling. All that on top of smeared mascara and wrinkled clothes. Will definitely wasn't feeling the same kick of attraction she was. Not ever, but especially not at the moment.

So, instead of going up on her tiptoes and kissing him, which was what she would do if this were the movie version of her life, she sat down and ate her soup.

"You have to stop this."

"Stop what? I'm eating my soup."

"You have to stop going to find all your exes."

"You have to stop telling me what to do." Alex scowled at him, even though the soup was really good. Possibly the best soup she'd ever had. She would not tell him that, though.

"Well, someone has to keep you safe." She didn't like that he was implying that she couldn't keep herself safe. She'd been keeping herself safe long before she'd met Will.

"I wasn't at risk when I went to go see Andrew."

Will leaned back against the counter opposite her and crossed his arms over his chest. When had he started doing that all the time? Or had she just noticed that he did that all the time because she was allowing herself to see him as a man and not the first guy who had thrown her over for The One.

"I don't like that guy." Well, there went any hope of a business deal with Andrew. Once Will decided he didn't like someone, he was done with them. That's why any thoughts she had about how well he filled out a T-shirt were futile. He had never really started with her, but that didn't matter. He'd shut her down. "I don't like the way he looks at you."

"Oh please. You seem to forget that you are not my actual male relative. Even if you were, you'd have no business telling me who I can't go talk to."

"And what about the dentist?" Will gave her a meaningful look. "Did you go in expecting not to be able to walk yourself out?"

Okay, maybe he had a point. That she was sitting here was a testament to how wrong her visit to Lyle's office had gone. On the one hand, she was glad that her tooth was fixed. On the other, she'd had to rely on Will Harkness for an extraction.

"I still haven't figured out why every man I date ends up with the next person they date after me."

"Which proves that this is pointless." She hated how smug he sounded.

"I have gotten a couple of useful insights." Her head might still be foggy, but she couldn't help but notice that both Andrew and Lyle had had a certain look in their eye when they talked about their wives—gratitude.

Will looked skeptical. "And?"

"I think that dating me is such a harrowing experience that they are so grateful they find a nice person after me. So they marry them." It almost felt better to think of herself as a bitch on wheels than it did to think that she might be intentionally self-destructive.

"Fuck that." Will grimaced.

"Well, what do you think it is?" Alex took another spoonful of soup because this conversation was making her hungry. And she thought she'd said enough.

"Dudes are dumb. All of us." There was a hint of something on his face that she had never seen before. Will had always been resolute—a pain in the ass, but he'd never seemed unsure of himself. "And you're very much not dumb. You see right through the games and shit that we try to play with you. I can't imagine very many guys want to deal with that."

"So I should just give up? Like you?" That wasn't fair, but he'd just called her essentially undatable, and she was desperate to turn things around on him. "You haven't dated anyone since separating."

"No time," he grunted at her, and she knew that she'd made a direct hit. "I don't want you going around on your own anymore, talking to these guys."

"Of all the patriarchal, bullshi—"

"I'll go with you."

Alex stood up and walked close to him, getting into his space. "I don't need to have some big strong man to protect me."

"I'm not saying that you're weak." His words were quiet, but she knew that they were meant to soothe her, and she was in no mood to be soothed. "I'm saying that guys get weird when you throw failure in their face. And"—he tucked one of the many pieces of hair that had fallen out of her ponytail behind her ear— "any man that's ever lost you is going to view that as a failure."

A lump formed in Alex's throat. That was maybe the nicest thing he'd ever said to her. And after having him touch her in the most tender way he'd ever touched her—the most intentional way he'd ever touched her—she wasn't sure what to say. She stepped back out of his space, the fight gone from her.

"You'll really go with me?"

Will looked down, but she could tell that he was fighting not to smile. "If you insist on doing this, then sure. But I have one condition."

Alex had been in negotiations with a lot of hard-ass lawyers before. She'd sat across courtrooms and conference rooms, facing off against guys who thought she was nothing but a cream puff because she was pretty and had a recognizable family name. When they looked at her like a confection and not a honey badger ready to rip their faces off, that's when she'd always known she'd won.

But with Will, she'd made the mistake that those geezers had—underestimating him. "What's the condition?"

He looked up at her, and the vulnerable look was back. She wasn't sure if it was genuine or if he was using it to manipulate the situation. Maybe he was going to put a condition so onerous on teaming up that she would agree to halt the entire initiative. Sometimes spouses did that at the end of the divorce process, trying to win their spouse back by inserting a poison pill into the final agreement.

Alex wouldn't have guessed that Will would do that, but she

wouldn't have guessed that she'd find herself alone with him, in his apartment, wanting to kiss him after all these years of trying to pretend that he didn't exist to her in that way.

She took another step back before she did anything stupid, like try to taste his mouth. When did his lips start to look as tasty as his food? Maybe she shouldn't have made fun of him when *GQ* named him America's Sexiest Chef after his Instagram Live videos blew up.

"We have to go interview my wife."

"Your *ex*-wife, you mean?"

Will just grunted. Alex didn't want to talk to the woman, but she didn't even really know April all that well. Although April had started dating Will shortly after he'd started apprenticing in his first kitchen, Alex hadn't taken the time to get to know her. At first, she'd assumed that April was just a convenient girlfriend for him to have. He'd worked long hours, and she'd been available. But once their relationship had stretched for more than a year, Alex had deliberately ignored April because she didn't want to know anything about a person who could snag Will's romantic affection.

Now, after they were divorced, Alex was curious. If this attraction to Will didn't go away, they'd have to do something about it eventually. Otherwise, it would turn ugly and make their run-ins when they crossed paths because of Lexi complicated.

"Fine." Alex stuck her hand out so they could shake on it.

Will raised his eyebrows before extending his. Alex knew she'd made a mistake when their skin made contact and she felt as though she'd gotten a shock—but just to her lower abdomen.

Him having this kind of effect on her after all these years was concerning, but she had the perfect person for them to track down, one who would make her weird pants feelings for Will pale in comparison.

"Who are we talking to first?"

"James Faherghty is having a party at his house on Saturday night. I thought we'd go there next."

Will's face dropped.

THIRTEEN

WILL HADN'T BEEN ABLE TO IGNORE ALEX'S INVOLVE-
ment with James Faherghty—the teen star turned
grown-up movie idol—because it was all over the gossip blog that
his girlfriend at the time had been obsessed with. Will had hated
the guy on sight. Probably because there was nothing wrong with
him. He was wildly handsome, filthy rich, and shockingly well-
adjusted. If Will was into dudes, he would definitely date James,
but that didn't change the fact that he hated the guy.

And James had been crazy about Alex for about six months
when she was eighteen. After Will had tried and failed to let Alex
down easy, he hadn't heard about her dating anyone else for a
while. And this was not for lack of trying to pump Lexi for information. Come to think of it, that was probably how Lexi got the
idea that he and Alex were fated mates or some shit.

But the summer before Alex started college, she'd gotten a fake ID, used it to get into some Hollywood club, and met James Faherghty. The dude had been mobbed everywhere he went, even picking up beers at the Bristol Farms. He'd just been cast as a superhero in a major franchise and was followed by paparazzi even going to take a leak. The paps caught James and Alex on the night of their meet-cute at a valet stand. He'd been smooth about asking for her number—smoother than Will had ever been in his life. He'd touched Alex's elbow, said something that made her laugh, put her number into his phone, and trotted back to his car.

Thinking about Faherghty touching Alex still made Will grind his teeth, but he couldn't say anything about it. He'd rejected Alex—for her own good, but he'd still rejected her. She could date whomever she wanted. And, for that summer, they were a tabloid golden couple.

People on gossip blogs had even gotten it wrong and said they were engaged once. One of the servers mentioned it when he was on the fish station, and he'd had to go into the walk-in and take several deep breaths. He hadn't cried, but it was a close one.

Actually, April had found him there and made a joke about the chef de cuisine that had gotten him out of his head about Alex. It was the first time he'd noticed the woman who would later become his wife.

He should probably think about that more. But later, not when he was currently hoping that Alex's friend Jane wouldn't get them killed on the way to James Faherghty's Mulholland Drive mansion.

"I can't believe you talked me into going to this party with you. His agent is going to think that I'm trying to poach him," Jane hissed as she took a curve in the road on two wheels. "As if I would try to poach the whitest actor on the planet."

"He's actually really great. I'm excited for you all to meet him." Will wanted to throw up listening to Alex talk about her ex like that. "And he's more of a spicy white than white-white, you know?"

"There was that photo of him getting his hair cut at the Dominican barber," Jane mused. "And he does wear a chain."

"He also dated me," Alex said. "And the woman he married in Vegas the weekend after we broke up was also biracial."

"If a spicy white is color struck, does he still count as spicy?" Jane asked.

Will thought their back-and-forth was charming, and he was kind of curious about what kind of white Jane saw him as, but also kind of afraid of her opinion. "Can we just come up with a strategy for getting in and out of here?"

Jane looked at him through her rearview mirror with a smirk. "You're fun at a party. I don't understand why Alex has never invited you out with us before."

"Be nice, he's usually working." He hadn't expected Alex to defend him to her friend but was heartened when she did. He waited for her to look back at him. She didn't. She just scrolled through her phone. "This is going to be fun. I haven't gone to a party at an actor's house in years."

"That's because we're in our thirties now, and these kinds of parties are for people young enough to do mushrooms with strangers." Will decided he liked Jane. She was funny and direct.

Lana was quieter than Alex's other friend, but she said, "I feel like if you're too old to try cocaine for the first time, you're too old to party at an actor's house."

"I think this is more like a dinner-party vibe, not as much a coke-and-banging type of thing." Will did not like how wistful Alex sounded about "coke and banging." Although they'd made every effort to avoid each other after that first summer, he'd known that she'd gone a little wild in college. It had never showed up in her grades, and she'd kept it from Lexi mostly, but he'd always known when she came into the restaurant with boyfriends like James.

"I can't believe you lost your virginity to James Faherghty," Lana said from across the back seat, prompting Will to start hoping for death. He would never get the picture of James Faherghty touching Alex out of his mind now. He had no right to hate it, but he hated it.

"He was the first guy to ever finger me," Alex said wistfully, and Will wanted to scream. "And he was so good at it. He really set the standard. Not all guys are good at that. I think it's because he had to study piano for that one role." Alex turned and looked at Lana. "Do your kids want piano lessons for Christmas? I'm sure their future partners will thank them."

Lana couldn't keep a laugh in, and Alex looked at him then with a devilish gleam in her eye. He realized then that they were fucking with him. Lana looked at him and winked. "Too fucking easy." She turned to Alex. "I still can't believe the first time you had penetrative sex, it was with an actual superhero."

"He's not even the best superhero," Will grumbled.

---

lex didn't know why she was nervous to see James. Maybe because it had been ten years since they'd seen each other, and she'd probably changed more than he had. Or maybe it was because men in the public eye were allowed to age, and women—in or out of the public eye—faced scrutiny for the same thing.

It wasn't that she thought she looked haggard at thirty, but she definitely wasn't twenty anymore. She was probably just nervous to see James because he was one of the first men who dove head-first into a new, committed relationship after they'd broken up.

And she wasn't sure why they'd broken up. Their relationship hadn't been that deep—she wasn't expecting that back then—but she'd felt a real connection with him. She'd snuck into the VIP area of some club to find a ride home because said club was lame and full of people who'd had too many drugs, too much to drink, or both. She'd thought that area of the club was empty—it was an off night—when she heard his voice.

She'd jumped and he'd laughed, but in a way that said he was making fun of himself more than he was making fun of her. There was something charming about him, which made sense. Even back then, she'd known he was going to be a huge movie star. And now he was one of the biggest stars on Earth.

When Jane pulled up to James's house, there was a valet. As they were stepping out of the car, Alex pulled Jane aside.

"How did you pull off an invite?" Alex hadn't asked questions when Jane had texted and told her that they were going. She just assumed that it was some sort of Jane magic—or that Jane had some piece of information or a piece of a project that James was interested in. "And does he know I'm coming?"

She hadn't asked in front of Will. He was skeptical enough of her whole deal right now, and she didn't think it was a good idea to express her reservations in front of him. Besides, James was truly a decent guy. If Will got a creepy vibe off him, it would be because that's what he wanted to see.

Will and Lana headed inside the huge contemporary mansion James had bought a few years earlier. He and his wife had renovated the place completely, and it had been featured in *Architectural Digest* just before they split up.

Jane and Alex made their way toward the front at a much more leisurely place.

"James's agent is the fuckboy that I was seeing."

That was a surprise. Jane usually kept business and pleasure very separate. As her divorce attorney, Alex approved of that policy. If she ever got married again and married someone in the same business, it would be a complete disaster if and when they split up. She'd probably have to write in which restaurants each of them could make reservations for lunch at on which days so that they were guaranteed never to cross paths.

"Am I going to meet your new boyfriend tonight?"

Jane made a screwed-up face at her. "He's not my boyfriend. He *was* my fuck buddy. And it's over."

"Are you sure it's not going to be awkward?" Jane had spiraled the first time she'd seen her ex-wife out and about after their divorce decree was signed. It was the first time that Alex had glimpsed any vulnerability in her client turned friend.

But Jane shook her head. "Nah. I never caught feelings. I find it's much easier to fuck a dude without feelings involved for some reason."

"For you." Alex had dated men her whole life, and she'd tried to do it without feelings most of the time. But it never seemed to work out the way she planned. Seeing Andrew, Lyle, and even Brody had stirred up all the feelings that she'd tried to keep buried when she was dating each of them. It was strange how much she'd forgotten why she'd been drawn to each of them and how it had come rushing back to her when she saw them.

But she'd also remembered the feeling that she was going to suffocate if any of them got too close. As though she was going to lose control, and that feeling always made her dizzy.

She should probably talk to someone about that.

Alex stayed quiet until they walked into the house. From outside, they'd seen that it was full of people—adult people, chatting and drinking champagne and nibbling on passed hors d'oeuvres.

When had they gone from wild clubbing to sedate parties with appetizers that you didn't just pull out of a bag?

"Don't get dazzled by James's charm and catch feelings for him. That way lies madness." Jane must have taken her silence for something other than what it was.

"No danger of that happening. I mean, I like him. But I don't have feelings for him anymore." Alex shook her head. "He was so much fun, but he could never sit still. Like he was always anxious to move on to the next thing."

"Honestly, I think you could use some of that energy right now."

"What do you mean?"

"I think that you should consider moving forward into an unknown future instead of spending all this time revisiting the past."

Jane was doubting her now, too? "I thought you were support-ive of this whole thing."

"I was, but then you got all quiet and pensive. This should be the best time of your life. You have so many options and possibili-ties. Why would you want to spend so much time talking to guys who weren't the ones for you?"

"Because I'm curious about why I wasn't the one for them. I need to know what mistakes I made so that I can avoid making them in the future." And just maybe excavating old shit was part of her DNA. That's what her mother did for a living, after all. How would she understand her past and be able to move forward if she didn't look at all the mistakes she'd made? If she didn't spread them out on a plastic tarp, examine them closely, document them, and file them away?

"There is one guy from your past that I think you should be interested in." Jane inclined her head toward Will, who was talk-ing to Lana and not paying attention to anyone else. He wasn't flirting with her, and that filled Alex with relief for some reason.

"Will doesn't want to be a part of my future. Trust me."

"Why not?" Part of what made Jane good at her job was that she took rejection as a personal challenge rather than a flat-out no. If the answer wasn't what she wanted the first time, she pushed harder or went at the problem from a different direction. Alex didn't have the words to tell her that Will wasn't a challenge, that his whole essence was a giant, unequivocal no. "He certainly doesn't look at you like you're a part of the past. And I don't think he'd be picking you up at the dentist or trailing you all over the city if he didn't care about you a whole lot."

"He only cares because of Lexi."

Jane grabbed a glass of champagne and a seltzer off a tray and handed the champagne to Alex. "Okay, whatever you say."

Her friend didn't believe her at all. Alex didn't know how to explain that this wasn't a case of "the lady doth protest too much" but a fully litigated piece of her history. They'd never talked about it after it had happened, but Will had been clear.

His answer wouldn't change just because her pants feelings for him had reawakened with a vengeance. She started to doubt agreeing to have him tag along when she talked to her exes. He wanted her to be safe, even though his overprotectiveness was completely misguided.

She just wanted to be around him.

She took a swallow of champagne and chanced another glance in his direction. Someone else had approached them, and she recognized his friend Charlee.

W hat are you doing here?" Charlee slapped Will on his back. They looked great tonight, dressed in something other than chef's whites. They were wearing a black dress and heels and neon pink eyeliner.

"What are you doing here?" Because of their profession, it was so strange to see another chef out on a Saturday night doing anything other than working a catering job. Sure, some chefs went out after their shifts to bars that were open late and drank and partied. But that had never been Will's deal. And he didn't think it was Charlee's.

"I'm trying to get a brief heaux phase in before the restaurant opens and I don't have time for anything but work."

That made sense. Will should probably do the same, but he knew he wouldn't. He looked back at Alex, who was still deep in conversation with Jane.

Charlee's gaze followed his. "I suppose she explains your presence."

"Shut up." Will didn't want to talk about Alex in front of Lana, but it was too late when he saw the look on Alex's friend's face. "Charlee, this is Lana. Lana, this is Charlee. They're my chef de cuisine at the new restaurant."

Charlee took Lana's hand. "Charmed, I'm sure. I'm also Will's only true friend. He actually got me in the divorce."

Lana smiled at Charlee. "Well, clearly he got the only friend that mattered." She drained her champagne and grabbed another. "Luckily, I would get all of my husband's friends in a divorce. They rely on me for dating advice. I'm a therapist. And I'm not planning on a divorce."

If Will had his druthers, he'd back out of that conversation. He had no intention of entertaining dating advice from Alex's friend. He probably could have used Lana's take before his marriage fell apart. He wondered what she would have thought about April calling him a "taciturn ogre with a God complex."

"You'd probably have a more productive heaux phase than this one if you did get divorced," Charlee said, pointing at Will. "I mean, I don't know you, but you are totally hot."

Lana perked up. "You know, no one has told me I'm hot in years."

"Not even your husband?" Charlee flicked their shoulder-length hair behind their ear. "That sounds like he's snoozing on the job."

Lana grabbed Charlee's hand again. "Thank you." Then, she looked around the room. "I'm going to go flirt with someone famous. Then I'm going to go home and jump on my husband."

Lana wandered off. And Will and Charlee were alone, like usual, then.

"Why are you so tense? You're at a party." Charlee's gaze trailed after Will's, and they noticed that Will was following Alex around the party with his eyes. "You know that brooding at her across the room is not going to let her know that you like her."

"Stop." Will wasn't sure about his feelings about Alex anymore. After talking to Lexi and the moment they'd had in his apartment, he'd started to allow some of his more possessive urges about Alex to come to the surface. If he'd ever really pushed them down all that deep.

"Who is she with?" Will was so focused on what Alex was doing—drinking champagne and talking to the guy who'd played the main villain in Faherghty's last movie—that he didn't respond to Charlee right away. But their sort of moony-eyed tone made him pause. "Who?"

"The tall, beautiful Black person in a killer suit next to her."

Will looked away from Alex and back at Charlee, who had pulled out a lip gloss and was freshening up. "Oh, you mean Jane?" When Charlee nodded, Will elaborated. "She's one of Alex's best friends. Alex handled her divorce."

"Divorced?" Charlee's immaculate brows went up. "So, you mean she's single?"

"I think Alex mentioned that she's pan." Contrary to popular belief among his ex-wife and Alex, he didn't tune everything out when he was cooking. He might not talk very much, but he listened. "You should go for it. She's really cool."

Charlee pulled themself together and leveled a hard look at Will. "I'll do it if you will."

FOURTEEN

ALEX COULD FEEL WILL LOOKING AT HER FROM ACROSS the room as she made her way through the party, looking for James. Like any Leo / Hollywood A-lister, he knew how to make an entrance to his own party. And that was late, after almost everyone was relatively sauced.

James's house had an open layout through the living and dining rooms, and she wasn't tall enough to see over the clutch once she got to the corridor. But she pressed on, even though Jane fell back to talk to someone she knew from one of the studios. She'd probably walk out of here by the end of the night with a deal to have one of her clients star in something. Alex should probably take time management and professional networking lessons from her. She was sure that plenty of the people she was currently rubbing against not on purpose were in the market for a divorce attorney.

Maybe the next time someone groped her ass, she would just turn around and give them her card. She'd make a mint.

She found James in a study off the corridor. It shocked her that he was alone.

"James?"

He looked up at her and his face immediately changed. One of the reasons she no longer dated actors was because some of them—#notallactors—could change their whole being on a dime. It was kind of wild, and it fucked with Alex before she'd become aware of it. However, from what she could tell, James was happy to see her.

"I hope it's okay that I came." This was so awkward. How was she ever going to get the 'nads to ask James why he'd fucked off to Vegas and married the next biracial woman to smile at him after they'd broken up? He was going to think she was sniffing around to see if he'd give it another go. And that wasn't happening.

First of all, she didn't want any of the publicity that would come along with dating one of the most famous people on the planet. She was sure that was why at least three of Lexi's marriages had ended. Sure, Alex had had a moment in the gossip blogs during the late aughts when she was dating James—he'd definitely been more of a "who?" but he'd had star quality even back then—but she'd never been regular celebrity gossip fodder. And she couldn't imagine being picked apart every time she left the house anymore.

That was assuming James would be interested in starting things up with her. She was here to find out why she wasn't The One for him, or even one of the few, not see if she could be next on his whosdatedwho.com page. She was already there once, in a mortifying short skirt.

James stood up and hugged her. "Of course I'm glad you're here. You're about the only person I'm happy to see." He still smelled good. And he'd filled out after playing a superhero for a decade.

"Why are you having a party if you don't want to see any of the guests?" Alex looked up at him. Jesus Christ, his eyes were blue. It was almost alien. Fuck. And he had a beard now. When had she started liking beards so much? Beards made her think of Will, and that must have made her face change.

"Do I have something on my face?" James's question shocked her out of thinking about Will.

"Oh no." Alex stepped back.

James smiled again at her. "You know, I never expected to see you again."

"Really?" Alex didn't remember their breakup as being that acrimonious, but what did she know?

James laughed, and she remembered how annoying his honking laugh had been to her when they were dating. But only when he was laughing at something that was important to her.

"Yeah, really." James motioned for her to sit and pulled a bottle of champagne out of a bucket that seemed to appear out of nowhere—how did champagne appear out of nowhere?—before refilling her glass and his. "You were so mad when I broke things off."

"I was?" Now that they were face-to-face, she remembered being irritated and telling him to suck on a bag of dicks. But that was because he'd broken up with her right before they were supposed to go to Bali for the three weeks after her fall term exams. "That was probably mostly about the trip."

"You always were kind of cold like that." He nodded. "I think that was mostly what attracted me to you. You didn't demand a whole lot from me. Not at first."

"Are you saying that I was easy?" None of this was the way she remembered things. She'd tried so hard not to need James. He was the kind of man, even back then, before he became as famous as he was now, who was like a planet. The people around him were the satellites. The best one could hope for when being with a man like James was that you could be a moon. You might get to gaze at him half the time and affect his gravitational pull. But you weren't the sun. You could never be the sun.

"Oh no, I remember you made me work for everything I got with you." He looked down into his champagne glass before lifting it to his full lips, and she remembered why she'd fucked him even though he didn't have a box spring in the house he'd shared with, like, five other young actors. "I just thought that if I got in your pants, you'd give me something else."

It was Alex's turn to laugh derisively. "You're honestly telling me that you wanted my heart?"

He gave her the puppy-dog eyes. Those were probably kryptonite to most women, but Alex had known him since before the whole world knew the puppy-dog eyes. It wasn't to say that they weren't genuine, but they got him what he wanted. He wouldn't use them if they didn't. And the circumstances of his life were such that people catered to him. The puppy-dog eyes weren't necessary anymore, but they were almost a reflex.

Will never gave her puppy-dog eyes. There was a steely determination in his gaze that rarely faltered. He might be susceptible to puppy-dog eyes or seductive glances, but he wasn't giving them out. Will himself was sort of the seduction. But it wasn't flashy the way James's was.

She needed to stop comparing the men she'd dated to Will. It wasn't like she could phone James out of the blue and ask him her questions next week, once she'd successfully sublimated her attraction to Will again. She needed to focus and get her answers now.

"Did you ever really want my heart?" Alex didn't remember having deep conversations with James. They'd had some romantic moments, but he'd never asked her about how she felt about her family situation. That was a lie. He'd once asked her why she hadn't decided to take up acting or singing like Lexi—given that nepotism was a leg up in the entertainment business, and James couldn't understand why she wouldn't take that leap. "You never really knew me."

He looked her up and down like she was a full snack. Alex couldn't help but feel the ghost of the flutter that she'd felt the first time he'd looked at her like that. There was a reason that he was a big star. The looks, the charisma, the ability to project what other people most wanted to feel about themselves.

"What was dating me like?" Alex couldn't believe that she'd never asked one of her exes that question point-blank. All her exes had cited circumstances instead of actual values, and it was the values that broke most people up. She should know, given what she did for a living.

James looked down, and she couldn't tell what he was thinking. Probably nothing good. The longer he paused, the more she was seeing the sense in Will's suggestion that she give all this up and just move on without investigating.

"It was kind of like when I was training to play Major Maximus." Alex furrowed her brow at him, so he added, "It's like after a training session, when I was empty and hollowed out and then right after my blazing-hot shower, my trainer made me sit in an ice bath."

"So I made your balls shrivel up?" This was terrible for her ego.

James laughed again. "You always were direct. That's what I meant. Dating you was painful, but also sort of refreshing."

"But you didn't want that for the long term?" It sounded like James didn't want to be with anyone who would tell him the truth about his shit. And Alex could never be with anyone who expected her to lie to them.

"Not back then."

She was on the cusp of asking if he wanted it now when she felt Will's presence behind her. It was funny that she could tell that it was him and not any of the other hundred or so people at the party. She didn't know if it was because she could pick up his smell or what. She didn't want to think about that.

"We're trying to have a conversation here." Alex didn't have to turn around, and she knew that didn't go over well when Will made a noise that she'd never heard from him before.

Will growled—not like his usual nonverbal grumbling, but an actual growl.

Alex knew she needed to smooth things over so that Will didn't punch a face that she was sure was insured for several million dollars. She didn't understand why he was acting like this. For as long as they'd known each other, almost half his life, she'd been a huge pain in his ass. And now he was growling at movie stars?

"James, this is Will Harkness. He's . . . a family friend," Alex said, trying to sound as breezy as possible. When Will didn't come farther into the room or say anything, she added, "I wish I could say that he's usually more effusive, but that would ruin my record of never lying to you."

"Champagne?" James lifted the half-empty bottle before returning his gaze to Alex. "Are you guys, like, together?"

At the same time that Alex said, "Absolutely not," Will said, "Nope," in a way that was sort of offensively decisive. It wasn't as though it would be inconceivable for them to get together. No one had ever made her put a bag over her head during sex.

"Do either of you need anything else? Uppers? Downers?" James stood up and approached a cabinet where she presumed he stored his drugs.

"I'm good. I think I'm officially too old for cocaine."

Will grunted again. It was a "no" grunt.

James nodded sagely. "Cool, cool, cool. I'm going out to smoke a cigarette."

"You should really quit. It's bad for your face, and that's the moneymaker." Alex knew then that she wouldn't have accepted the date she was almost sure that James was going to offer. They were way too old to still be smoking.

James pointed at her with finger guns that made Alex cringe. "See? Honest! I love it." He walked out the door. "Feel free to talk things out. If you need the drugs"—he pointed at his stash—"they're right over there."

"Thanks," Alex said when Will did not even turn to acknowledge him leaving. "It was great to catch up."

James walked out of the room, and Alex stalked toward Will until her eyes were level with his mouth. Bad idea.

"Why don't you just piss on my leg?"

"That wouldn't have gotten him to leave you alone." He leaned over so that he could look her in the eye.

Alex fought the urge to step back. "What if I didn't want him to leave me alone?"

"You wanted to kiss him?" Before she knew what exactly was happening, his lips ghosted against her ear. "You wanted to fuck Major Maximus like some groupie?"

"I'm not a groupie, Will. He's my ex-boyfriend. We shared milestones." Alex didn't know why she was taunting Will with this, placing an emphasis on the last word so he would remember that James had taken advantage of what Will himself had turned down. His posture was so tense, it seemed as though he would break in half if she made any sudden movements. "Why are you suddenly all up in my business?"

"He's not a good guy, Alex." Will still didn't pull away. If she wasn't mistaken, he was smelling her hair. Like a fucking were-wolf in a YA book. He didn't have the right to do that. He hadn't earned it, and as far as she knew, he didn't want it. "He's not good enough for you."

"That's it, isn't it?" Alex was done with this overprotective, jealous-seeming bullshit. It was childish and toxic. She put her hand on his chest, intending to pull away, until Will kept her hand there with his. The heat of his skin seeped through his T-shirt and into her palm. The way he smelled permeated her nostrils. His lemongrass and sage smell—intoxicating, like a strong martini on a summer day. He was dessert, and she was starting to forget why she didn't indulge. But it didn't change the facts on the ground. "You don't want me, but you don't think anyone else is good enough for me."

She dared a look into his face. It was almost impossible to tell what he was thinking; he didn't wear his feelings like a lot of people. Part of what had initially attracted her to him was the fact that he was the only person she knew who wasn't constantly spilling his emotions all over the place, regardless of whether she was in a place to receive them. He was a calm anchor in a storm. But not right now. There was a firefight behind his dark gaze. He was fighting something within himself.

His hand clenched on hers. She gasped, not because it hurt, but because she wanted to feel him grasping her other places that way. If either of them shifted a few centimeters, their lips would touch. But both of them were frozen. They both knew that they could lie about having impure thoughts about each other all they wanted; they could deny that they'd each thought about ripping each other's clothes off at times that didn't quite coincide. But if they kissed, there would be no going back. Both of them would know it had happened, and it would sit between them like a boulder in the middle of the road.

"Do you want that guy?" Will asked.

Alex sighed, and the movement from her breath ruffled the collar of his shirt. She wasn't sure, but she thought she felt him shiver. "No."

"Do you want me?" That question made Alex's breath catch. He knew that she'd wanted him as a teen, but he thought she might have gotten over it. She could hardly blame him, but she'd thought she'd gotten over it until quite recently.

Alex never lied. Apparently, with her exes, that was her brand. But she was tempted to lie this time, because the stakes were so high. If she told him the truth—that she felt as though she was on fire right now—there would be no denying it later. If he rejected her again, she didn't know how she'd deal with it. That kind of hurt as an adult was completely foreign to her.

She wanted him—of course she did—but she didn't want to be the one to say it first. Not this time.

"Do you want me?" Alex's voice was raspy. She hoped it made Will think of sin and sex.

Will didn't answer with his words, but he used his mouth. His lips ghosted over her forehead, and she thought he was going to pull away at that. But then he kissed her cheekbone, nibbled at her earlobe, ran his nose up and down her neck. He shifted and put his hands on each side of her head when it lolled over to the side.

Alex clutched his T-shirt for a long moment, until Will buried one hand in the hair at the nape of her neck. Then she let go of his clothes and ran one hand around his neck. She loved the texture of him, his warm skin, the silk of the close-shaved hair.

He lifted her head so that she looked at him. He stared down at her for a long moment, giving her time to tell him to slow down or stop. She wouldn't do that now unless the house started coming down around their ears. And she might not even stop him then.

A slow smile spread over his face. "You want me."

This time, it was Alex who didn't answer. Instead, she pulled him close with the hand at the back of his neck and tugged on the short hair of his beard with the other until their lips were aligned. She'd probably remember the instant she tasted champagne on Will Harkness's breath for the rest of her life. Even when all this ended in disaster and they were fighting over who got to see Lexi on which holidays because they could not stand to be in the same room together, she would remember the earthy taste of his mouth, the way he took over the kiss, the heat of his body against hers.

She would let the way she opened to him like an unlocked door remind her that she wasn't incapable of letting go, of being hungry for another human being. His kisses didn't slake her thirst, not when he delved into her mouth with his tongue or when his hands drifted down her body, ever so slowly, until he cupped her ass. She wished she could see how his long, skillful fingers shifted and moved her flesh the way his mouth against hers was altering her insides.

The only relief she felt was that he hadn't let her kiss him the night she'd told him that she loved him—before she knew that what she felt for him was a lie people told themselves so that they didn't feel so alone. If he'd kissed her before, she would have never left her room at Lexi's house again.

They pressed their lower bodies together, and Alex got her answer to the question of whether he truly wanted her. He was hard. She gasped when he pulled her off her feet so that the center of her was aligned with his hard-on. Through her silk slip dress, there was so little fabric between them that she could have been naked, rubbing herself all over his jeans.

A swarm of possession raged through her, and she wanted to leave her scent on him. She'd never felt that way before. When other boyfriends had flirted with other people—when a couple of them had cheated—she'd felt jealous. But she realized now that it was about how bad it made her look when her lover flirted with someone else—not because she felt some sort of claim over that other person.

But this was different. Will was hers. Even though that wasn't the truth, and he probably wouldn't agree to belonging to her, her body didn't care.

Their kiss seemed to go on and on. It was frankly sexual. She put her hand under his T-shirt and ran her fingers over the muscles on his abdomen and chest, teasing him. He hiked her dress up and grabbed her thighs.

They were still upright, but that was not going to last.

Or it wouldn't have lasted if the door to the study hadn't opened.

Will turned so that his back was facing the door. Alex didn't know if it was to protect her identity or because he didn't want anyone to know that he'd been kissing her. She thought it was probably the former, because Will only cared what Lexi thought of him. But the part of her mind that doubted that Will Harkness had really just kissed her believed that it was the latter.

"This is where the drugs are, right?" the voice from the door asked.

Lexi's hand was on Will's jaw, so she could feel it clench when he said, "Get out."

"Sorry, man." And Alex heard the door shut.

But the moment was broken. Will stepped back, and when

they weren't touching, Alex started thinking. They shouldn't have done that. Ever since he'd rejected her, they'd maintained their détente through a strict policy of bickering and no physical contact when they had absolutely no choice but to be in the same room together.

They'd shattered all that in the span of a few minutes. Alex waited to feel a pang of regret about it. She waited for the dread that they'd ruined something to rush in and make her nauseous. She waited for Will to turn on her and blame her for making him so crazy that he had to kiss her. Because he made her feel like a siren. What had happened in that room wasn't wrong—they were consenting adults who were not related—but it was definitely complicated.

And while she waited for all her regret to rush in, she refused to look at Will. He mattered to her. What he thought about her mattered to her. No matter what happened between the two of them, he was never going to be out of her life. Even when Lexi—hopefully a long way into the future—passed, Will Harkness would loom large.

"I'm sorry" were the first words he said to her after tipping her center over on its side with that kiss.

"Why?" She wasn't going to let him off the hook so easily. "For what?"

Then she ventured a look at him. How dare he look so good? He was a whole banquet of delicious man. A tasting menu of strength and heat and everything she desired. But he hadn't wanted her before. What had changed now?

"I shouldn't have been such a dick to that guy." Alex hoped she didn't show on her face how relieved she was that he wasn't sorry about the kiss. Because even though the idea of them together was folly, she wasn't sorry for kissing him at all.

"No, that was really rude. He should probably have kicked us out, not offered us drugs."

Will nodded, his lips pressed into a line. That made her want to walk up to him and kiss him again. But she shouldn't do that until they'd talked about it. And, knowing Will, he wouldn't want to talk about it until he'd rolled it around in his head so much that he'd turned it into a disaster. That was just how his brain worked.

Alex was going to say something—she wasn't sure what—when her phone chimed. Jane was looking for her, ready to leave the party. Alex was almost tempted to tell her that she and Will would call a car at some later point, but she knew that Will wasn't ready to do more kissing or talk about the kissing that had already taken place.

It was time to go home.

FIFTEEN

WILL TURNED HIS KISS WITH ALEX OVER IN HIS MIND
so many times that by the next time he saw her, a week
after the party at Major Maximus's house, he wasn't sure it had
happened. He'd known exactly what had come over him the night
it had happened. He'd heard Alex laugh in a room off the corridor
and been drawn to it. Spending so much time with her over the
past few weeks had worn down his shields against Alex.

They were completely shredded now.

When he saw her standing outside the comedy club in West
Hollywood where they were planning to see another of Alex's
exes perform, he wanted nothing more than to kiss her full on the
mouth. She looked beautiful. She always looked beautiful. But
now that he'd kissed her, he wanted to do it at every opportunity.

Even though he'd walked away from that kiss with blue balls
and a lot of unanswered questions, he was sort of relieved it had

happened. There had been over a decade of buildup to that kiss. He'd been wanting to kiss her and denying himself for so long that he'd stopped even imagining what it would be like. He'd stopped allowing himself to imagine how soft her skin was, how plush her lips would be when they opened under his. He'd never let himself imagine how she would sound when she was making little noises, how she would chase his lips with her own as he got to know her body as well as he knew her mind.

But he didn't let himself kiss her again. Not in public. Not until they talked about what had happened and figured out if they were both on board with doing it again. He'd been an overbearing jerk, and he wasn't sure she knew how sorry he was for that, even though he'd apologized.

They also had to figure out if and when to tell Lexi that they had a thing, although he didn't trust her not to divine it on her own if they were all in the same room together.

The final reason he didn't kiss Alex when he walked up to her was that she didn't look as though she wanted to be kissed. Although she looked gorgeous, she had her arms wrapped around herself, until she grabbed his arm and gave it a friendly squeeze.

The other night, he'd felt electricity running though his skin whenever she touched him. Tonight, there was none of that. With April, he would have waited for her to finally tell him what was bothering her. But that hadn't worked out so well for him in his marriage, and he had the feeling that it was an even worse idea when it came to Alex. She was probably the only person on the planet more stubborn than he was—as evidenced by the fact that she would rather continue interviewing her exes in light of all that had happened.

"Where are Jane and Lana?" he asked. This would be a lot less awkward if they had the buffer of her friends.

"Lana couldn't find a babysitter, and Jane said that she'd rather dip her left tit in acid than go see a stand-up show."

Will laughed but stopped when he noticed that Alex's smile was strained. And he really wished that Jane didn't hate stand-up as much as she seemingly did.

"Are you okay?" It probably wasn't the most articulate way to broach the subject, but she was the one with all the pretty words.

She furrowed her brow, and he fought the urge to press his lips to that crinkly spot to soothe her. He was starting to not recognize himself. She aroused a tenderness in him that he had never felt for anyone before. He knew she wouldn't appreciate it, though. She would be totally justified in being suspicious of his intentions.

"I'm fine." She looked down. "The plan is that we'll sit through the show, then go to the bar and wait for him to have two, maybe three drinks. That should be enough for him to slough off his comedy persona and be able to have a real conversation with a human being who is not a comedian."

That sounded like a whole production to get to the reason she wasn't The One for a stand-up comedian. He got finding someone you could laugh with—his whole marriage had been built on gallows humor about working in the restaurant industry—but having to douse their inner turmoil in alcohol before having a conversation with someone was a bit much.

"You're judging me for dating a stand-up comedian, aren't you?" Alex almost read his mind.

"Not judging you, but questioning his charm." Will had done

a little research on this guy. He was markedly less good-looking than James.

"Well, looks aren't everything." Alex shrugged. "He was great in bed." Before he could get jealous, which he shouldn't be doing because jealousy was bad, she added, "Well, he was great in the sack when he didn't have whiskey dick."

"It sounds like you two didn't work out because of alcoholism." If Alex decided to give up on talking to this guy, or there was a reason she hadn't worked out with this guy other than something she did, they could get back to kissing. If that's what she wanted after having a conversation about the kissing.

And if she was hesitant to continue kissing, he wasn't opposed to tempting and seducing her into it. He would be as underhanded as he needed to be to get more of Alex.

"I knew that I was likely getting some substance-abuse issues when I started dating a stand-up." Alex looked at the door to the club as though she was dreading seeing the dude again. "Best get it over with."

As they made their way through the club to the courtyard behind it where the show would be held, he stopped her. "Are you sure you're okay?"

"Why wouldn't I be?" she asked, and he felt like a jerk for asking. He didn't know where he stood with her, and he wasn't used to the feeling of caring about whether someone else was on the same page. "I mean, you only kissed me a week ago and then haven't talked to me since. Excuse me if I'm a little wary of that, given our history."

Oh shit. "I thought about calling you—"

"You know what?" She pulled her arm out of his grasp. "I'm glad you didn't. If you had called, I would have thought you cared about me."

He didn't have a good answer for that. Although he really had thought about calling, he didn't know if the kiss had meant anything to her. Instead of staying and talking to him, she'd suggested they leave with Jane as soon as she got a text from her friend. And when he'd assumed that she would get out of the car at his place so they could talk things out and possibly pick up where they'd left off, she'd stayed in the car and done an awkward salute at him.

She'd been unreadable, and he hadn't wanted to risk getting his olive branch slapped back into his face. It had happened too many times with Alex. She'd never forgiven him for rejecting her when they were lost teenagers. And every time he felt like they were making progress, she tripped him and kicked dirt in his face.

And even though all signs pointed to her enjoying the kiss, he didn't even think that she liked him very much. So he hadn't reached out. Like a coward. But he wasn't too cowardly to apologize. "I'm sorry. I should have called. I just assumed that we would talk about it when we were done here."

"It's fine," she said, but he wasn't sure he believed her. He was going to say something else, maybe emphasize his apology, when she said, "C'mon. The show's about to start."

The last thing he felt like doing was laughing.

Maybe Will was right, and it didn't matter why she was always the last one before The One. It wasn't like she wanted to be The One for any of the guys she'd dated—not really. She had very good reasons for eschewing marriage altogether. But in the week since she'd kissed Will, it suddenly mattered more that she couldn't seem to find someone who would think about her feelings. She knew that it could seem—at times—like she didn't have any, but it hurt to share an OMG-mazing kiss with someone and then not hear from him other than a "Still on for Friday?" text around midweek.

What could she read into about that? Maybe someone more compelling to him had asked him out on a date. Maybe he'd rather work on stuff for the opening of the new restaurant, which was coming up in a few weeks. Maybe he felt so awkward about the kiss that he couldn't look her in the face anymore. The possibilities—at least the ones in which he was on the precipice of rejecting her yet again—were endless.

This was why she'd set out to get answers from her exes. None of them had worked out, and some of them had even bruised her heart. But none of them had left the ache that Will had. And she was more annoyed that she was the last straw to being in the dating world for them anyway. She needed to know why she was such a trial that they committed themselves permanently to the very next person they met.

She was in a really bad mood, but a strong vodka soda and a funny feature act before her ex Ace's set helped loosen her up. The woman who came on before him told a lot of humorous and relatable stories about planning a wedding while pregnant—or at least Alex could imagine relating to them in a universe where she wanted kids.

Will sat next to her in the dim evening air, lit by a string of white Christmas lights. It was warm out, so he'd taken off his leather jacket to reveal another of his endless supply of plain T-shirts. It was black this time. Faded, with little holes at the edges. It had been well loved.

That was the thing about Will. Once he loved something, he kept it. He loved Lexi, and he took that love seriously, even after she and his father were long divorced. Will's own divorce had to have been so hard on him.

At the wedding, she'd forced herself to keep her eyes open the whole time and really look at the way Will had looked at April. She wanted for there to be no doubt in her own mind that Will was never going to be hers. And he'd looked at April as though she was the whole world. He hadn't cried, at least not that she could see from halfway back in the sanctuary.

If Will had broken her heart when she was a teenager, he'd shattered it when he'd gotten married. The feeling of pain and hollowness in her chest had taken her by surprise. She'd thought she'd been over it. But she hadn't been, so she'd hardened her heart toward him even further.

The trouble was, the more she hardened her heart toward Will, the harder it was to feel anything for someone new.

Oddly enough, she'd been at the wedding with Ace. She'd only started dating the stand-up because she'd been pretty drunk at a comedy club—not this one—when she'd met him and he'd laughed when she'd given him the finger and told him she'd rather suck on a dumpster full of dicks than let him buy her a drink.

That had actually made him a little more interested. Although she hadn't been lying when she'd told Will that Ace was great in the sack, she'd left off the part about how he could only get off if she was insulting him while he came. And that it kind of turned her on, too. Until it didn't.

But she'd kept seeing him for a while after that had stopped being fun. She just hadn't heard from him when he returned from the road once. Alex had left a few messages, but he'd never returned them, and eventually she'd given up.

A few months later, she saw—via Twitter, of course—that he'd met a woman on the road trip after he'd ghosted her and married her in a very tasteful ceremony on Martha's Vineyard.

The comic finished her set, and the emcee introduced Ace. The courtyard was packed. Ace's career had just been starting out when they'd started dating. He was doing shows all over town five nights a week, so she'd seen it a lot. He was an incredibly funny guy, but those jokes had gotten really stale.

But he had new material now that he was married. His wife was still performing as a comic, too, although it seemed like she was pregnant every time she filmed a special on Netflix. It had become part of her gag, but having a baby for a bit seemed a little much to Alex.

But she wasn't a professional entertainer.

Alex joined the crowd in clapping for Ace when he came up onstage. She looked over at Will, and he joined in.

Ace still looked good, though marriage had softened his edges and degraded his fashion sense. He was wearing pleated khakis, which she would have burned if she were his wife. Although comics were legendarily all cads, so maybe his wife kept him in ugly clothes so no one else wanted to fuck him.

Alex really couldn't speak to the effectiveness of that strategy, but no women had thrown their panties on the stage when he came out, like they had when he was with Alex.

Ace started his act with the usual "How's everybody doing tonight?" He scanned the crowd and Alex felt his gaze on her and Will's table. She had a sinking feeling for a moment, in the pit of her stomach. But he didn't say anything directly to or about them, so she breathed a sigh of relief.

Will did look over at her and mouth, "He saw you, right?"

Alex nodded and shrugged. She couldn't think of anything more embarrassing than being called out by a comedian doing crowd work, but he really didn't have anything to say about her that was bad enough to turn into a bit. Did he?

He then turned to some jokes she recognized from when they were in their nascent forms—things he'd said when they were hanging out and laughed at to himself. She hadn't gotten them then, but he seemed to have worked them into something funny. She found herself laughing and almost forgetting that this was a man she'd dated who had ghosted her.

Until the spotlight hit her and Will. Alex froze. Will looked ready to make a run for it. Alex shot him a look that said she would eviscerate him painfully and slowly if he dared to move a muscle in the direction of the door—at least if he didn't throw her over his shoulder before escaping.

"My ex-girlfriend is here." The crowd wasn't sure what to do with that, so they stayed quiet other than a few stray laughs from people who couldn't sense that shit was about to go down. "How are you doing, Alex?"

Oh shit, he was naming names. She could feel more than hear the grumble coming from Will. It seemed to vibrate through the table, amping up her own sense of unease. Hoping that being a good sport would make this horror pass more quickly, she smiled brightly and gave a thumbs-up.

There was more nervous laughter after that. She should have known this was a terrible idea. Ace had always prided himself on how edgy his comedy was. Alex was pretty sure it was just mean.

"You know my wife hates your guts, right?" Alex shook her head, smile firmly in place. She put her hand on Will's arm then. She couldn't physically tie him to his chair, but Will hated bullies. Ace's bit hadn't strayed into bullying territory yet, but the tone was there.

"Yeah, she says you broke me." Ace looked away from them and made a face at the crowd that was meant to put a button on that. Then he continued. "This sweet-as-pie-looking light-skinned girl used to insult me during our"—he paused for dramatic effect—"lovemaking."

Alex wanted the floor to swallow her up. And she wanted to take Will somewhere after this and wipe out the memory of this whole debacle. Even though she was pissed that he hadn't called her all week after the kiss, she didn't want him to think that she had a kink that made her want to degrade her partners. Will just didn't seem like he would be into that. The way he'd taken control of the kiss, and the way he liked to control everything in general, told her that he was definitely a toppy-toppy top.

And that was more than great for her. Thinking about Will topping her allowed her to dissociate from the whole debacle when Ace started talking about how she used to call him a pencil dick.

And he left out the part about him asking her to call him names during sex.

True to her policy, she'd refused to insult him in ways that were not true, and he did have a pencil dick. But it was fine. While they'd been dating, she'd done plenty of Kegels and brought toys into the equation.

All of this was fine, but it was beyond mortifying to have it all laid out for an audience. And then for them to think it was the funniest thing they'd ever heard. She wanted to die. She legitimately wanted to die. She also wanted to know what Will thought, but he could tell her when she was dead. She was sure that Lexi would hold a séance in lieu of a funeral, and he could tell her then.

Even in profile, she could tell that the look on Will's face was just shy of murderous. But she knew, and she hoped that he knew, that walking out now would only bring more attention to the problem. Right now, the audience was paying attention to the fact that Ace was holding a pen perpendicular to the floor in front of the placket of his jeans and galloping around the stage. The spotlight was off her and Will, and the crowd was not paying them any attention. If they left, Alex didn't doubt for a moment that the spotlight would return to them and Ace would improvise another bit.

She wouldn't give him the satisfaction. Alex just hoped that Will didn't want to tear out Ace's entrails after the show. When Will was murderous, he looked sort of like a Viking. A half-Italian Viking, but still.

So, they sat through the rest of the show, but they didn't laugh after the pencil-dick debacle.

Alex tried to rush Will out as soon as Ace left the stage. She didn't want them running into each other, and she didn't think she needed to talk to Ace about why they'd broken up. He was a mean drunk, and that was really enough of an answer for her at this point. She would probably be better served by talking to a licensed therapist about why she was drawn to a mean drunk.

But Will stopped her short of the exit. "You dated that guy?"

"It wasn't my finest moment, but yeah." She wasn't going to defend the choice. It was a bad choice.

Will smirked at her, and she stopped worrying that he was too mad for public consumption. "Did he really have a pencil dick?" But he said it too loud, and several other people who'd been at the show turned to see if they could hear her answer.

"Never mind." She gave the stragglers some pointed looks. "Can we get out of here?"

"Oh no, I want to meet this guy." Will cracked his knuckles. "I have some things to say to him."

"Would you stop it? You are acting like some sort of wise guy, and I'm not going to let you menace that man. You can't punch people, and you know this."

Will started scanning the room above Alex's head, likely looking for Ace. "Why not? He put you on the spot, and I just want to have a few words."

"Listen, Fredo. Let's get out of here and we can talk about what happened last week."

That got Will's attention. He looked down at her. And then he looked down at her body suggestively. More suggestively than he'd ever looked at her. She felt the heat under her skin from her hairline to her toes. That low tug in her belly was making her languid . . . and stupid. They had to leave. She didn't need to interview Ace. She didn't need to talk to him. He wasn't a nice man, and it was a good thing he'd ghosted her. Even if he'd been telling the truth onstage and his wife did hate her guts, Alex hoped he was nicer to the woman he'd married than the character he played onstage would suggest.

"The only way we can leave before I have a few words with that asshole is if you give me more of what happened last week."

She was going to tell him that she'd give him a lot more. She wanted more than a few furtive grabs under clothing. She wanted him sprawled out on a bed. Naked. She wanted his fingers and cock inside her, his mouth doing more than glancing over her skin. There was nothing that she didn't want to do with him. Nothing off-limits.

But that would probably take more intimacy and communication than a quick chat. She might be direct to a fault, but this whole odyssey told her that intimacy was a problem for her. He might be able to commit, but he couldn't talk about his feelings worth a damn.

They were quite the pair.

They didn't get a chance to even have a quick chat, though. Because Ace found them. And from the look of his gait as he approached them, he'd found a bottle of whiskey before he found them.

When he reached them, Ace grabbed her arm and moved her closer to him. The playful, flirtatious version of Will that she'd been working with moments earlier disappeared, and the taciturn, stubborn bastard she knew better than the calculation to determine community property took his place. Because it wouldn't be fair for Will to knock out a drunk person, she feigned friendliness.

"I didn't realize when I came to the show that you would expect audience participation."

Ace just looked at her blankly before turning to Will. "I know you."

"I doubt you know your ABCs at the moment, and we've never met. So I'm not sure how that can be true." Will's face was impassive, but he kept looking at where Ace was touching her. It didn't frustrate her like it normally would. She knew that Will just wanted to keep her safe at the moment. He didn't think that she was weak or needed saving. He just would never be the type to intervene, because he hated bullies.

"I know where I know him from," Ace said, pointing his drink at Alex. "You made me go to his wedding."

"Oh yeah, you did meet that one time." Alex wanted to end this conversation immediately. She didn't want to think about Will's wedding. She'd been so distraught after the ceremony that she'd made Ace do car bombs before the reception. There had been very few times in her life when she'd been puking drunk, but that had been one of them. Ace had complained the whole time. He hadn't even fetched her crackers or Gatorade the next morning.

And he'd ghosted her not long after that, so maybe her behavior at the wedding had been the turnoff. She could empathize with that.

"You were so in love with this guy." Ace pointed at Will, but both she and Will froze. Ace didn't notice. "You got shit-faced, and then I had to bounce."

Alex wanted to make what Ace had said go away. "I mean, people commonly get drunk at weddings. Open bars."

"You made me buy you six shots before the reception." Oh shit! He was like Drunkstradamus now? Except, instead of telling the future, he had perfect recall while drunk. Maybe she should ask him to investigate some unsolved murders for her before he sobered up.

She could feel Will staring at her. The last thing she wanted him to know was how sad she'd been watching him get married to someone else. The last thing she wanted him to think was that she'd been in love with him since she was fifteen years old.

And that was what he had to know and think right now. It was the logical conclusion.

Even with the knowledge that Alex had been a wreck for him ten years after he'd rejected her, he recovered more quickly than Alex did. He stepped between her and Ace until the other man had to let go of her arm and gently turned Alex toward the door.

Over his shoulder, he said, "Great show, buddy. Lay off the sauce, though. More booze isn't going to help the pencil-dick situation."

Both of them had taken a car over, so they both took out their phones to summon a ride share. She just stared blankly at the interface, not wanting to talk to Will about what Ace had said. She was mortified. If it was possible, she wanted to sink into the concrete on the sidewalk more than she'd wanted to be snapped out of existence in the courtyard.

She had to face the music when Will grabbed her phone and tucked it into her purse. He took one finger and tipped her chin up until she met his gaze. "That guy"—he pointed at the front of the club—"was never ever good enough for you."

Alex searched for words for a long moment, sure he could see her inner turmoil all over her face. But for once, it was convenient that he was a man of few words and all action, because he didn't say anything else until the car showed up.

And when they got in the car, he didn't ask her if it was okay that the car pointed toward her place and only her place. He assumed that she'd recover her ability to speak at some point and would need to talk to him. And she was sure that if she asked him to leave when they got to her place, he would.

But she didn't want him to leave. Not when he pulled her to the middle seat in the back and grabbed her thigh on the ride home. Not when he said, "Makes sense that you would be that mean and bitter if the best thing you could come up with to joke about was the piece of spaghetti you had for junk. He should have just joked about his stupid-looking pants."

Alex huffed in laughter, and the silence wasn't as loaded after that. The driver didn't talk either and the car was totally quiet except for the sounds of a podcast about a gruesome murder in the background.

SIXTEEN

WHEN THEY WERE YOUNGER, WILL HAD BEEN SURE
that Alex would find someone better than him when she
went back to stay with her mom for high school. And he'd been
sure that she would dump that guy for an even better guy during
college. And he'd been utterly certain that she'd meet some dude
in law school who checked all her boxes—someone who looked
good next to her in a Sunday *New York Times* wedding announce-
ment.

But from what he could tell, none of the guys she dated were
worth shit. Of course, he probably could have guessed that any
guy who let Alex go had a couple of screws loose, but he'd had no
idea what kind of flotsam and jetsam she'd been wading through
in the dating pool all these years. And he wasn't mad at that.

If Alex had found a great guy after he'd rejected her, he never
would have had a chance with her once he'd realized his mistake.

And then he'd have to wade into the dating pool and hope he came out alive.

He hadn't known that his wedding had upset her. And he hadn't noticed her absence from the reception. Since they'd no longer been related by marriage at that point, she'd come with Lexi—and, he guessed, Ace.

As they climbed the stairs to Alex's condo, it occurred to him that he might not have gone through with the marriage had he met Ace before the ceremony. Even though he'd been happy with April, he might have made a different decision if he'd known that Alex had feelings for him. If he'd known that Alex hadn't met someone better and still felt something for him, he might have been sorely tempted to pursue it.

But then again, he might not. He'd been sure about absolutely everything back then. He'd never wavered in his decisions, which April had claimed made him the most stubborn being in existence. He'd thought that if he dug in his heels enough, April would do it, too, and they'd make their marriage work. But he hadn't realized that their marriage was quicksand. By the time they realized that they didn't want to be together and work so hard anymore, they'd already been up to their necks.

When they got to Alex's door, off the open colonnade that overlooked a pool, she got the keys out and in the door without any fuss. He was relieved.

He hesitated before following her in.

Alex dropped her keys on a side table and hung her jacket on a hook. He'd been over to her place when Lexi had made him help move her in, but he hadn't been there in years.

It was almost a miniature of Lexi's Spanish-style home, with soft white walls and wood floors. The furniture was all white as well. But somehow it still had personality. Everything was obviously chosen with care. He was so used to thinking of him and Alex as opposites that he might have guessed that her home was going to be cluttered and messy instead of curated and ordered.

"Do you want something to drink?" Alex was looking at him expectantly.

He cleared his throat. "Uh, sure."

"Any guidance as to what you want?" she asked. There was a hint of humor in her voice and it made him less worried that she was traumatized by the events of the evening.

"I'll have what you're having."

He followed Alex when she walked into the kitchen. It looked a lot different than when he'd been here at first. "You did a lot of work in here." As she took out a bottle of wine and two glasses, he looked at all the finishes. She had the kitchen of someone who could really cook.

She caught him out examining her stove. "You know that you're not the only one in the family who can cook."

"Yeah?" He quirked up one brow, wanting to play with her.

She winked at him, and he felt that. "You're just the sucker who does it all the time so Lexi and I don't have to."

Testing out the waters, he reached out and put a strand of her hair behind her ear, pulling on the lobe. She leaned into his touch for a moment and then headed to the living room. He followed her.

When she sat on the couch, he decided to hope for the best and sit next to her. She turned to face him.

He wasn't quite sure what to say. If her ex had been telling the truth, Alex's feelings for him had been a lot deeper for a lot longer than he'd known. He didn't know how to feel about it, but the last thing that he wanted was to hurt her. He cared about Alex, and he was attracted to her, but he wasn't sure that he could be what Alex needed. He wasn't sure that Alex wanted to commit to anyone, even him.

This thing between them was so much more complicated than an ordinary dating situation. There was so much more history and family and drama wrapped up in the story of the two of them. The attraction wasn't new, but they'd both forced it to simmer under the surface for so long, it had ebbed and flowed in differing proportions and might overpower them.

And what if it was just the sexual attraction between them? What would happen when they'd slaked it? Would they be able to go back to being friends—sort of? And would one or both of them get hurt?

Will still couldn't imagine losing the only family he had left.

"You're thinking pretty hard." Alex searched his face, and he knew he owed her some answers. Her ex had revealed more about her than she was comfortable with. He'd known her long enough to know that.

"Ace is a real asshole." He smiled, but it felt creaky. "I hope you got the answers you need about why the two of you didn't work out."

Alex raised her glass and brought it to her lips. "Good luck to his wife, who apparently hates me."

"I don't know how she thinks you 'broke him.'"

"I think he was broken before we ever met," Alex said. "I mean, I might have thought to send him back to the factory for repairs."

They were silent for a moment. Will looked at her, deciding that he had to try to do something he was bad at. "I want to kiss you again."

Alex looked up at him, seemingly startled by the confession, because her eyes got wide. "I would have thought you'd run screaming after what Ace said at the club."

"Was any of it true?" He probably shouldn't have asked that question, but he had to know for some reason.

Alex looked down. "Sort of. I'd put any feelings I had for you out of my mind for so long before the wedding that I didn't realize that I'd care about seeing you promise to spend the rest of your life with someone right in front of me." She put down her wine and fully turned toward him, resting her head on her arm over the back of the couch. She looked sweet and vulnerable like that, and it didn't help his growing desire to kiss her, to strip her out of her clothes and explore every crevice and curve with his mouth. He wanted to bathe in the scent of her. It was a jarring thing to go from trying to tolerate someone to wanting to be inside them. "And yeah, I got super drunk after the ceremony and spent the evening sending my regrets through the plumbing system."

"I wish I would have known before I met April." He'd always thought that Alex had regretted trying to kiss him as much as he'd regretted rejecting her. They'd been so young back then. And she'd always acted like she didn't care at all about him. So he'd moved on with April.

"I wish I'd known, too." Alex shook her head and her hair fell over her face. "I wouldn't have gone to the wedding."

Will pulled her hair back from her face again. Now that they'd broken the seal on touching each other, he wanted to touch her all the time.

"What are we going to do about this?" He had to give Alex credit. She always had a plan for everything. Even if it was totally cockamamie like her mission to talk to all her exes.

Too bad this was the kind of thing that was hard to plan for.

W ill sitting on her couch, drinking wine, talking about feelings. This was like a Bigfoot sighting, only rarer. It felt like a first date, but it wasn't a first date. Was it?

"I put you out of my mind after that." Alex probably needed to clarify. "I don't fuck with married men." In her line of work, she saw that married men were usually too complicated to consider. And Will assuming that she was in Andrew's office for prurient purposes was still a fresh wound.

Will started touching the inside of her wrist with the tip of his finger, tracing lazy patterns. She suppressed a shiver. "I know that."

"So?" In a role reversal, it was Alex who couldn't get the words out.

"Are we going to give this thing a try?" He leaned over, close enough for her to move a few inches and catch his mouth with hers. It was clear what he wanted her answer to be. "It doesn't have to be anything serious until we want it to be. Lexi doesn't even need to know."

Alex sat up and moved back on the couch.

Will looked confused. "What?"

"You want to keep me a secret?" If Will only wanted to have a few secret hookups, then she wasn't interested at all. She wasn't going to be his booty call. She might have been that for a few guys on her list, but she wouldn't do it with Will. He'd meant too much to her for too long. She'd loved him, hated him, lusted after him, for half her life.

"I can't do that with you." She fought to keep her voice calm, even though there was a lump in her throat the size of the Hope Diamond. "I think you'd better go."

Alex stood up and found Will's shoes and coat. She opened the door and set them carefully on the ground outside the door.

"Wait. I'm not trying to keep you a secret. I know how I feel about you." Alex turned toward Will but kept the door open. Because he might know how he felt about her, but she wasn't sure what they were even doing. After talking to her exes, she wasn't sure that she could even be in a relationship, but what she felt for him felt so much bigger than what she'd felt for anyone else. Could she even be what he needed her to be?

When Alex was silent for a long moment, Will's face and posture hardened. "We're not even going to talk about this?"

"You know what?" she said, motioning for him to take his exit. "I think I'm all talked out for the night. I need a break from talking."

"Don't push me away." It was wild how he knew exactly what she was trying to do. "I'm not like those other guys. I care about you, and I know you. I see you."

That punched her in the gut. He did see her, and that was terrifying. "I know. I care about you, too," Alex heard the emotion in her own voice and paused. "I just need a little more time. Tonight was a lot."

He stepped up to her, and she was enveloped by his smell again. She almost changed her mind when he cupped her face with his hand. "I'll give you all the time you need. Just don't need too much."

SEVENTEEN

ALEX WAS LUCKY. FOR THE NEXT FEW WEEKS, SHE WAS busy negotiating a divorce settlement for a repeat client. That always made things more complicated, because she had to consider the terms of their previous divorces when drafting the new settlement. Sort of like nesting dolls, and people got antsy as the settlements inside the nesting dolls got smaller.

The only good thing—other than all the hours she'd billed—about working a hundred hours a week was that it left little time to think about the fact that not only did Will want to have a physical relationship with her, he also wanted more of her. That was everything she'd wanted when she'd thrown herself at him. And maybe she wouldn't have been so afraid when he'd gotten married. But the older she got, the more she had to lose from risking her heart. She wished she was still as openhearted as she had been when she'd first met Will. But her job and her life experiences made it too hard. She already hurt thinking about how aw-ful she would feel if things ended with Will.

It sucked. And Alex wasn't sure how to proceed.

By the final day of mediation, which felt more like a Monday than a Friday, all she wanted to do was wash her face and get into bed with a big glass of wine and an *SVU* marathon. She was half-way through an episode in which the sexual tension between Sta-bler and Benson was at its juiciest—her favorite time period of the show—when her bed started shaking.

She really hadn't lived through many earthquakes during her time in California. Most of them were small. The ones during which she was at her office were the worst—the building was on rollers, which kept it from falling down during the shaking but made her really nauseous.

Her condo building was old, even though they'd retrofitted it to meet the codes. But it was a disorienting thing to have the bed shaking when she wasn't being railed. She tried to remember the rules when it came to earthquakes, and she rolled off her bed and made her way to the doorway.

It seemed to go on forever, and her entire life flashed before her eyes. She couldn't believe that she'd spent the last few weeks sad about a man. A man she'd already spent time being sad about.

By the time it stopped, Alex was back to being pissed at Will. The lights had flickered for most of the quake, but they were def-initely off now. Stabler and Benson were silent, and she was alone in her dark apartment, the one that probably had broken glass all over the floor. Barefoot.

———

Will lived in an old warehouse, so he'd barely woken up during the earthquake. He usually didn't even turn over during the minor ones, so he knew it had to be major for the light fixtures in his tank of a building to sway above him.

Once it stopped, he immediately went into worry mode. Charlee lived close to the restaurant and they texted him before he even got his phone out to let him know that the restaurant was undamaged and hadn't lost power. Thank goodness none of the glassware had been delivered yet.

Then he remembered that Lexi was in Seoul for three weeks. Her music had resurged in popularity in Asia after a K-pop group had sampled one of her songs. His mind immediately turned to Alex. He wanted to make sure she was okay, but he also didn't know whether she wanted to hear from him yet.

The instant he'd walked out of her place, he'd wanted to turn around and make her see that they didn't need any more time. But his pride had kicked in. He knew how she felt about relationships. If she didn't see that he was better for her than any of the other guys she'd been with, there was nothing he could say to convince her.

If she'd taken a beat and talked to him instead of asking him to leave, he would have told her that he didn't want to keep their thing under wraps at all, that he'd only offered that because he knew how skittish she was about relationships. He'd been willing to take her on any terms she would accept.

But now he realized that he wouldn't accept keeping a relationship with Alex a secret. They were both too old for that. And she needed to talk to him instead of putting up walls between them. Maybe that was the difference between him and the other guys she'd been with. Now that he knew he wanted her, he wasn't going to let her walls stop him. He would climb over them.

As soon as she decided to talk to him.

He was fumbling around his room for something to wear—he'd probably have to file something with insurance for the restaurant even if there wasn't damage, and he wanted to verify that all was well himself—when there was a knock on his door.

Only a few people had the security code for his building. Somehow, he knew it was Alex. Only she would elect to be a pain in the ass during a natural disaster.

He found pants and opened the door without his shirt. Part of it was that he'd put a load of shirts in the dryer before bed, and part of it was that he wanted her to see what she'd been missing.

The way her eyes widened when he opened the door told him that he'd succeeded.

"What are you doing here?" He probably shouldn't be such a dick, but he was mad that she'd put herself at risk by driving around the city in the immediate aftermath of an earthquake.

"My power's out, and I was scared." The Alex he knew didn't easily admit to being scared of anything. Maybe he wouldn't have to climb quite as high as he'd thought.

"You came here first." He liked that she came to him before going to her friends. That never would have happened before her stupid quest.

"Jane's not answering her phone, and Lana's kids have the stomach flu." He'd definitely still have to climb over some walls, but he stepped aside and motioned for her to come in.

Alex trailed into his living space and stared at the couch. It was the old one from his study at the house he'd shared with

April. He could attest from the last few months of his marriage that it wasn't comfortable enough to sleep on. "I have a king-sized bed."

A few weeks ago, the thought of sharing a bed with Alex would have been enticing, but now it would just be torture. They couldn't even kiss once without things getting irrevocably weird, and now they were going to be bunking together. He wasn't going to sleep with her until they'd had a real conversation. He pressed the heels of his hands on his eyes and let out a sigh.

"I'm sorry." Alex hitched up her overnight bag in her hand and turned to the door. "I can just get a hotel."

Will put up a hand. Now that she was here, he didn't want her to leave. And she might be ready to talk if she was here. "You're okay?"

Alex bit her bottom lip, and he wanted to touch her. Even though he was still irritated with her, he wanted to pull her into his arms. When he was touching her, he would forget all the very good reasons why this was a probably a terrible idea. He wished that they could just give in and save the questions and conversations for later.

But he knew better than anyone that surrendering to the sexual pull between them wouldn't solve their complications. It would only make them worse. He knew it didn't fit with the expectations that most people had of him—guy's guy and hard-ass chef—but having sex with Alex would mean something to him. He knew it would mean something to her—why else would she have kicked him out of her home instead having a fucking conversation with him?

"I was sitting on the floor, waiting for the shaking to stop, and

I felt like I needed to say some things to you if it was really the end of the world," she said. "But my power really is out, and I don't know when it's coming back on. I didn't want to be alone."

"Is everything else in your apartment safe? No broken gas lines?"

"I turned off the gas before I left."

"Good girl."

Her eyes fluttered when he said that, and the air in the room changed. He was suddenly conscious of being shirtless and her standing across the room in deceptively modest pajamas that were so thin they didn't leave anything to the imagination.

She licked her bottom lip.

"It wasn't safe to drive over here." He added a little remonstration in his tone.

"We should talk about this." Alex dropped her bag on the floor, and he heard some bottles—probably cosmetics—jangle together. But that didn't break the tension between them. He took a step toward her. She took a step back. He stopped.

They were dancing. They'd been dancing for as long as they'd known each other. He wanted to be done with this dance and move on to another.

Alex was not afraid of Will. She knew for a fact that if she told him that she didn't want him, that they shouldn't be together, he would respect that. He would respect her. But at the moment, she didn't particularly want to be respected.

She wanted him to call her a "good girl," but not just because she'd remembered to turn off the gas after an earthquake. She wanted to please him on an elemental level. But, after she stepped back, he turned and went to the kitchen. Not asking if she wanted something stronger, he grabbed two glasses and filled them with water. When he offered her one, she moved closer to him to grab it.

Their fingers brushed, and she gasped.

"This isn't going away, is it?" He whispered as though he was trying to gentle her to his whims. She wanted to hate it, but she didn't. Mostly, she was done fighting her attraction to him. It was complicated and probably ill-advised, but he was right—it wasn't going away. They were drawn to each other, whether they liked it or not.

And maybe they had all this tension because they'd never given in to it. He was like an ultra-decadent ice cream when she was on a diet. The only reason she couldn't stop thinking about it was that she wasn't going to let herself have it. Maybe, if they'd ever allowed themselves to give in, it wouldn't be as good as what they built up in their minds.

"No, it isn't," she said. "Maybe if we just do it once, to get it out of our systems, then we won't be at each other's throats all the time?"

Will laughed softly, and it was as though he'd blown over her clit. "You think I'm going to be done with you after one time?"

Alex shook her head.

"Good. Because it's going to take at least three times."

"Three times?" That seemed random.

Will took a sip of water and nodded. "Once, to get the lay of the land. I can't promise to last long. I haven't been with anyone since my divorce."

Alex hated that she liked that. She tried her best not to put morals around sex—as long as someone didn't harm others while expressing their sexuality, she was all for it. That was why she didn't sleep with married men. No matter what a guy said about whether his wife was okay with it, she could never trust it.

But a part of her was thrilled at the idea that she would be the first woman that Will had after his divorce. It was like he was starting over brand-new with her. It had also been months and months. He was a beautiful man and had likely had plenty of opportunity to fall into bed with any number of other beautiful people. That he chose her made her feel special.

That was the thing about being human. There were things that shouldn't matter that did, and things that should matter that didn't. And judging herself for the fact that she liked being the only one for Will wasn't going to make her like it any less.

"What are you thinking?" He moved closer to her and took the water glass out of her hand. She didn't say anything but pressed the side of her face into his chest, which told him that it was okay to put his arms around her.

"I don't seem to do a lot of thinking when I'm around you. I just react to things, and I can't seem to stop myself." She was trying to apologize, but she wasn't doing a very good job of it. "I shouldn't have thrown you out of my place without listening to why you didn't want to tell people we were seeing each other."

"I understand why you would react that way." She could feel his voice through his skin as well as hear it. She'd missed this kind of intimacy after Jason, hadn't realized how much she craved physical closeness with another person. She could have gone out and found sex, but she wouldn't feel comfortable letting someone she was just having sex with hold her while she apologized to him.

"I didn't say the right things when we were younger." She knew he was referring to him rejecting her that first summer. "It wasn't that you weren't beautiful or that I didn't want you. Even if I hadn't been a constantly horned-up teen, I would have wanted you."

"It's probably better that you flat-out rejected me. It's not easy on my pride to say that, but both of us were too young for anything serious."

"Are we old enough now?" he asked in a faux-serious tone.

She buried her laugh in his chest hair and let her fingers roam the muscles of his back. "I don't know."

"What do you know?"

That was a real question. She only knew that she wanted him now, that he was the first person that she'd thought of when she needed a soft place to land tonight. He was the only man she'd ever been involved with in any capacity that she'd been willing to rely on. If it had been any of her other lovers, she would have gone to a hotel and sent them a text letting them know she was okay.

But tonight—even though the last time they saw each other was what it was—she knew that he would open the door and let her be here. He would understand why she needed him instead of a stupid hotel room. Even though he didn't have cable and she wouldn't be able to finish her *SVU* marathon.

Who needed Stabler and Benson when she and Will had a "will they or won't they?" that had gone on almost as long?

"I know that I've been thinking about the way you kiss since before you stopped kissing me."

Will smiled. "I'm glad I didn't forget how."

She lifted up onto her tiptoes and planted her lips against his, taking his implied invitation. He didn't leave her hanging on whether the kiss was welcome. He grabbed her hips and pulled them into the cradle of his, not making a secret of the fact that his body had responded to her nearness.

The kiss from a month ago had been a gentle exploration at first—tentative. This one was nothing like that. He owned her mouth with his, kissing her as though he was headed out to war the next morning. She moaned into his mouth and wrapped her arms around his neck, pressing her breasts against his chest.

When he stopped kissing her on her mouth, considerately allowing her to breathe, she said, "Are you sure we should be doing this?"

His body froze, and he lifted her onto the counter in one fluid motion. She wasn't a lightweight, and it felt so nice that he was strong enough to lift her. His hands bracketed her hips on the cool marble. "I'm honestly not sure if this is a good idea, but I'm so hard that there's not a lot of blood flow to my brain right now."

Alex looked down, appreciating the tent in his pajama pants. "It's not as obvious on my end, but I'm having a similar blood-flow issue."

"This might not be a good idea, but I think it's inevitable." Will picked up a hand and trailed one finger over her collarbone. "Even if we crash and burn, at least we actually tried it. At least we'll know if it's as good as it has been when it was all in our heads."

Alex copied him and ran her fingers over his chest. She couldn't stop touching him. Didn't want to. "You've thought about me?"

Will grunted, slipping seamlessly from his perfectly cogent—to her vagina at least—argument for why they should at least give sex with each other a shot to his usual mode of communication.

"Tell me what you've thought about."

He looked at her then, his deep, green eyes fathomless. She couldn't possibly know what was behind them, but she knew it was dark and dirty and dangerous. "Every time you wear a tight skirt, I think about bending you over the nearest couch or chair and peeling it up until I can see if you're wearing underwear or not."

His deep voice unfurled another wave of desire, and she wanted to tease him. All that came out, though, was, "They're usually thongs."

Will bit into his lower lip and grunted. "When you wear a sundress, I bet you're wearing a thong, too. Whenever you move, the dress gets caught between your cheeks."

"You have an obsession with my ass." Hearing Will say that after waiting for so long to hear desire for her coming out of him was more arousing than any other foreplay she'd ever had. She wasn't particularly vain, but hearing this man tell her what he found sexy about her was intoxicating.

"Who the fuck wouldn't?" he asked before nuzzling her neck with his nose. "I want to know every inch of your body, Alex. I want to know if you're that juicy and ripe everywhere. I want to lick you until you scream and curl into me like a kitten and I want to fuck you like I hate you and have you leave scratches all up and down my back."

All that sounded very good, and she wanted to start right

away. She had her hand halfway down his torso when he asked, "What have you thought about doing with me?"

She was a little embarrassed to admit it, but he'd been so forthcoming that it was only fair. "Every time there's a sex scene in a movie or a television show, I think about you and me acting it out. But not like a full-on role-play. I just want the real thing, with you. I want to have every kind of sex with you, and I want you to go feral for me."

As soon as she got the last word out, his mouth was on hers. His hands held her face still as he kissed her until she was breathless again. His chest was heaving, and his skin was flushed by the time he ended the kiss. Knowing that he would probably be hesitant to rip her clothes off in his kitchen the first time they had sex, she grabbed the hem of her pajama top and pulled it over her head. She'd been so rushed to get over here that she hadn't put on a bra.

Will looked down at her breasts and licked his lips. He didn't wait for her to ask him—beg him—to touch her there. He cupped her and brushed her skin, his hands both gentle and firm. He bent his head and licked at her nipples until she squirmed on the counter. This was what she'd wanted the day she'd skinned her knee outside his restaurant.

She mussed his hair with her fingers while he tasted her. And even though he said that he wanted them to fuck each other like they were enemies, his lips and tongue were gentle and reverent. It was good until she got restless and couldn't wait to be skin to skin with him from head to toe.

"I need more." She didn't have to ask him twice. He put his

hands under her ass and carried her the dozen feet or so between the kitchen and his bedroom. He set her on her feet long enough to pull down her pajama pants and panties and then nudged her backward, until the backs of her legs and then her whole body hit the bed.

She tried to sit up and kiss him, but he knelt on the floor next to the bed, between her dangling legs.

Somewhere in the back of her mind, she'd always known that Will Harkness really liked to eat pussy. She didn't know anyone who liked raw sea urchin as much as he did. Sure enough, when she looked down at him, he was looking at the center of her like she was a nineteen-course tasting menu. Knowing that he wanted her as much as he seemed to made her lower belly clench. The air over the core of her gave her a chill, and he stopped in his descent. She nearly moaned in frustration. She'd been waiting over a decade for him to touch her like this. She'd thought about it nearly every time she'd looked at his mouth at a teenager. If she didn't get her moment of seeing stars with him between her legs, she might actually die.

"Are you cold?" While it was very kind and considerate of him to think of her comfort, she didn't care if she was cold if he could make her legs shake.

"Just my vulva. It would help if you put your mouth there." He laughed, a teasing sound that caressed her legs when his body moved between her thighs. "Seriously, Will."

"Say please."

He expected her to use her manners now? When she was nearly feral for satisfaction? The bastard. "Please eat my pussy, Will."

If he had any idea how much it cost her to ask him that, when the ghost of his rejection had haunted her most of her adult life, he wouldn't have asked that of her. But even though they'd opened up to each other quite a lot over the past couple of months, there was still a part of herself she hadn't shared with him. She'd shared the angry bits about him and the sad bits about the other men she'd been with. But she'd never shared how sad she'd been when he'd told her no. She'd just pretended to be pissed at him and decided to hate him forever.

But she couldn't pretend that she hated him now—well, maybe as a sex thing, but not in real life. He could make her beg. He could bring her to her knees—and probably would.

He might know that without her telling him because he gave her what she begged for. He licked and sucked and gradually zeroed in on her clit before she was forced to rip a clump of his hair out. He teased her entrance with his fingers until her hips started dancing for him. She grabbed his perfect white sheets so hard she might have shredded them, but she didn't care. He coaxed her body to the edge of orgasm and then slowed down what felt like ten times, until she was sweaty and writhing, and less verbal than he was before his coffee.

And when she finally went over, either because he took her there or her body demanded what he'd been refusing to give, he was still looking at her with the same level of awe that he'd started with. And that made her hungry for him again. She didn't know that she'd ever get enough of him.

"I want you inside me," she said, once she'd recovered the power of speech.

He stood up and pulled off his pajama pants, but she didn't get to see his cock because he crawled over her body. "Condom?" he asked.

"I have an IUD," she said. "If you really haven't been with anyone else—"

"I haven't."

"We can—"

"Are you sure?"

She would never trust anyone else like this. He might have been a dick sometimes over the years, but he'd never lied to her. So she nodded. And opened her legs to him. When he was inside her, it felt so right that tears came to her eyes. She liked everything about being with him, and it felt like being young again. Like when she'd first met him and had gripped on to every word he said as though it had been a shiny agate that she could keep to admire later.

It was first-time sex. He rolled on her hair when they changed positions; she had to tell him how to touch her clit when he was behind her so that she would come again. But he didn't seem invested in performing well as a salve to his ego. He genuinely wanted it to be good for her so that it would be good for them. It was so different from sex with her exes, when she always felt as though she was performing a role for their benefit.

She came again while he was behind her, so they moved again until he was on his back and she straddled his thighs. "This is one of the things I've pictured again and again."

"What?" She took him inside her and rolled her hips until he groaned and started steering her. She liked that she'd made him

lose control. He normally didn't let anyone see him close to un-
done. She knew that she was one of the intimate few.

After he came, he cleaned her up. Another first. And they
cuddled, yet another first after first-time sex. Most of her relationships had started out as hookups, so she'd usually been calling an
Uber as the guy had been rolling off her the first time. She was
back in her panties and looking for shoes by the time the app
found her a car.

Before this, she'd had her postcoital escape plan down to a
science. Hell, even the hookup had been science. But sex with
Will was art. It was music. He was literature.

She shook her head. Will's dick was not literature. It had just
been a long time for both of them, and that's why it was so good.
They'd also gone without a condom—another first—and knew
each other really well. It was just more intimate because of a
whole host of circumstances. That's why it felt different. They still
hadn't talked about where they were going, and she shouldn't read
too much into what had just happened. Even if it was the best
she'd ever had.

Just because they'd had sex, that didn't mean she could start
planning a whole future with the guy, as much as her heart was
telling her to. To be fair, her vulva was singing along with that
chorus. She hadn't felt so relaxed, maybe ever. This sex-with-trust
thing was not overrated.

Will pulled her so that she was on her back, and he was on his
side looming over her. Like, a sexy loom, and not a creepy loom.
"You're thinking a whole lot."

"How can you tell?"

He gave her a sexy smile and then kissed her on the tip of her nose. She might have been wrung out, but she felt a tingle of desire when his lips touched her. "I don't know, but I know. It's like your brain has a rhythm and I can tell that it's moving fast."

"You're so weird," Alex said. "Cute, but weird."

"You never made me feel weird when I was a teenager," Will said. "I never thanked you for that."

"You were the coolest guy that I'd ever met. It wouldn't have done me any good to make you feel weird. I had a giant crush on you from the moment that we met." He looked different now. He was broader and manly in a way that wouldn't have appealed to her when she was a teen. He might be a chef, but he had the look of a biker about him. When he was younger, he hadn't had a baby face. But he'd been sort of an insouciant bad boy to her. It hadn't struck her until this moment that her memory might be faulty—that she might have been wrong about him.

She'd thought that because he hadn't shown any vulnerability to her back then, he didn't have any. But knowing how rarely he let people in, she knew that he'd been feeling her out. And she'd tried to kiss him like some creeper. If the tables were turned, he'd be rightly labeled a sex pervert.

"I'm so sorry," she said, and he looked at her with a scrunched brow. Even that was cute, though it would be menacing if he looked at one of his staff like that. "I came on to you when you weren't wanting it. And all these years, I've been so angry and upset that you rejected me."

"I regretted turning you down, and my dick punished me for it. But I'd found a home for the first time since I was really little. After my mom left, my dad got married a bunch of times. You know that, but I really felt like you couldn't understand what it was like not to have roots."

"I was lucky. My mom wasn't a marriage junkie. She had to pawn me off on Lexi every summer because she needed to go on academic trips and make discoveries like it was her job," she said with sarcasm. She rubbed the forearm that he'd slung over her body. Even his veins were appealing to her. "But I was plopped in a completely different world every summer. I adapted. And I am so lucky and so privileged. My whole life, I've wanted for very little."

"You were kind of a brat." His voice was teasing, so she only pinched his arm a little.

"It's true." She could admit that much about herself. Although she was privileged, she tried to see herself clearly. "But to be fair, I've never reacted quite so poorly to not getting what I wanted as I did when you said you would absolutely not consider kissing me or being my boyfriend or anything of the sort."

"I wasn't nice about it. I didn't know how to be. I'd never had a girl actually approach me before."

"Understandable. You probably just crooked your finger when you were at school."

"That's a laugh. I didn't have a real girlfriend until April. I was so scared to become my dad, the chronic philanderer, that I just sort of avoided the whole thing."

Alex let that sink in. She wanted to be his second and only girlfriend. And she wasn't terrified.

Jesus. She was glad that she hadn't realized that before they'd fallen into bed. It might have made her terribly nervous about her performance.

"So I'm the—"

"The second girlfriend," Will said. "You technically have a lot more dating experience than I do."

"But you were with April for so long that you got a lot more sex reps in than I have." Will looked behind him. "What are you doing?"

"Making sure there's not a football coach in my bedroom." They both laughed, but his face sobered. "Can I ask you something? What was it about your relationship with Jason that made you freak out when he decided to marry someone else?"

"Right after me." She thought that was the most important part.

"Yeah, right after you."

"It just came as a shock to me that he wanted more with her." She wasn't quite sure how to put this in a way that wouldn't make it seem like things weren't right with Will now. "We're both lawyers, so we understood the hours involved. We're both biracial, and we both feel the same way about it."

"And what way do you feel about it?"

"I mean, I grew up with a white mom and my dad wasn't around most of the time. The summers I spent with Lexi made me feel at home in my Blackness. But I've never wanted to erase pieces of myself just to belong with one side or the other."

"That makes sense."

"It doesn't make sense to a lot of people right now. But I'm not going to go around feeling that half the people who made me who I am don't matter and that my light skin and wavy hair aren't part of my privilege. That would be delusional. I'm no authority on Blackness. I'm only an authority on me.

"You've met my mom. As an anthropology professor, she was always talking about how race—just like gender, sexuality, social class—was made up by people to keep us sorted into our own groups. And, while it's significant, it means something to people, it's not real. Or it's both real and not real at the same time. Whenever someone asks me what my race is, I tell them I'm biracial, and their response is more of a reflection of who they are than it says anything about me. But it took time to get there.

"Anyway, Jason's dad was a Republican. So me with my anthropology-professor mom and him with his misguided father had a whole lot to sort out for ourselves about race before we met. He was easy to spend time with. It was a nice feeling."

"Do you miss him?"

"Jason? Not really. Sometimes. Maybe." There he went having the vulnerable face on.

As much as she didn't want to hurt him, she knew that it was important to be honest with him. "I miss talking to him sometimes. It was nice to have someone with whom I could leave so many things unspoken, who would get me if I gave the shorthand version of how my day went. But it also didn't really leave space for growth. We never had a serious disagreement, not even when we broke up. I was always sure where I stood with him. Until I wasn't.

"But I don't miss feeling like someone was only half listening to me. The problem with shorthand is that you don't have to learn someone."

"I like learning you," Will said as his hand crept under the sheet and found the warm skin of her belly. "I think I'd like to learn more about what's . . . here."

EIGHTEEN

I T HAD TAKEN ABOUT FORTY-EIGHT HOURS FOR THE POWER
company to get her electricity back on and for the city to ensure that there hadn't been any gas leaks during the earthquake.
Selfishly, Alex wished that everyone else on her block had gotten
power but something in her unit had proven stubborn. She would
have had an excuse to stay in bed with Will through the whole
weekend, but no one else in her building would be dealing with
spoiled food and lack of AC.

And just to spend time with him without their mutual habit of
taking jibes at each other constantly. The jibes that remained
were usually aimed at getting the other person to reveal something kinky to do. And it was always worth it.

It didn't totally suck to have a trained chef on call, either. Alex
could put together a brunch, but her hollandaise was nowhere
near professional.

As long as they were together in his apartment, Lexi on another continent, and their friends out of reach, they didn't have to talk about whether they were *together* together and whether they were going to tell the people in their lives.

After feeling how big the feelings were between her and Will, she was starting to see the wisdom in keeping it under wraps until they figured out whether it would burn out with time. They lived vastly different lifestyles, though she had a tiny bit more control over her schedule now that she was a partner with her own book of business. That just meant that she could sometimes delegate time-consuming and tedious work, not that she could have court dates scheduled on nights and weekends when Will was busy with his new restaurant.

It was slightly unhinged that she was planning in her head for a future with Will, even though she didn't know if he was ready to plan a future with anyone. She hoped he was. Hell, she hoped she was. When she'd asked him about his favorite food cities, he'd talked about hole-in-the-wall restaurants in Milan that he wanted to show her. The idea of traveling the world with him was really appealing.

And even though she'd returned to her apartment, they'd spent every night this week together. Will had come with her to make sure her place was safe the Monday after the earthquake, and he'd still been there when she got home from work. She'd been in such a rush that she hadn't had time to finish cleaning up the broken glass, but everything had been in perfect order by the time she got home.

In addition to being great with his hands, he was handy to have around. She tried to resist getting used to it, but she was starting to rely on him to be there not just in times of crisis, but when she wanted to send him a funny TikTok that would make him mad based on his fervent belief that lettuce wasn't a good substitute for bread in sandwiches. He was also weirded out by her liberal use of mayonnaise on both sides.

But she didn't know precisely where they stood with each other, and she didn't know if she was going to tell Jane and Lana when she sat down to brunch with them and Lexi the following Sunday. She wasn't sure how they would react, and she wasn't sure how she wanted them to react.

They were already at the restaurant and had probably already ordered her whole wheat pancakes, bacon, and a bottomless mimosa.

Alex had the choice about whether to tell her grandmother and her friends that she was seeing Will taken away from her when Lexi looked her up and down and said, "You finally did it." Lexi's voice was so loud that other diners looked at them. Although she didn't want to be a spectacle, she wasn't going to admonish her grandmother in public. And Lexi knew that, so she didn't modulate her tone or volume.

Instead, she went with pure denial. It wasn't as though she was wearing a sign that said she'd slept with Will. There was absolutely no way that Lexi could know that for sure. "I have no idea what you're talking about."

She took her seat. Jane and Lana stared at her, wide-eyed. Lexi was undeterred. "Young lady." Lexi never did the "young lady" move, so this had to be serious. "You know exactly what I'm talking about. You finally put poor Will out of his misery."

"Poor Will?" Alex was dumbfounded. Lexi was prone to revisionist history when it made her ex-husbands look bad or herself more glamorous, but any suggestion that Will was some sort of victim in their decades-long animosity was strictly out-of-bounds. "Now neither of us knows what you're talking about."

"Your problem is that you're not a romantic like he is," Lexi said. She took a bread roll from the basket at the center of the table and started smearing it with butter rather aggressively. Given that Lexi had come of age before body positivity was even a glimmer of a thing in Hollywood, the fact that she was eating carbs in public was a sign that Alex had upset her.

But Lexi was right. Alex was not a romantic. "How could you expect me to be a romantic given what I do for work and where I came from?"

She literally spent her whole life steeped in unhappy couples. Most of them had started out with a romantic idea of what their lives would be together, and just like fifty percent of other couples, they failed. There was no way she would come out of that unscathed.

Jane and Lana both looked around as though they deeply regretted accepting the invitation for brunch. "And look at these two: Jane's divorce was messy and expensive. And I give Lana and Greg five years tops before they start going to key parties."

"Key parties" distracted Lexi. Her "Oh, how fun!" was at her original volume. She might be aging, but she could still project her voice, God love her.

Through gritted teeth, Lana said, "We're never going to key parties, Alex. That was in the vows." She smiled at the diners at the tables around them, who were suddenly interested in eating their food again.

"And I'm happy that I'm divorced, but I don't regret getting married," Jane said, draining her mimosa and motioning the server over for a refill. "I learned a lot from my ex, and we have nothing but love for each other now that we're not living in the same house. Sometimes you have to try something out before you decide that it's not for you."

"You're still paying for the woman's yoga classes and bikini waxes, and you have nothing but love for her?" Alex always thought that Jane was more sensible about these things. She felt as though she was being ganged up on, and she didn't like it.

"Lexi, whether or not I'm a romantic is beside the point. I don't know what Will I are even doing together. Not yet."

"So you admit that you are seeing each other?" Lexi looked over her readers at her. When the server had come over to refill Jane's mimosa, Lexi had apparently decided to change her order.

"Yes. Although it really freaks me out that you could tell by looking at me." It was that kind of witchy shit that prevented Alex from completely discounting Lexi's reliance on tarot card readers and other mystics, even though it didn't fit with Alex's generally nonspiritual vibe. Most of the time, it felt like one of Lexi's many quirks, but every so often . . .

"We don't have to talk about the details, but I think you should be careful," Lexi said. She never warned people to be careful. When people left her house, she told them to "drive fast and take chances." It was ironic, but barely. Alex had never been able to figure out why Lexi was so willing to take risks and chances, especially in love, after so many losses.

But the fact that she was telling Alex to be careful now must mean that she thought Alex was doing something foolhardy. That there was a high probability that her heart would end up broken.

"I know it probably won't work out, Lexi," Alex said. "But when we break up, you have to promise not to hold it against Will. This is probably just something that we're both getting out of our systems."

"I'm not worried about you. I'm worried about him," Lexi said with a sniff. "You chew men up and spit them out. They're sad and broken when you finish with them."

"Hello, pot. Meet kettle." For someone who'd been married more times than she'd had a colonoscopy, Lexi sure was being judgmental about Alex's approach to her love life.

"I always leave them better than I found them." When Alex gave her a look, Lexi added, "If not financially, at least spiritually."

"I do not destroy men. If anything, I leave them in good enough condition that the very next person they date snaps them up to make a long-term commitment."

"Or you wound them so severely that they vow never to date another person with an avoidant attachment style." Lana threw that grenade on the center of the table.

"Avoidant attachment style?" Alex was really sick of people telling her that. "I don't have an avoidant attachment style. If I did, I would never even get in relationships in the first place."

"Oh, cut the shit, of course you do," Jane said.

Okay, so they were definitely ganging up on her. The only thing that kept her from getting up and walking out of the restaurant was that it would be a very avoidant attachment style thing to do.

"It's totally understandable, of course," Lana said in her therapist voice. "Your mother supported you financially, but she could never give you what you needed emotionally. And your father was neither physically nor emotionally available to you. So, even though you had Lexi every summer, you got used to managing your own emotions. You essentially raised yourself. Because you couldn't rely on either of your parents, you can't allow yourself to rely on romantic partners. You rarely even rely on your friends."

"I rely on my friends. I rely on the two of you." Alex didn't know why she was starting to cry. She definitely needed to go back to therapy if Lana telling her things she already knew about herself was going to get the waterworks going in public. "I made you help me interview my ex-boyfriends. And you did it. I couldn't believe that you did, but you did."

"And we did it because you never ask for anything," Jane said. "We literally could have told you that all of your relationships end because you have an avoidant attachment style and you date men—the vast majority of them are real dumb and think that your pathological indifference toward their feelings is sexy for a minute until they get too close. You get afraid, and then you shut down."

"You date fuckboys, too, Jane." Alex really didn't have a rhetorical leg to stand on. She had always had a secret pride that she wasn't like other women in this one respect. She didn't need anyone to feel like she was complete. She was fine on her own. Men were dessert, and there was no point in catching feelings for any of them, because they would always let her down.

But she was exactly like other women. She needed. She needed a lot. And now that she'd gotten just a fraction of her needs met by Will, she was afraid that she'd grow addicted to it. That was why she'd hesitated about whether to tell Lexi and her friends. She didn't want to be made a fool of. She didn't want to have that feeling that she'd always had, waiting in baggage claim at LAX at the beginning of every summer.

Every year, she'd waited to see if her dad would show up and at least drop her off at Lexi's. He did it once. The whole ride to his mother's house, he'd listed off things that they were going to do for the summer. But when she'd called him the following Saturday to ask when he was going to pick her up for their trip to Disneyland, he'd told her that he was busy working on a paper. And she didn't see him until about a month later. When she was sullen and borderline rude to him, he'd yelled at her and told her that she couldn't speak to her father that way.

After that summer, when she was ten or eleven, she hadn't bothered hoping to have her dad pick her up, or even spend time with her or ask about her life. She'd learned to assume that all men were self-absorbed and could only care about her to the extent that she made them look good.

"None of this is meant to hurt you," Lana said.

Lexi rolled her eyes. "You actually could stand to risk getting hurt a little more. I know your dad was not a good father. And one of my major regrets in life is that I didn't hold him accountable for the way that he treated you. I tried to make up for it, but—"

Alex put her hand over her grandmother's, doing her best to ignore how fragile the bones in her grandmother's hands felt. She didn't want the woman who had helped her come out of her childhood whole feel like any of her emotional shit was her fault. "He was an adult, and he needed to know that on his own."

"Jesus Christ. You should have told me that this was going to be emotional before I put on non-waterproof mascara," Jane said, dabbing her eyes at the other side of the table. That made Alex's tears flow, and Lana was close to full-out sobbing.

"Well, since we're making announcements, you all should know that I'm dating Will's friend Charlee," Jane said. "So Alex's very silly quest actually did something good."

At least there was that. And when she thought about it, Charlee was pretty perfect for Jane. They were fun and loud and up for anything. Charlee had the kind of personality that could stand up to Jane's brashness. And they lived their life unapologetically, just like Jane. They were also very, very hot.

"I'm glad my stupidity bore fruit."

"Neither of us thinks that it was stupid for you to look at your past and why a certain pattern shows up," Lana said. "The way you went about it was flat-out crazy, though."

"Is that your clinical opinion?" Jane asked. And they all laughed.

"So, Lexi, did you meet anyone cool in Seoul?" They'd had enough heavy for breakfast. Alex was now sufficiently scared that she would repeat her avoidant pattern with Will and that she would probably ruin the relationship because of it. Or at least rack up a new batch of therapy bills so she could white-knuckle her way through the urge to flee.

Luckily, Lexi decided it was time to let the heavy stuff go, too. "I had a lot of fun, but the K-pop boys were a little too young for me."

NINETEEN

WILL SHOULD HAVE KNOWN THAT EVERYTHING WAS
going to go to shit. His life was going too well for it not
to. He was spending almost every night with Alex, and she'd
given up her stupid project of talking to all her exes. According to
her, she'd had an illuminating conversation with Lexi and her
friends that made her think about a lot of things.

He'd been surprised when she'd told him that Lexi had
guessed they were together. But he knew that Lexi would be
happy about it. And she'd interfere, but that couldn't be avoided.
He'd thought that the fact that Alex had shared with friends that
they were together meant that she thought this was something
more serious than just "getting things out of their systems," but
he couldn't help but notice that she'd pulled away from him after
the fateful brunch with Lexi.

They hadn't had any more deep conversations after sex. He felt like there was still so much that he wanted to learn about her, but Alex seemed to want to keep their conversation light. He wasn't used to trying to parse out mixed messages from a romantic partner—he was usually the one doling them out.

But he didn't have the time to focus on his nascent relationship with Alex as the restaurant opening date got closer. Every day was filled with finalizing menus and orders and giving tours to and cooking meals for his investors. He was up to his ears and overwhelmed from the time he woke up until the time he slipped into bed with Alex every night.

By the time he curled up next to her, all he could do was lose himself inside her. And she seemed to welcome it. But he couldn't stop the sinking feeling that she was using the sexual connection between them—the one that only seemed to get stronger every time they were together—to hide from any growing intimacy.

It was familiar to him, too familiar. It was the same feeling that he'd had at the end of his marriage. He wished the way that relationship had turned out had taught him lessons that he could use to avoid something similar with Alex, but he was coming up blank.

Maybe that was why he was irritated that his publicist had scheduled another meeting with Alex's ex Andrew. Apparently, Will's rudeness hadn't scared the guy off, and he still wanted to do a show with Will.

And maybe that's why Will snapped at Andrew when the meeting time actually arrived.

"Is this a bad time?" the other man asked as he walked through the door.

Will tried his best to answer in full sentences rather than grunts, because his manager had asked him to be on his best behavior. He knew that a show would bring publicity to his restaurant, which would lead to other restaurants. It would lead to the kind of financial security that would allow him to build the kind of life with Alex that she truly deserved.

"No, it's as good a time as any." Will watched as Andrew took in the kitchen, which was finally full of chefs setting up their stations and putting everything in place so that they could do a soft open with critics that night.

"I wish we'd gotten started earlier, because this would be fantastic on film."

"I don't think you'd say that if you heard the kind of salty language that usually gets thrown around. Everyone's minding their p's and q's right now."

Andrew laughed and clapped Will on the back. "I actually had an idea for how to spice up our project, if you're into it."

Will didn't roll his eyes, but it was a close call. One of the reasons he was hesitant to do reality TV was that the gimmicks were often cringeworthy. "All right. Shoot."

"Are you still in contact with your ex-wife?" Will must not have controlled his face quite as well this time because Andrew stepped back a little. "I think it would be great television if she came to work here as your head sommelier and we set up a little 'will they or won't they?'"

"'Will they or won't they?' what?" Will had a sinking feeling that they were going to try to gin up viewership with a showmance between him and his ex-wife. The very idea made him a little nauseous, and he was doubtful that April would go for it.

"I think people love a second-chance romance. It has everything—lust, tension, redemption."

He could have been describing the run-up to him and Alex sleeping together, but it would be awkward to say that right now, considering Will's current relationship with Andrew's ex-girlfriend.

"I don't think that's going to work. I doubt April would even be interested. She's moved on." She'd been seeing someone new the last time he'd stopped by the house they'd shared to pick up the last of his stuff. That had been a few months ago, so who knew?

"Her agent said that she might be interested, given the right terms. She got some bad publicity when that web channel she was doing wine content for fell apart. I think she's looking to freshen up her image."

Will had heard about it, but he'd empathized from afar because the ink had still been wet on their divorce papers.

"Even if April is willing to do it, I'm not."

Andrew quirked his head. He probably didn't have many people wanting to turn down a dose of publicity very often.

"I have a new girlfriend."

Andrew's brows went up. "Is she also in the business? If so, we can slot her in where we'd planned to use April."

Will didn't like how this guy talked about people. But he was used to not liking everyone he worked with. Some of his investors worked in the oil and gas industry, and he'd learned to keep his mouth shut when they talked about his farm-to-table ethic as a way to greenwash their dirty hands.

Capitalism sucked, but it was the water they were all swimming in for the time being. Until the oceans rose so high from climate change that they were actually all just swimming. And Andrew was a capitalist who had seen a way to make money.

"Actually, no. You know her," Will said. Even though he was feeling unsure of what was going on in Alex's head, he was willing to disclose their relationship if it got him out of pantomiming a reconciliation with April for the sake of good television. "I'm dating Alex."

Andrew blinked a couple of times in seeming disbelief. "You're dating Alex? Why?"

That was when Will got angry. The back of his neck got hot, and his gut tightened. "Why not?"

"She's kind of a cold fish." Andrew's words were scoffing and dismissive. Will's hands curled into fists, and he stepped around a prep table to be away from this guy. "She was so much fun when we started dating—just cool and sexy and I never had to guess at what she was thinking. It was exciting to be with someone who didn't ask very much of me. But after a few months, it was like there was just no softness to her. Zero tenderness."

If this guy was interested in tenderness, Will had a meat mallet with which he could tenderize his balls. He wanted to throttle him for making such broad proclamations about Alex. He didn't even know her that well. There were so many arguments that he could make for why Alex wasn't a cold fish. But given how little emotion Alex had expressed since they'd spent the weekend sequestered in his loft, he could see how someone could assume she was cold in a romantic relationship.

The only reason Will held out hope that they could weather whatever hesitation she was having about them was because he'd known her so long. They'd been falling in and out of love since they were teenagers. Oh shit—did he love her? He certainly wasn't going to waste his time listing Alex's attributes to this guy. But he wasn't going to fake angst with his ex-wife for the sake of ratings, either.

"Well, she's my cold fish." He'd leave it at that.

"Good luck, man." Will barely suppressed a growl at that, but Andrew seemed to get that the topic was closed because he moved on to other format and story ideas, and they had a productive meeting for the rest of the hour.

When Andrew left, though, Will thought about what he'd said about Alex. Will was still angry at Andrew. He thought he was definitely wrong, but maybe Alex got cold in romantic relationships. Maybe the only reason she ran hot with him before they'd slept together was that there wasn't any risk involved in the relationship. He couldn't force her to let him in, to let him know her. The only thing he could do was let her know that he wanted inside her heart and hope that she gave him the key.

TWENTY

O N THE LAST MONDAY BEFORE HIS RESTAURANT
opened, Will hosted a soft opening for the one person
whose opinion mattered to him most. Over the past week, he'd had
to deal with final health inspections from the city; hosting a dinner
for reviewers local, national, and international; and another meeting with Andrew. Luckily, the producer didn't mention Alex again.

However, Andrew's words had stayed with him. And he hadn't
even been able to sleep in Alex's bed every night that week. She'd
taken a trip to San Francisco to take a series of depositions in a
contentious child custody case, so he'd had to settle for a couple
of sleepy FaceTime conversations. She'd seemed distracted the
whole time, but when he'd asked her what was wrong, she'd just
said that she was tired.

He found himself growing unsure and anxious about whether
she even really liked him. And it was a huge head trip.

When she arrived at the restaurant that night, though, he finally let the tension that he'd been holding the whole week go. If she didn't care about making their relationship work, she wouldn't have gotten off a plane and then put on a dress that made his heart beat faster. She wouldn't smile at him like she'd been waiting to see him all day. And she wouldn't have melted in his arms and given him a kiss that screamed through his bloodstream, almost making him forget that he needed to take fresh focaccia out of the oven so that it would be warm when she dipped it in olive oil.

"You look beautiful," he said. He knew the words weren't adequate. When she'd walked in, he'd been tempted to say "I love you," but he didn't know for sure that she felt the same way. He didn't know if she'd had enough of him and was ready to say that they were out of each other's systems. Maybe she'd dressed up to trample all over his heart.

He felt a moment of sympathy for the stand-up who had ghosted her. Even though he'd been out of order when Alex had gone to see him, Will was beginning to understand the particular category of hurt that he'd felt.

Before they'd gotten involved, he'd been able to read Alex like a book. But after they slept together, it was as though a wall had come down between them. He couldn't see through the good face that she was putting on—he finally understood what it was like when someone's smile didn't reach their eyes.

"Is everything okay?" he asked her, and she dipped her head.

"Everything's great." She put her hair behind her ear. They stared at each other for a long moment before he moved closer to her and grabbed her jacket. "It's chilly outside."

Great. They were now reduced to talking about the weather. "How did your depositions go?"

She stopped smiling at him then, and he knew he'd said the wrong thing.

Alex froze when he asked about the depositions. She hated working cases where child custody was contentious, but she wouldn't have many clients if she turned those cases down. This one made her particularly sad, because the divorcing couple's daughters had tried to parent trap them into getting back together, and it had backfired spectacularly into a domestic violence incident.

The couple and their children lived—separately now—in Los Angeles. But she'd had to go to San Francisco because the incident had happened while they were traveling. She'd needed to depose members of the hotel staff where the incident had occurred. Alex represented the mother, who was now seeking sole physical and legal custody. Since the father was famous, and the incident had been all over the papers, it was highly sensationalized.

Alex's father had always been either absent or hypercritical, but he'd never gotten violent. Whenever Alex came home proud of accomplishing something—straight As, making the dance team at school, beating a class track record—her father had done his best to belittle her.

When she'd gotten into her first-choice law school, he'd said, "I'm sure there are some interesting things that you can do in the law," which heavily implied that he found her boring. And whenever she'd stood up to him and told him about how his absence made her feel, he hung up the phone or disappeared for weeks or months on end.

Eventually she spoke to him as little as possible. As hurt as she'd been when her parents had split up suddenly, she was grateful that they hadn't stayed together for her or her sister's sake.

She'd realized this week that she'd never let herself entertain the idea of having children because she didn't want to open herself up to be hurt through another person. It was a kind of enviable courage that she didn't believe she had in her.

But Alex certainly did not envy her client, who was trying her best to keep her daughters out of the press and away from reports that their father was a monster. He would probably mess up as a parent on his own enough during visitation and when they were adults that their mother wouldn't need to tell them that she'd saved them from spending time with an asshole who would tear them down and ruin their adult relationships.

She'd wanted to forget all about her work when she saw Will tonight. His arms were a solace to her. The only time she wasn't thinking about running was when he was touching her in a way that made it impossible to think.

When she wasn't with him, it was so easy for her to think about how she'd messed up all her previous relationships because she hadn't trusted anyone to really see her. They were all so superficial. Because she'd known Will for so long, it felt so much deeper so much sooner.

She was afraid that she didn't have it in her to stay, and she could feel herself pulling away from him. But she knew, based on her work with the therapist she'd started talking to immediately after brunch with Lexi and her friends, that she needed to fight the urge to keep things at the surface with Will. She could trust him not to tear her down if she let him in. Even though they'd bickered over the years, they both respected each other.

Instead of reiterating that she was fine, telling him that the depositions had been fine when they'd opened a wound that she thought had closed up long ago, she said, "It was really rough on me, to be honest."

The tenderness in Will's expression almost wrecked her again. "What happened?" He'd been pouring them both wine, but he crossed the kitchen to hug her. He rubbed his hand up and down her back, and she shivered.

She fought tears and refused to start sobbing. Even though they'd known each other for a long time, it was too soon for her to just lay all her shit on him. He had enough to worry about. Opening a restaurant was a big, difficult thing. Most of them failed. That was just a fact. And the last thing Will needed to be thinking about right now, mere days before they opened, was that she was going to fall apart on him. It wasn't fair.

Still, he didn't rush her. "Shhhhhh. It's okay."

"I should be used to this by now. I handle custody cases all the time." Now that she was speaking in full sentences, he led her over to the prep table where he'd put place settings. They were still finishing setting up the dining room, according to his texts, and she liked that they were eating in the kitchen. Empty and lit by candles, it was intimate and romantic.

"Tell me." He pushed her glass of wine toward her and waited until she took a sip to plate their first course.

"It was just that the girls remind me of myself and my sister when we were their age. My sister was little, so I don't think it was quite as hard on Francesca, but I remember wanting so much for my parents to get back together and feeling like I was a failure because they didn't.

"I had no idea why they broke up, and I didn't understand what kind of person my father was until much later. I was just so angry at my mom for making it impossible for him to stay close to us. I even blamed her for when she left me with Lexi that first summer. I had no idea that it was because my father no longer had any use for us once he could no longer use us to manipulate my mother."

"None of that was your fault, Alex. None of it." Alex's whole nervous system calmed down after he said that. He seemed to sense it, because he moved her to a stool near the counter and left her for a brief moment.

It gave her a few moments to collect her thoughts, which she needed. She appreciated him for giving her that.

Will was back with a gorgeous, perfect caprese salad with watermelon and balsamic vinegar that he'd sourced himself from a farm in the Central Valley. Even though Will made simple dishes, he did it with intention and such careful precision that they sang.

He was such a great chef. He didn't get all that viral social media fame just because of his good looks. She really hoped that he went through with the reality show. From what he'd said on FaceTime this week, it sounded like he was pushing to be able to teach simple principles in the kitchen and how they could be iterated through more complicated dishes.

Women would go crazy for him. Probably ones who weren't scared that they'd fuck up a relationship with him.

After she'd taken a few bites and he was satisfied that she was enjoying the food, he said, "You never met my mom. She sounds a lot like your dad in a lot of ways."

"I didn't, but I know that Lexi didn't have anything nice to say about her. And she can usually find something nice to say about anyone. Including her ex-husbands. She's particularly fond of your father."

"I don't think she ever wanted to have a kid, but she and my dad had me to save their marriage. She was raised in this old-school Italian family that expected her to get married at eighteen and pop out as many babies as possible until she couldn't anymore and became a nonna to take care of her babies' babies. Or so she told it. She resented having to take care of me, and having a kid didn't make her fall back in love with my dad. She just kind of bounced after that."

This was more than Will had said about his mother since she'd known him. She didn't know what to do other than listen and hope he shared more. Hearing him talk about his mother made her feel less vulnerable, less like she was exposing her internal organs. "But I had my nonna until I was fifteen. She just up and moved to the States from Italy after my mom left and took care of me until my dad got married again."

"I knew that was why you cooked Italian food, but I didn't know that she was with you that long." It had to have had an impact, if he made his whole life's work about his grandmother's cooking.

"It was only for a few years. I inherited some of her recipes, but I never feel like they have the same magic." Alex wanted to reach out to the little boy who had been comforted by his grandma's food. She wanted to wrap him up and hug him and tell him that everything would be okay.

"But she went back to Italy when your father got married to Lexi?"

Will's father had been married almost as many times as Lexi. She remembered him as an okay guy, but looking back he probably could have used a therapist instead of six wives.

"As an adult who made the wrong choice in partners at first, I get it now. Sometimes things just don't work out. But after my mom, I don't think he had it in him to fight for another relationship. He didn't want to put work into a thing only to have it fall apart on him. So they all fell apart on him anyway."

Did Will think that he was just like his father in that way? Could he not see that he had more perseverance in his pinky finger than his father had in his whole body?

"You're nothing like him," Alex said. He needed to know how special and wonderful he was. She wouldn't allow him not to know that. "I barely remember what it was like to be in a room with him. He's not the kind of man that you think about all the time, even when he's not around. I think Lexi married him because she needed a break from intense love affairs. And then, of course, you came along as part of the package with your dad. She apparently collects a specific brand of stray."

Will laughed. He got up to refill their wine and dish up their main course from the Dutch oven on the stove. The scent hit her nostrils immediately, and her mouth started watering. It had a little to do with Will's very fine backside, but it was mostly about the fact that he'd made osso buco for her. She hadn't had his rendition of the dish in years but had fallen in love with it because she'd stolen some leftovers from Lexi's fridge when she'd been low on grocery money during law school.

It had been during the time period when Will had started dating April, so she'd been doing her best to avoid him. But she'd never tried to pretend she didn't enjoy his food.

"Lexi said you were really into this."

Alex took a sip of wine. She would have expected him to serve a red with this, but it was a crisp white to cut the richness. "She usually hid it from me after I cleaned her out once."

"I wish I had known. I would have made sure you got some more."

"You were with April then."

Will put down her dish in front of her and shrugged. "But I still could have fed you."

"No. No way." Alex shook her head. "If you would have fed me on a regular basis, I would have been so in love with you that I would have tried to stop your wedding."

After taking her first bite, she knew it was true. She moaned, and Will blushed. She loved how he could be so gruff and tough, but also so sweet like this. He infuriated her when he tried to interfere or when they butted heads, but he backed off eventually. The way he took care of her, always checking to make sure she wasn't working through lunch, should annoy her. She was an adult. And it was so foreign that she was shocked at how quickly she'd gotten used to it.

"Nothing standing in our way now." His eyes were dark, but she was pretty sure she could see clearly into his soul at that moment. He was trying to tell her that he loved her without saying the words. She knew that she wasn't ready to hear them. She wouldn't believe him if he said it. It was hard to believe that anyone loved her in the romantic sense.

It scared her how quickly and easily she'd come to rely on him, and she was scared that she couldn't withstand the growing pressure inside her to run far away from the magnitude of her feelings. It had been so much easier to love him when he was nothing more than an idea of the man she couldn't have. The fact that he wanted her now terrified her, even though she knew he wouldn't abuse her trust. Some part of her knew her heart was safe with him.

"You seem to have ended up so well-adjusted." Alex narrowed her gaze at him. "How did that happen?"

"According to my ex, I'm an android with my emotions features disabled."

"Then she doesn't see who you are."

Will shrugged again. "I guess that I was probably that with her. I loved her, but not enough. It's only recently that I've been feeling a lot."

There was that look again, the one that had the whole world in it.

Instead of dwelling on her fears or delving deeper into the terror of intimacy, Alex asked him about the restaurant and all the preparations for the opening. Will followed her lead, and he had plenty to say about it. She couldn't believe that she'd ever thought he was as taciturn as she had. She'd merely not been looking at him through the right lenses.

After they finished eating and Alex helped him clean up, he took her out front and mixed them both Negronis. Then he took her on a tour of the parts of the restaurant that had been completed in the last week.

Before she'd left for her San Francisco trip, they'd christened his office, and she could feel a blush come over her cheeks when they passed by that room. She was still blushing when he opened the door to one of the four gender-neutral bathrooms.

"Why are you showing me the bathroom?" she asked right before he closed the door and pushed her up against it. "Oh."

He moved her hair off her neck and nuzzled there. They hadn't been together long, but she knew that it was his favorite place on her body. When he kissed her there, she knew that he was craving her. And she responded instantly. Their dinner conversation had been so heavy that her mind had been completely off sex, which was a feat when she was around Will.

But as soon as he touched her, the energy between them changed and she could put her week from hell and her worries about their relationship longevity out of her mind. It was like meditation when his mouth met hers.

That was a great idea. Maybe she'd give up her law practice to become a wellness influencer spreading the gospel of kissing meditation. She didn't consider it for more than a moment, but it made her laugh.

Will pulled back and said, "Is something funny, woman?" He sounded like a growly caveman, and she pulled him back by his hair.

"I was just thinking that kissing you erases everything bad roaming around in my brain. I feel like I'm addicted to your mouth," she said, stroking one finger under the neckline of his

T-shirt. After they'd eaten, he'd taken off his chef's whites and was down to his uniform of jeans and T-shirt. Her response to the clothes he wore every day was also conditioned. She wasn't sure she'd be able to get it up for a guy in a suit anymore. "It's almost transcendent, like meditation."

"Too bad there's only one of me, and I won't share my gift with the masses." His tone was sarcastic, which was good. Because the thought of him kissing anyone else, even for the sake of her mental health, had her feeling murderous. "I only want to kiss you to enlightenment."

His mouth descended on her jaw and her neck. He had one strap of her dress down when she regained a modicum of thought. "Should we be doing this here? It's so public. Could someone come in? Like Charlee?"

"Charlee is out with Jane tonight. I sent the rest of the staff home to spend one last Friday night with their families and friends before the onslaught." He looked down at her with a feral and lascivious look on his face that made her pulse jump and her body soften and open to him. That look on his face usually meant multiple orgasms, so she was inclined to believe him. She probably would also have been inclined to have her way with him even if there was a risk of someone dropping by.

"I've never done it in a public bathroom," Alex said, scrunching up her nose. "It always seemed so unsanitary." She didn't really need to be convinced, but she liked for Will to seduce her into things. It was a fun game for them to play, when in truth she was ready to take Will inside her at any time and in any place.

"Well, no one has used this bathroom for its intended purpose yet, and I'm pretty sure people will fuck in it eventually." While

Will was talking, he hiked up her dress and found the edge of her lacy panties.

"So we'll be the first. We have to make sure the energy is good so it's clear when people walk in that this bathroom fucks." She'd spent too much time with Lexi's collection of healers to not believe that places had energy. This whole restaurant had good energy because Will built it. They were just enhancing its charisma.

"That's pretty woo-woo, even for you." She bit his bottom lip, so he stepped back on that statement. "I mean, you're right. I had better make you come more than once."

With that, he knelt on the floor and pulled her panties down. He adjusted her stance so she was wide open to him. Every time they had sex, it got better. But tonight, there was an edge to it. They'd revealed things to each other, and both of them knew that this was about more than getting their rocks off. Sex with Will was about connecting to each other, reassuring each other, taking care of each other.

Will knew exactly how to take care of her, and he was faster than her fastest sex toy at making her come at this point. When she was done, he moved them both to the sink. She tried to turn into his arms, thinking that he would boost her onto the counter and fuck her that way, but he kept her facing the mirror.

His hands were rough, but she liked that. She liked that he took control of her body during sex. It helped that he knew what he was doing. He pulled the top of her dress down so that he could palm the skin of her breasts while making her watch. It was lewd and raw but also fantastic.

Alex didn't know the woman looking back at her in the mirror. She was wild and ravenous, open and vulnerable. She was in the arms of a man who meant everything to her. But she wasn't afraid of loving him.

If she saw that, Will—with his watchful eyes—had to see it, too. She willed him to see it.

Will hiked up her skirt again, and she heard the sound of buttons popping on the fly of his jeans. If she hadn't already been drenched from his mouth on her, she would have been then. She dipped her head so that her hair hung over her face just as she felt his cock at her entrance. But he wouldn't let her escape that way. He gently cupped his hand around her throat and lifted her head up so that their gazes met in the mirror.

"Baby, I've got to see you. Let me look at you." She knew he wasn't just talking about her face right then. She gave him something when she let him see her when she was not at her best. When she felt tears well up again, he pinched her ass and smiled softly. "You don't want me to see you, but I do. I hate it when you cry, but I'll never look away."

Instead of entering her and putting them both out of their misery, he laid an open-mouthed kiss on her neck and teased her by almost coming inside her. "You want me." It wasn't a question but a statement by a man gratified by her need for him.

For so long, she'd been afraid to need anyone. He gave her more by being happy with her desire than he could possibly know. She whimpered something unintelligible, and he entered her. He didn't last long, but neither did she. It was quick and rough and desperate, but he held out until she came, bucking and breaking at her center.

And he held her, standing in that bathroom, which definitely had good energy after that.

TWENTY-ONE

THE NEXT MORNING, WILL LET ALEX SLEEP IN AT HIS LOFT. He woke intending to cook breakfast for them and then head to the restaurant, but he found himself watching Alex while she dozed. Her face was soft this morning, but he'd noticed that she wasn't always restful in sleep. She sometimes tossed and turned and talked in fragments of sentences that he didn't understand. He wondered if her work had anything to do with it. Anyone who bothered to really see her would know that she wasn't cold—quite the contrary, she cared too much sometimes.

It satisfied him that he could give her that respite from the world. It made him feel a level of peace that he'd never felt. It was something that he thought he'd find in his marriage but hadn't.

When she woke up, it was all at once, faster than a brand-new cell phone. "What are you still doing in bed? Don't you need to be at work?" Even though she was completely awake, her eyes were still sleepy, and it was completely adorable.

"I'd rather be with you when you wake up," he said. "I don't want you to think I've gone off slinking into the night."

Alex sat up then. "Seriously? I cry one time during sex and you think I'm a fragile flower who can't wake up on my own?" She slid out of bed so unexpectedly that he didn't make a move to stop her. He was so perplexed by her change in attitude from last night. "You know I've lived on my own and taken care of myself for yeeeeaaars, and I don't need some man swooping in to save me from myself."

"I wasn't saying that—"

"Don't." She held up a hand. "I saw the way you were looking at me. Like I was some sort of sad, pathetic thing who needs a lollipop because I had a hard week."

Will knew why Alex was freaking out. Their years-long dance toward a relationship was moving too fast for her. She'd shared too much the previous evening, and now she was trying to push him away. It wasn't anything he'd done; it was reflexive. If he didn't let her see how much it bothered him and didn't let her get away with it, she would stop. Maybe.

Just because he realized that this wasn't about anything that he'd done didn't mean that it didn't irritate him.

Also she hadn't had her coffee. He got out of bed and went toward the kitchen to remedy that at least.

"Where are you going?" Alex followed him naked. "I wasn't done talking to you."

"Well, I'm done talking to you until you've had some caffeine and an attitude adjustment." He wanted to laugh at her, but he knew that would only make her angrier.

He made coffee, feeling her seething behind him the whole time as she found her clothes from the night before and one of his T-shirts to wear over her satin slip dress. "I wish you'd told me that we were going to stay here last night. I would have packed a bag."

She was really just going to complain about anything she could think of. When she stomped into the kitchen, he pushed a mug across the counter at her and nodded. She would take anything he said in that moment as an attack, so he wasn't going to give her any ammunition.

"Stop smiling at me like you think it's cute."

"Stop being so cute when you're cranky."

She muttered something that sounded a lot like "Fuck you" as she brought the mug to her lips, but then she fell silent. Since she didn't want him looking at her like she was cute when she was cranky—and he was just lust addled enough to think that she was supremely cute when she was cranky—he went back to his espresso machine to make himself a latte.

He'd made an Americano with no sugar and a touch of cream, just the way she liked it. It only took until he turned around with his drink for her to say, "Thank you."

"You're welcome," he said before taking a sip. "Feel better?"

She said "Yes," but the word sounded grudging. If she didn't want to admit that she'd been hell on wheels this morning, he wasn't going to make her grovel when he could see the remorse on her face.

They enjoyed their beverages in silence—his experience working as a barista as a teen really came in handy when dealing with a pissed-off Alex—until she started staring at him as though he were cute.

"What?"

She reached out her hand and wiped foam off of his top lip and mustache and then sucked her finger into her mouth. It made him want to drag her back to bed and demonstrate the benefits of intimate mornings that weren't plagued by drama, when his apartment buzzer went off.

He waggled his eyebrows at her and said, "I'm going to get rid of this person and then make you come a couple times to make sure your good mood sticks."

She licked her finger, even though she'd cleaned it off on the first try, and said, "Hurry."

But when Will saw who was at the door, his plans for a sexy morning quickie with his girl went out the window.

Alex knew that she wasn't going to be getting any of those promised orgasms when Will turned from the little video feed on his phone and mouthed "Sorry" at her as he buzzed the person at the door in. And she thought he should probably be a whole lot more apologetic when he let his ex-wife in the door.

The insecure parts of Alex's mind started to sound panic alarms that blared inside her brain and curtailed rational thought. Why would April be dropping over to Will's place on a Saturday morning? Was this a frequent occurrence? Alex didn't even know that they still spoke. She dealt with some couples who had fast and friendly divorces, but she hadn't thought that was Will and April. She'd seemed so angry the last few times that they were together that Alex wouldn't have thought she'd ever want to see Will again unless absolutely necessary.

And April looked no less surprised to see Alex sitting in Will's kitchen drinking coffee. With sex hair and part of last night's outfit sticking out from under Will's T-shirt. It was more obvious why Alex was here than why April was.

Will, for his part, seemed unbothered by the whole thing. As though it was normal to be hosting a coffee klatch with his ex-wife and his current girlfriend, who'd been very much infatuated with him while he was still with his ex-wife.

"April, you remember Alex, right?" Will asked, as breezy as could be.

The other woman recovered her ability to speak first. "Little early in the morning for your stepsister to be here, isn't it?"

"Ew, I was never his stepsister," Alex said. And then she remembered why she hadn't liked April, aside from the fact that she'd been jealous that Will had fallen in love with a woman who wasn't her. She'd definitely always been too petty to want to see him happy. But she also thought that April was rude and sort of intentionally obtuse. "His father was married to my grandmother for about a minute over a decade ago."

Will looked at her as though he was taken by surprise at the exchange. And then he looked back to April. "What's going on, April? What are you doing here?"

"I need to speak with you in private." April turned to Will and apparently decided to pretend that Alex wasn't even there anymore.

Will looked concerned rather than irritated with his ex, and that pissed Alex off. She knew it wasn't fair that she wanted him to stand up for her, but she couldn't help it. She also wondered if she should just leave them to talk whatever this was out. She didn't want to insert herself into the situation in a way that would make it contentious. Maybe he could get rid of April more quickly if she made her exit now.

"What you have to say to me, you can say in front of Alex." Will's voice was emphatic.

April did not react well to that. "This is private. It's between you and me."

Alex figured that Will's ex wasn't going to bend. Because he had a thing for Alex, and April seemed to be her own brand of iconoclast, she figured that he had a thing for obstinate women.

Her coffee had cooled enough that she could down it without burning her throat, so she swallowed the rest of it. Will had been right; her mood had vastly improved with coffee. When she walked toward the bedroom to get her purse, April said, "Oh, so she's sleeping here now?"

Alex stopped in her tracks when Will said, "That's none of your business, April."

"Did you have a thing for her the whole time we were together?" April asked, her voice rising at least two octaves. "Is that why you wouldn't try marriage counseling one more time? I always knew you had a thing for her. And it was painfully obvious that she was in love with you. I just didn't think either of you were gross assholes enough to act on it. It's disgusting. You're practically related. You can just look at each other and know what the other one is thinking."

"April—" Will's voice held a warning, but April barely paused in her tirade.

"I came over here to talk about business, Will." The hairs on the back of Alex's neck went up. They were legally divorced, which meant that April should have no interest or say in Will's business. When Will's lawyer had brought the tentative final settlement on their assets to him, he'd asked Alex to look over it. It had made her a little uncomfortable to look at another lawyer's work because she had been conflicted out of the case, but Alex hadn't been able to say no.

It was a solid agreement, and they shouldn't have any business to discuss. But Alex didn't have a chance to say any of that.

"April, if this is about that stupid idea for the reality show . . ." Alex didn't know anything about an idea for a reality show that included April. If Andrew wanted a wine expert on the show, he could pretty easily find one. And he could probably hire someone a lot easier to work with than April. If he was stuck on Will's ex-wife, it would be because he wanted to insert a romantic story-line.

And she could suddenly see why April wasn't happy to see her there. It wasn't just about Alex and her history with Will. It was about the fact that he'd moved on and it might cost her an opportunity.

But Will was looking at her as though he was planning to earnestly hear her out. Alex couldn't say anything because she would sound unhinged and jealous. She'd already used up any credits she had on being unhinged with her pre-coffee tirade.

"Are you just going to stand there, or are you going to leave so that I can talk to my husband?"

It was clear that April wanted Alex to respond to her leaving the "ex" off of "husband," but Alex refused to take the bait. Instead, she went into the bedroom and grabbed her purse.

Will moved away from his ex to try to keep Alex from walking out the door. The thing was, Alex wanted to talk to him alone as well. She was pissed that he hadn't mentioned the direction Andrew wanted to go in with the show, or even if he'd met with him again. Sure, he'd wanted her to spill her guts to him last night about her work, but he didn't think it was important to share this. She wouldn't have put it past Andrew to announce April's appearance on the show, even if the parties hadn't agreed to appear, just to gauge whether people would be interested.

And people would be interested. Will and April were both beautiful people, and people would tune in for tension and fighting and drama. But then the show wouldn't be about Will's approach to food as much as it would be about the interpersonal drama. It wasn't like people watched *Vanderpump Rules* to get an education on how the restaurant industry worked. And they hadn't watched the Kardashians to learn how to become an influencer.

But when he asked her, "Are you mad?" she couldn't quite get herself to tell him the truth.

He expected her to share with him, but he was only going to give her so much back. She wanted to tell him that yes, she was so angry she could spit fire, but it didn't make sense. They'd only been hooking up for a few weeks, and they only felt as close as they were because they'd both been in Lexi's orbit for so long.

She knew that she would cool off once she got back into her own space and processed this. That it wasn't a big deal in the long run. Even if they both did the show, reality television had a very loose relationship with reality.

It didn't spell the end of her relationship with Will. It just felt like it did.

So instead of throwing a fit, Alex smiled brightly. "Of course not. Everything is fine. Have your talk with April, and I'll see you later."

"I have to be at the restaurant tonight, so it probably won't be until the opening."

It hurt Alex more than she could admit that they wouldn't be able to connect until his big public opening. She'd come to count on their private moments together, even though she was scared of depending on them. On him.

She thought that maybe Lexi had been wrong about her acting skills after that commercial when she was five—the one where she'd set a backdrop on fire while blowing out birthday candles—when she was able to keep her smile affixed. "See you then."

And because she couldn't resist rubbing the fact that Will was with her now in April's face just a little, she went up on her toes and kissed Will on the mouth.

TWENTY-TWO

WILL INTENDED TO GET RID OF APRIL AS SOON AS possible—her dropping by at his apartment was seriously not cool, especially when the visit definitely could have been a phone call. Apparently, she wanted to do the reality show and keep the fact that they weren't going to get back together secret. Apparently, she'd had extensive talks with Andrew about a show that was supposed to be featuring him.

When she said this, he laughed at her, and that made her angry. "What the hell are you doing with that woman?"

"I don't think what I'm doing with Alex is any of your business."

"Well, it's hurting my plans for my business, and I don't like her for you."

Will started to get a headache from trying to figure out what women wanted this morning and accounting for the ways in which he'd pissed them off. He didn't care that his ex-wife didn't like his new girlfriend. He squeezed the bridge of his nose between two fingers. "I don't think you understand what divorce means."

"I didn't want to be married to you anymore, but that doesn't mean that I don't care about you."

That was nice, and he was glad that they could be in a room together without wanting to kill each other—that had never been their problem anyway—but he didn't need her making judgments on his life choices. Especially whom he dated and when.

"I'm glad you care about me, but we can't do the show together. And we can't work in the same restaurant. It wouldn't be good for either of us. If there is any other way for me to help you with your business, I will. But I'm not pretending to still be in a relationship with you for the publicity."

April sighed and stepped back from him. "You're in love with her, aren't you?"

"I'm not talking about this with you." Will shook his head and walked toward the kitchen to snag his coffee. "Can I get you a coffee?"

He hoped that she wouldn't say yes, but she did. As he fixed her a latte, she looked around his new place. For obvious reasons, she hadn't visited before. "You really like things bare-bones, don't you?"

Will just didn't like to have a thing unless it was meaningful or useful. He could think more clearly when he wasn't surrounded by stuff. It was the same reason he wore the same clothes pretty much every day. It made things simple. Maybe it was because he'd grown up amid chaos that he craved order, but it was just something about him.

"I just like what I like." He shrugged. April had never appreciated his penchant for simplicity. She came from the "more is more" school of home decorating, and that seemed to be part of her philosophy of life. He'd been attracted to how voracious she was for new experiences, but they'd never been able to come into agreement on their differing desires for things.

It had made it easy for him to walk away from their shared home after the divorce, though.

He didn't see the use for rehashing that now, so he decided to ask about her business in order to keep things simple. "Tell me about this new business."

"I'm starting a wine club that will serve both individuals and businesses. I'm sick of staying in one place all the time, and I want to travel more."

For the first time, he thought that maybe the end of their marriage had been good for both of them. Even though she'd initiated the divorce, it was only after she'd begged him multiple times to go back to couple's therapy. He really didn't see the use of it. They'd talked and talked about their problems until there were no words left and nothing seemed worth discussing anymore.

"I'm glad you'll get to do that." Will put down his cup of coffee and met her gaze. "I do really want you to be happy."

"That's a change from during our marriage when you just wanted me to be Alex."

Will shook his head. "That's not true, and you know it. There was nothing between me and Alex while I was married to you.

Unlike my father, I took that commitment seriously. But I think we got married way too young, before we really knew ourselves."

"But I always sensed that there was this crackling thing"—she made a motion with her hands—"between you and her."

"For a long time, it wasn't crackling. I was committed to you." Will wasn't going to deny his feelings for Alex now, but he didn't have anything to feel guilty about during his marriage. He'd been committed to his wife from the time they'd started dating seriously until the very end. "And neither of us ever acted on it. I'm not sure that either of us knew that there was anything else underneath all the stuff that we'd been through together."

"So how'd you get together now?" April seemed genuinely curious. And since the energy had calmed down considerably since she'd come in, he told her the story. Minus the really intimate details.

When he was finished, she blew out a stream of air that was half whistle. "None of her relationships have worked out because she's just as emotionally constipated as you are. I get why her exes called her a cold fish, and I get why she was cold with them." April knew enough about Alex's family from fragments of history she'd gathered through Lexi. "You realize that she's going to use my showing up here to clam up on you. Just like you used to punish me with silence when you felt like I was asking too much. Honestly, I find it astonishing that you two ever ended up getting together in the first place."

It was funny, but Will didn't feel the pressure to run away when it was Alex. He wouldn't say that to April, because that would be hurtful. But it was true. "I think maybe she's just benefiting from all the therapy that we had."

"Or you should have been with her to start with." There was a wisp of hurt in April's voice, and he didn't want her to feel that way. But another thing he'd learned in therapy was that you can't control other people's feelings.

"I'm grateful that I got to misspend my youth with you," he said, knowing that it wasn't adequate. But he needed to say it, and it made April smile.

"I should go." She got up and grabbed her purse. "I'm sorry if I caused any problems with Alex. I just—"

Will gave her a hug and kissed her on the top of her head. It was friendly and didn't hold any sexual tension. A showmance between the two of them would not have played well on television anyway. Too much water under the bridge.

"Good luck with the restaurant," she said as she opened the door. "And with Alex."

As risky and uncertain as the restaurant business was, Will felt as though he probably needed more luck to make things work with Alex.

TWENTY-THREE

WILL DIDN'T CONNECT WITH ALEX FOR THE NEXT FEW days. The run-up to opening a restaurant was all-consuming, and he didn't think much of it for the first two days. They texted about a few things, but he found himself checking his phone whenever he had a minute to breathe, hoping to hear from her.

He didn't like how they'd left things when April had shown up at his place, but there were so many decisions to be made that he was dead tired when he returned to his place for three or four hours of sleep every night.

What was so frustrating was that he knew what she was doing. He knew she was afraid that he would disappear on her, like almost everyone else in her life had. But he couldn't make her share her feelings instead of putting up a wall.

But they would have to talk about that after the opening of the restaurant, which was tonight. He was able to push his uncertainty about his relationship with Alex out of his mind as he oversaw the work in the kitchen. He was extremely proud of the team they'd put together and the menu they'd created.

When he walked through the kitchen to get to his office to check his phone one more time, he caught Charlee's eye. They handed off their prep to one of the other cooks and followed him.

"You okay, boss?" They looked concerned for him, and he didn't want to say that he was agitated about a girl. That would be pretty fucking pathetic, but there he was.

"Yeah, I'm fine." He nodded toward the kitchen. "How is Diaz working out on sauces?"

Charlee crossed their arms over their chest. "It's Alex, isn't it?"

"What about Alex?" Will knew he wasn't going to get away with not talking about it, but he was still going to try. "Don't you have work to do? We are opening a restaurant tonight."

Charlee looked back to the kitchen. "Everything will be fine for a minute. They all know what they're doing."

Will leaned against his desk. "I had better go check with the bar. Neither of us has worked with this sommelier before." Because they'd always worked with April. "I want to make sure that they ordered enough prosecco for that silly signature drink they recommended."

"Oh, so April interfered." Will had no idea how Charlee had intuited that from him mentioning checking on the bar, but they did. "That's why Alex made a weird face when we were at dinner the other night."

"You got dinner with Alex?" Will didn't even know that Alex

and Charlee were friends. They'd never said two words to each other until that night at James Faherghty's house.

"Well, I'm dating her best friend, so yeah."

So Alex had time for dinner with her best friend, but no time to text him back. He didn't know why he was so upset about this. He and Alex hadn't even dated that long. There was so much shared history that it would be challenging for her to ghost him on their romantic relationship. But that didn't mean that she wasn't running scared and trying.

That didn't mean that he didn't like Charlee and Jane together. If he were the type to fix people up, he might have thought of the two of them. "I like Jane. She's good people."

"Yeah, she is. And a total babe." Charlee smiled at him with a shit-eating grin.

Will shook his head. "We gotta get back to work."

As they turned to walk out the door, Charlee said, "You're going to work things out with Alex, right? It's the only way we'll get to go on double dates."

"I mean, that's really up to her." Will didn't like it, but he'd hooked up with a woman who had just as many communication issues as he had. "She's the one who can't tell me how she feels."

"One of you is going to have to bend," Charlee said.

"That's what I'm afraid of."

Alex was embarrassed. That was the crux of why she hadn't talked to Will very much this week. Her petty jealousy about a visit from his ex-wife was not a good reason to throw a fit.

And she knew Will. They'd grown close enough that deep down she was sure that he would never do anything to hurt her intentionally.

When she showed up at the opening of his restaurant, with Lexi, there were some photographers outside. He'd canceled the red carpet—that just wasn't Will's style—although there was also a photographer inside snapping pictures of celebrities.

Over the past few days, she'd missed the kinds of growls and glares that Will could give when he was mad. She hated that she was the one to put distance between them, but she'd had to think.

One night, she'd gone over to Jane's house for dinner. Jane had a kitchen that would make Nancy Meyers green with jealousy, but Charlee had done the cooking. It was always hit or miss when Jane did the cooking. The hits were delicious, but the misses sometimes required the fire department or Pepto-Bismol.

Looking at Charlee and Jane together made Alex crave the same easy closeness with Will. It also made her doubt whether they would ever have it. It seemed like one of them was always running from the other. Did that mean that it wasn't real or sustainable?

Alex wanted things to work, but she also doubted whether she had it in her.

When they got inside the restaurant, their table—which Will had specifically told the front of the house belonged to them—was still occupied. Alex and Lexi waited at the bar. There was a signature cocktail, a twist on an Aperol spritz, that tasted great. The bar also allowed Lexi to hold court. It was easier to walk up to a celebrity to ask for a picture there than when they were sitting at a table.

Alex faded into the background and looked around at what

Will had created. She was so freaking proud of him. It was cool without being trendy—simple, bare, minimalist, but everything had its perfect place. It was so essentially Will that he permeated everything about the restaurant.

Her gaze was meandering when it hit the sommelier, whom she instantly recognized as one of her exes. She hadn't even planned to talk to Gilles as part of her aborted ex-boyfriend project, because she knew exactly why they broke up. Gilles had told her he loved her after three months of a very intense affair, and she had never spoken to him again.

It had been right after Ace, the stand-up comedian. She'd been sure that he was lying to her, that he had said it while he was drunk and would ghost her. He'd said it right after strenuous sex, so she'd assumed that he'd been addled by the loss of blood to his brain. So she'd snuck out and never returned his calls.

Shame filled her gut, and Alex wanted to run and hide again. But if she did that, she would never be able to come back here while Gilles was working here. And she was going to try to resist doing her avoidant shit with Will, so maybe facing up to it with Gilles would help her keep that commitment.

The Frenchman looked fantastic. She'd never figured out how the cowlicks in his hair always managed to make it sit in a carelessly tousled sexy way. He had craggy, gray-stubble-covered cheeks that dipped in fascinating ways as his expression changed. It had been the first time she'd dated a man significantly older than her. He wasn't old enough to be her father, but he was too old to be her older brother. Strands of silver threaded through his dark hair, making him look hopelessly distinguished. He was still tall and lean.

If she wasn't pretty sure that she was in love with Will, she would definitely still be wildly attracted to Gilles. That was what had scared her away. Someone who devastated her senses every time he was near, who treated her well and was in love with her, had been too terrifying to contemplate and too good to believe.

She remembered that she'd been happy that he'd married the next woman he'd dated—an Instagram fitness influencer whom he'd started working out with after their breakup. Apparently, she'd made him quit smoking.

Their gazes tangled. To her shock, he smiled at her. He spoke some words into the ear of the server whom he'd been giving instructions to and approached her. She didn't pull back when he kissed her on both cheeks. She found herself smiling back at him.

"Alex. It's a surprise to see you here." Although he'd been born and raised in Paris, he spoke English without a discernable accent. "You look beautiful."

"You don't look so bad yourself," Alex said. "I'm here because . . . uh . . . well, Will is close with my family." She didn't know where she and Will stood, so she didn't want to tell one of his employees that they were together. That was for Will to decide after he decided whether to forgive her for her childish fit over April's visit.

Gilles accepted her explanation and looked at her empty drink. He motioned to the bartender. "Champagne for my friend." Alex knew it would be perfect and smiled back at him.

"Listen." She put her hand on his arm, taking the opportunity to apologize gracefully. "I'm so sorry how things ended between us. You were lovely. Our time together was lovely. I just—"

"No need to explain," he said. "You were not ready for me to say the things I said. And I'm not sure that I was ready to say them. And if you had not dropped me like last year's jeans trend, I would not have found Harmony." His wife's name was Harmony, and it was a testament to Alex's growth that she refrained from rolling her eyes.

"I'm so glad you're happy."

With that, he handed her champagne with a kiss on her cheek. If she had been looking at their tableau from the outside, their affection might have appeared to be something else. Like a dance that would lead to hot, sweaty groping in the coat room.

It was likely the worst time for Will to see them, Gilles's hand on her waist and them toasting. But if Alex didn't have bad luck with men, she'd have none at all. And Will walked out of his kitchen to see them in that moment.

TWENTY-FOUR

WHY WAS ALEX EMBRACING HIS NEW SOMMELIER? AT
first, he didn't get mad or jealous, just curious. Maybe it
was because Alex had gotten so jealous when April had showed
up at his place, but he was slammed with irritation seeing another
man touching her as though he had a right to. He was pissed that
she was smiling at another man when she'd denied him that for
almost a week.

He'd come out of the kitchen to see what the holdup was with
Alex and Lexi's table and because he wanted to see Alex. He'd
almost expected her to come seek him out in the kitchen, and he
would have welcomed that. Not from anyone else—he'd snapped
at his publicist when she'd interrupted them during prep today to
take some pictures for Instagram—but he craved Alex. He'd just
wanted to hold her for a minute. Even a chaste kiss on the lips.

Instead, she was out front, flirting with his sommelier.

The moment she saw him, her face fell and she stepped back from the other man as though she had something to feel guilty about.

Gilles didn't seem to notice any weirdness, because he held out his arm. "Will, I didn't know you were family friends with Alex." The sommelier put his hand on his chest. "I used to think that she was the love of my life."

Will was one of a crowd, then? Thinking that Alex was the love of his life. Alex's eyes grew wide. She stepped farther away from Gilles. "Can we talk for a minute?"

Will felt himself turn to stone. He didn't want to talk to Alex right now, because he wasn't feeling reasonable about things. He didn't want to do the dance where they hurt each other and then reconciled again. He didn't have the time for it tonight, and he didn't have the energy for it in the long run.

But the past week had shown him that it wasn't just about getting Alex to trust him enough. She would never trust him enough. He was just part of her pattern with men. His first thought was that she'd made him fall in love with her, and now she was done with him. His first instinct was to shut her out and shut down.

But that's what he would have done while he was married. So he caught himself. He didn't want to play these kinds of games with Alex. He was way too old for that shit. He was too in love with her for that shit.

"I don't think there's anything to talk about right now," Will said, trying to sound as calm as possible. "I just missed you this week."

"This is not what it looks like." Alex stepped closer to him, and Will took a step back, almost taking out a server with a tray.

"I know. I know." That was true, but he put extra tenderness in his voice. If he talked to Alex now, he wouldn't get to say all the things he wanted to say. "Let's just leave it until later."

He could see the uncertainty in her eyes, and it made him ache. But the ache now was nothing compared to how it would feel if they kept hurting each other. If they were truly going to let each other in, they had to learn to trust each other. To trust that they didn't need to sink their teeth into every conflict. He could love her all he wanted, but they both had work to do on being good at relationships. He saw that now.

He wasn't even upset about seeing her with Gilles, but he wished she'd sought him out first. She wasn't sure of him yet. If she needed him, all she would have to do was call. And he knew that she could crook her finger and he'd come running. But she didn't know that yet.

He had to be sure that she was all in this with him. He would do absolutely anything it took to love her. But he had to take care of himself. If she couldn't just stay put with him for a minute, if she couldn't listen to him instead of jumping to conclusions, if she couldn't keep her heart open to him, what was the point?

He was done waiting.

The host found them and let them know that Lexi's table was ready. Will looked right at Alex and said, "We'll talk later."

TWENTY-FIVE

ALEX WAS SORELY TEMPTED TO WAIT AFTER THE RES-
taurant closed and force Will to talk to her. The vibe had
been so totally weird when Will had come out of the kitchen. She
didn't know if he was jealous or mad. But she didn't like leaving
things unresolved with him. That's when she knew that what she
had with Will was truly different from what she'd had with any
previous boyfriend. She was only grateful that Lexi had been talking to a fan and missed the whole thing.

Will disappeared back into the kitchen after they were seated,
and Alex put on a good face, making agreeable noises as Lexi ex-
claimed over the décor and the drinks and the appetizers.

When Jane and Lana arrived, they were seated with them.
And they noticed that Alex was off, if their increasingly concerned glances were anything to go by. Alex pleaded with them
with her gaze not to say anything, and she could only hope they

understood. If she told Lexi things were weird with Will, her grandmother would march them both into a room and demand they work things out.

The problem was, both of them were so stubborn that Alex wasn't sure they could work things out. What was there to work out when they would get in the same kind of stupid fight/standoff next week and want to kill each other until they could rip each other's clothes off? It would be an endless cycle.

The food was excellent, and there was plenty of it—of course Will would take care of Lexi—but it all tasted like cardboard to Alex. There was a burrata and peach salad that all melted together in her mouth. And the osso buco that he served her was just as perfect as it had been the other night. But Alex couldn't taste any of it, not even the panna cotta.

When they'd finished the meal, and Lexi had licked the last bit of custard off her spoon and everyone else had wiped out their espressos, Alex got up to leave with her grandmother and friends.

But Lexi put a hand on her arm. "You should stay and help Will celebrate a successful night," she said with a wink.

Alex tried to come up with a reason why she couldn't stay that wouldn't reveal that she and Will weren't getting along but only came up with, "I'm sure he wants to celebrate with his team."

It was Jane who sealed her fate. "Lana and I will drop Lexi at home. You should spend some time with Will."

Alex gave her a dirty look, but she knew that she'd lost. She was going to have to stay and face the music. Even if the music involved working through things instead of getting angry or running.

She waited at the bar for the last table to leave, but she didn't have any more cocktails. She sipped on seltzer and ripped up a napkin until it disintegrated. The bartender recognized her from the times she had visited before they opened, so he closed out his till and left as the last patrons cleared out.

The dining room was dim except for some lights above the bar when Will came out and found her there. "I thought you would have left to take Lexi home."

Alex looked up at him but couldn't tell from the look on his face how he felt about her being there. He looked tired, but that was to be expected given that he was probably coming down from a huge adrenaline high at the moment.

"Jane and Lana got her home." Alex looked down at the pile of dust that had previously been a napkin. "I thought that you and I had some shit to talk about."

Will gave her an affirmative grunt before asking, "Did you enjoy the meal?"

She wasn't going to tell him the truth, that she'd barely tasted it, but she didn't want to lie to him, either. "I don't think I've ever seen Lexi enjoy a meal so much in her life. She's so proud of you."

"Good." That made Will smile slightly.

"You know. Even if we don't work this out, she'll still love you. She'll still be yours."

Will nodded and then turned to peruse the liquor bottles. The only sounds for those few moments were the last few people clanging around in the kitchen, working cleanup duty. When Will turned back around, he had a bottle of brown liquor and two glasses, so she guessed they were going talk.

Alex lifted up two fingers and he gave her a hefty pour, himself a lighter one. Although he could probably use more than she had. She switched their glasses and his lips twitched. Alex sighed. She wasn't sure what to say, so she started out with, "I'm sorry."

"For what, exactly?" Will raised his eyebrows. He had a point. She had a lot to apologize for.

"I'm sorry I was weird about April coming over." She supposed that had started this round of Alex's signature fuckups.

"You know that I'd never do a reality show with her where I have to pretend to be romantic with her. She and I are really over."

Alex believed him. "I know that, but I was just upset that you didn't tell me. It caught me by surprise."

"I didn't think it was important." Will leaned his elbows on the bar, and she caught the musky hardworking scent of him. They should be working off all his excess adrenaline in a dark corner somewhere, not having a heavy conversation. "But I should have known that you would want to know."

"I don't expect you to be a mind reader," Alex said, even though she kind of had been expecting him to read her mind. "I'm sorry for not just telling you that I was upset so we could move on."

"Is that what you want?" he asked. "Do you want to move on to the next guy?"

Alex shook her head. "That's not what I meant. I should have said that I want to move forward. I want us to have a future, but it seems like we're always tripping ourselves up."

Will quirked his head to one side and finished his drink. "I know that you and Gilles weren't flirting."

"Oh, he was flirting with me. But that's just Gilles. He's a flirt."

"Such a small world, you dating my sommelier." Will shook his head, pouring himself another drink. "What happened there, since I assume you did the postmortem this evening?"

"We didn't have to. He told me he loved me too fast." Alex was not proud of that bullshit move. "And I ghosted him. Hard. Blocked his number and made sure the doorman at my old building didn't let him up."

Will winced. But then he recovered and surprised the hell out of her. "Would you run away from me if I told you that I loved you?"

If he was telling her he loved her now, she couldn't imagine why. She'd been acting like a spoiled, selfish brat for almost a week. He hadn't even been able to fully enjoy his big night because of her. If he loved her, it would be a miracle. And she would feel guilty that it came out this way.

"I don't want you to say it tonight."

"Because you'll make sure you never see me again?" His question was only semi-serious, because he was still half smiling.

"No, I just don't think I deserve it."

"Love isn't something you deserve, Alex." He reached out and gripped the side of her face. She leaned into his warm palm. "Tell you what."

"What?" He rubbed his thumb against her bottom lip, and she wanted to bite it, but this wasn't that kind of party. She had a feeling that turning this into a sexual thing now would ruin their chances of ever making this relationship work.

"I think you need to decide that you deserve for me to say it before I say it to you. Because if you don't know it, deep in your soul, that you don't have to earn anything with me, you're going to find a way to fuck things up."

"How did you—Mr. 'I don't express my feelings and I only speak in grunts half the time'—become so wise and together? Especially about me? I always drove you crazy before."

"You still drive me crazy. That's not in doubt." Will shrugged. "I don't know."

Alex looked down at the liquid in her glass, which she'd barely touched. "What if I take too long?"

Will tipped up her chin and his mouth was on hers before she could say anything else. His kiss stole her breath and any protests or doubts about whether he would wait for her.

He poured promises and the words she hadn't let him say into her with that kiss. When his mouth left hers, she had no doubt about what he said next. "Then I'll wait for you."

TWENTY-SIX

ALEX HAD NO IDEA HOW SHE WAS GOING TO CONVINCE herself that she deserved to be loved by Will. She was so used to working hard for everything, especially love. She'd worked so hard that she'd burned herself out. And it wasn't like she didn't know where that came from. Fucking daddy issues. She wished he was still alive so that she could make him pay for her therapy.

She was still thinking about how she could show Will that she was ready to let go of the past a few days later, when the last person in the world she thought she'd ever see again walked into her office. Since the night at the restaurant, she hadn't kept a close eye on her schedule, but she would have noticed Jason and his fiancée as a new client meeting.

When her ex and the woman she recognized as his fiancée

walked in the room, she was speechless for a second. She tried not to let her surprise show, but it was very hard. And she also tried not to compare herself to the curvy biracial woman standing next to her ex-boyfriend and also failed.

They could honestly be sisters. The woman—Danielle—looked more like Alex than her own sister did.

Unsure what else she could do, Alex rose and offered her hand to Danielle and then Jason. "I'm Alex Turner."

Danielle giggled. "Oh, Jason's told me all about you."

Alex wasn't sure whether that was a good thing, "I saw you on *Say Yes to the Dress*." Then Alex turned to Jason. "I hope your visit isn't a sign that you won't get to wear such a beautiful gown." Alex was pretty sure from the things she'd said on the show that Danielle wasn't going to pick up on the sarcasm of her last statement.

But Jason did. His hand flexed, and a wispy cloud of irritation crossed his face before he recovered. "No, we're here because we think it's wise to have a prenuptial agreement."

Alex would have advised one for anyone with Jason's assets, but she still wasn't sure why they were here. "I'm not the only family law attorney in the city, Jason."

"But you are one of the best." The empty flattery with a tinge of mild condescension grated against her nerves. In the year since they'd broken up, she'd forgotten that. Probably along with a million other things that used to irritate her about him.

"I'm actually the best according to that list that came out last month. Where were you on the M&A list?" Alex asked, knowing that Jason wasn't on it. It wasn't his fault; mergers and acquisitions was a popular legal specialty among Ivy League grads. The pool was stacked. Family law was less shiny and sexy, and so she'd risen through the ranks more quickly.

"Well, we were hoping you would draft the agreement for us."

Alex didn't want to do this and wondered if it was Jason's way of rubbing in her face that he'd chosen someone else to spend his life with. Or maybe it was his way of letting his fiancée know that she could be replaced if she didn't behave in exactly the way he expected her to.

Either way, it smelled fishy. And Alex wasn't going to agree to anything before getting to the bottom of it. She turned to Danielle, who was playing with one of her paperweights. "Would you give us a minute? My assistant can show you the new espresso machine or grab you a bottle of water." Before Jason had shown up, she'd been thinking about a third latte. But now she needed a bottle of Valium and a handle of Tito's. "I just want to talk to Jason privately for a minute."

"Sure." Danielle jumped up. She was certainly eager.

Alex didn't let her smile slip until the other woman had cleared the doorway. "What are you really doing here?"

Jason leaned back and unbuttoned his Brioni suit jacket so she would see his very flat abs. He wanted her to salivate over what was no longer hers. She'd rather be looking at Will's abs underneath a white T-shirt. Or just bare.

"I told you that I need a prenuptial agreement."

"You also know that we could have done this with a phone call, Danielle needs her own lawyer, and it's probably a conflict of interest for us to work together or on opposite sides of this matter." Alex took a breath but continued before Jason had a chance to interject with any bullshit. "Now, tell me why you're really here so that I can give you a referral and you can leave."

Jason, for his part, did not turn to dust from the way she glared at him. Damn it. "You're right. I wanted to see you."

"You seem to have found a reasonable facsimile of me to look at. Try again."

They were probably running out of time to talk in private, and Jason knew that because he looked over his shoulder before he said, "I just wanted to be sure."

"Sure of what?"

"That I was right about you."

Alex hated the way he said that. "Right about me how?"

"That you really wouldn't care that I was getting married to someone else. That what we had didn't mean anything to you."

"I mean . . . I did care. But then I took a good, long look at myself." She left out the part about seeking out her exes. "And we were never right for each other. We looked good on paper, but I didn't feel for you how I needed to feel."

When she was done, Jason narrowed his gaze.

Alex sighed. Jason had a huge ego that nothing she said would likely penetrate. Maybe that's why they'd lasted for almost a year. She hadn't been able to push him away using her usual methods. If she didn't call him for a week, he wasn't the kind of person who was sensitive enough to think she was upset about something. He would believe her if she just said she was busy.

Totally different from Will. She had to stop comparing him with Will. Because she'd never loved Jason. They had just seemed like a good fit. They looked good together, and that was all that Jason was ultimately looking for.

He didn't want to deal with a real person who had real feelings. Everything was a negotiation with him, and Alex didn't want to live like that now that she knew it could be different.

But she couldn't tell Jason all that, and he wasn't really the person she needed to tell. And she didn't have time to get into it, because Danielle came into the room with a cup of coffee.

Alex waited until Danielle sat down to say, "It was lovely to meet you, though it's unfortunate that we won't be able to work together. But I'm giving you and Jason a list of attorneys I think would be a good fit."

Danielle was definitely getting the better list.

TWENTY-SEVEN

WILL FOUND ALEX OUT BY THE POOL. HE'D WAITED ALmost a week for her to come to him, and he'd been patient enough. He hadn't wanted to bring Lexi into it, but he'd broken. He'd missed Alex and would deal with her running away from him.

It was late evening, after the restaurant closed, and the pool lights put a blue cast over everything. Including Alex's face, which made her look especially sad.

She turned when his feet hit the concrete and looked at him until he dropped into the pool chair next to her.

"You came after me," she said softly.

"Yup." He'd told her he would. He had many faults, but he always did what he said he'd do. "Said I would."

"I'm pretty sure I deserve you, but I'm not sure what you screwed up in a past life to deserve me."

He wasn't going to touch that. He was sure he'd purchased enough trouble in his current life to deserve an irksome woman. Especially one who made him laugh and loved his food and had wanted him since before he could grow a beard.

"This is where it happened," Alex said, and he immediately knew what she was talking about.

They'd spent all summer together, and she'd finally kissed him a few days before she was set to go back to her mother's house. He'd frozen at first, so shocked that she was kissing him that he couldn't move. And then he'd pushed her away, because his first thought after realizing that she liked him like that was that he didn't want to lose the only home he'd ever had.

"I'm really sorry about that," Will said. "I could have been more sensitive."

Instead of pushing her away and wiping off his mouth, he probably could have explained why he didn't want to risk raising Lexi's ire by kissing her back instead of saying that it was gross that they were kissing and she was like his sister.

"It would have been gross for us to hook up while your dad was married to my grandma. You were my step-uncle. And it would have gotten grosser had they stayed married."

She had a point, but he still felt bad about hurting her. Until she'd started trying to interview her exes, he hadn't realized how deeply his careless words had cut her. He asked, "You don't think it's gross now, do you?"

She looked at him up and down, and he could feel a flush creep up his neck. "Definitely not." She paused for a moment and said, "I am a pain in the ass, and I'm not suddenly going to be the perfect girlfriend anytime soon, you know that, right?"

Will thought for a second before responding. "Well, I figure 'You broke it, you bought it.'"

"You didn't break me, Will," Alex said. "I might be broken, but you definitely didn't break me. And I'm not expecting you to put me back together, either."

Will took a deep breath and sighed. She'd taken a leap in telling him that she deserved him. And now he needed to take a leap and trust that she wouldn't run if he said the words that had been burning in his throat every time he saw her for a while now. "I love you, Alex. You can always come to me when you're falling apart."

She got up and came over to his pool chair. The metal creaked as she straddled him and kissed him on the mouth. It was a short kiss. A sweet kiss. A promise of more later.

"I love you, too."

Will wrapped his arms around her and pulled her closer to him so that he could take her mouth again. He soaked up her magic, relearning her body with his hands under the blanket that she'd draped over both of them.

He didn't know if it was because they were making out by Lexi's pool while she was presumably inside watching a movie or something, but he felt like a teenager again. This was what he would have done if he hadn't been so unsure of himself back then. If he'd known that his found family would love him no matter what, and that he'd find roots and his place in the world where he least expected it.

Alex had no idea how long their kiss went on, but it was a movie kiss. She felt like she was floating on a cloud, except where she and Will were connected to each other. When Will grabbed her face and pulled it down to his, his hands were so sure that she felt grounded again.

If he hadn't come for her tonight, she would have gone to him in the next few hours. After seeing Jason again, she realized that every man she'd ever been with had taught her something about herself that she'd needed to know before she could accept the kind of love that Will was offering her.

Jason had taught her that everything could be perfect on paper but still not fill her heart the way that a messed-up courtship with the right person could. She might always feel like she was getting the better part of the deal with Will. But she could tell that he felt the same, and wasn't that ideal?

They might have kissed forever if Lexi hadn't barged onto the patio playing a vuvuzela, with Star Sign tagging behind her.

"Finally!" Lexi cried out into the night. Alex was grateful, not for the first time, that Lexi's neighbors couldn't really hear anything that went on the backyard.

Will groaned into her neck, but he had a twinkle in his eye when Alex looked down at him. "We might as well get this over with," he said.

"You know that this is only the beginning, right?" They needed to brace for what was coming. "We have to present a united front to Lexi at all times. If she suspects we're have a problem in the bedroom, then she's going to send over a healer for that. You know she has a crystal guy on call, and I'm not sticking any jade eggs in my hooha to release bad energy."

Will laughed at that and Alex scrambled off his lap.

"Oh, you weren't having sex?" Lexi sounded almost disappointed.

Will put his arm around Alex's waist and pulled her close. She checked in with herself to make sure she wasn't feeling any urges to run away. And she was all clear.

"We are adults, Lexi. We don't need to utilize the back seats of cars or backyards to get our rocks off."

Her grandmother's reply was, "Don't knock it until you try it."

"What's Star Sign doing here?" Alex didn't really feel like they needed a story about one of Lexi's many escapades.

And Alex's question got her back on track. "Oh, I was going to tell you that I had called her when you were out here moping by the pool, but then Will showed up, and I got so excited that he'd finally decided to do something romantic involving you, and I wanted to leave the two of you alone, so I forgot."

Will asked the next, obvious question. "Yes, very excited that I finally learned what romance is. But why is this woman here?"

Lexi scowled at Will. "She's my personal tarot card reader, Will. Some respect."

Will gave Alex a look that said "God help me" before saying to Lexi, "Of course. So sorry."

Even if she hadn't been planning on getting it on with Will in Lexi's backyard, she was hoping to get to it at some point tonight, so she wanted to move this impromptu healing session along. "Why did you call Star Sign, Lexi?"

Through this whole exchange Star Sign had stayed silent, but apparently witches for hire had an end to their patience. "I never finished your reading," she said to Alex. "You weren't ready for it then, but I'm pretty sure that you are now."

"And it's really important to finish it now?" Alex asked. She barely believed in cards and astrology, and Star Sign seemed really nice. But a lot of water had traveled under the bridge between the night she'd fallen apart watching *Say Yes to the Dress* and now.

She was going to say all that to Star Sign, when Lexi blurted out, "Star Sign predicted it."

"Predicted what?" asked Will. Lexi hadn't noticed yet, but he'd been moving them ever so slowly closer to the gate between Lexi's back fence and the path that would bring them to the driveway. So they could leave and be alone and not hear anything about what the cards had in store for them.

"I predicted that the two of you would end up together," Star Sign said. "Well, the cards predicted it."

"Stop shuffling to the fence," Lexi said. "Sit down and let Star Sign explain this, and then you can get to fucking like bunnies. I won't even bother you about anything for a full week."

"You're not a bother," Will said.

Alex said, "I mean, a week of her not talking about the sex we're having would be good."

They looked at each other and sat down on the pool chaise they'd recently been making out on. Neither of them was a teen-ager anymore, not by any stretch of the imagination, but they sure as hell wanted to get back to making out and making up for lost time.

"The last card I pulled was the Lovers," said Star Sign, as if that was going to explain everything. When it was clear that they weren't jumping for joy at that information, Star Sign continued. "Because of the other cards in the spread, I knew that you were done with the Prince of Wands—the past—and were moving back toward someone you were in love with in the past. And Lexi said that you were in love in the past?"

Neither of them had been exactly ready for love in the past, but they weren't going to argue that the spark wasn't there. More important, they didn't want to spend any more time talking about divination.

Lexi could tell that their patience had run out, so she came over to them and kissed them both on the forehead. "If you only make it to the back seat of one of your cars, I won't even flick the lights on and off on you."

ACKNOWLEDGMENTS

First of all, I want to thank the readers who turned to romance novels for a shot of hope over the past two years. You're the reason I get up and write love stories instead of hiding under the covers. Thank you to my editor, Kristine Swartz, and my agent, Courtney Miller-Callihan, for pushing me to grow creatively. A huge thank-you to the Berkley art department for creating a gorgeous and distinct cover and look for this book. Thank you to Fareeda, Stephanie, and Keisha for getting my words into the right hands.

Frankly, I wouldn't be able to write books without my community of authors—Nisha Sharma, Sarah MacLean, Joanna Shupe, LaQuette, Adriana Herrera, Adriana Anders, Christina Lauren, Alexa Martin, Tracy Livesay, Alexis Daria, Sierra Simone, Jen DeLuca, Kate Clayborn, Michele Sandiford, Katie Dunneback, and Tara Kennedy. And I wouldn't know what to write about without my non-author friends. The conversations in this book would be much less entertaining without Michael Angelo, Nick Christianson, and Kim Miller. Thank you to Serena Golden and Sharone Carmona for welcoming me into your circle.

I would be remiss if I didn't thank my mom, who isn't anything like Alex's mother, and cooked for me while I was finishing copy edits on this book. And I have to thank my chosen family—Mike Halls, Kathy Zabawa, and Mary Lynn and Rennis McPherson. Your support means the world to me.

ONE

O N THE THIRD DAY OF NINTH GRADE, JACK NOLAN
asked Maggie Doonan to be his date to the Leo Catholic
freshman dance. He blackmailed his older brother, Michael,
into dressing up as a chauffeur and driving them in their father's
baby-shit-colored Lincoln Town Car. Then he sweet-talked
Mrs. Jankowski at the flower shop into finding lilacs in Chicago,
in September, just because Maggie's sister had told him that they
were Maggie's favorite flower.

After that, Maggie Doonan hadn't needed any more convinc-
ing that he was the perfect half-formed man for her. And the fact
that he was an actual, honest-to-God choirboy had convinced
Maggie's father not to even bother threatening him with the shot-
gun that still resided in the Doonans' front closet.

At the time, Jack had no idea what kind of power he had unlocked.

Two years later, he and Maggie had sullied the back seat of the baby-shit-colored Lincoln Town Car in unspeakable ways. And two years of near constant shagging after that, he'd watched her get in her parents' SUV to leave him for Harvard.

Watching Maggie's tearstained face drive into the distance had broken Jack's heart. But he'd been the only guy in his high school friend group to leave for college with valuable sexual experience not involving his right hand.

Still, he'd been sad.

Until he met Katie Leong during the third hour of freshman orientation at the University of Michigan. She'd winked at him while they'd learned the fight song at some stupid mixer for first-year students. That wink had hooked straight into Jack's dick and driven him to be the best college boyfriend ever—midnight burritos, romantic two a.m. walks to and from the library, and oral sex at least three times a week—six times during finals. Hell, he'd even started working for the school paper because Katie was going to be a journalist when she grew up.

The only things about his relationship with Katie that had stuck past her semester in Paris, and her subsequent new relationship with some French douche named Julian, were his career in journalism and a broken heart.

But the broken heart had lasted only a few months—until he'd met Lauren James, his favorite ex-girlfriend. She was off-the-wall funny and could suck the chrome off a trailer hitch.

He and Lauren had lasted through their senior year at Michigan and a shitty apartment with six roommates in the Bronx while he'd studied for his master's at Columbia and she'd waited tables at a craptastic Midtown tourist trap and raced to and from off-off-Broadway auditions.

Lauren hadn't even dumped him when he'd moved home to Chicago for a shiny new job. She'd saved her tips and flown out twice a month until she'd met a British director who wanted to cast her in an all-female West End production of *Waiting for Godot*.

You're the best man I know, Jack. Such a great guy. I'll never have another boyfriend like you.

No, she wouldn't. Because she married the prick director after the very brief run of the show. That British guy hadn't been a Boy Scout, and he for sure didn't know all the best sex knots to tie.

As he stood at the bar of a speakeasy in Wicker Park, after waiting fifteen minutes for an artisanal old-fashioned made with, like, artisanal cherries and orange peels scraped off with the bartender's artisanal hipster fingernails or some shit, he'd been without a girlfriend for six months. It was the longest he'd ever gone, and that was why his buddies had thought it was a good idea for him to leave his couch—and the Michigan–Notre Dame game—to sit around and talk to them in public.

He *should* be working tonight. In addition to not having a girlfriend, he didn't have the illustrious journalism career he'd dreamed of. In a recent pivot to video, he'd become the online magazine's how-to guy. His boss told him he was "too handsome to break real news," but more important, he would be laid off if he didn't shift with the times.

Now his father grumbled about him "not having a real job" every time he saw him, and Jack kept his mouth shut because he was living in a condo his family owned. If he lost his not-real job, not only would he have to hold his tongue around dear old Dad, he would have to wear a sandwich board on the corner. Or worse, work with his dad. While his father could deal with his working a job outside of the family construction business, he wouldn't be underwriting Jack's lifestyle if he got fired.

He loved his father—looked up to him—but they would kill each other if they had to work together.

So, he was here with his buddies, trolling for ideas for his next bullshit column. Chris and Joey could be his guinea pigs for whatever he came up with. He'd grown up with them; they'd all graduated from Leo together. Unlike him, they were knuckleheads about women. The idea that they would need to stage some sort of intervention with him over the nonexistent state of his love life was freaking preposterous. As demonstrated by the fact that they were wearing suits for a Saturday night out in the hipster hell that was Wicker Park, so they could stand around a bar that served overpriced, fussy drinks while looking at their phones and not talking to any of the women actually in the room.

Neither of them understood that for the first time since Maggie Doonan had put her hand down his pants under the bleachers at the freshman dance, he was kind of happy being alone. He could finally do the kind of shit that he liked—watch the game with a beer or five, sleep until noon, bring bread into the house without ruining someone's gluten-free cleanse.

For the first time in his adult life, he was figuring out what he liked instead of contorting himself into the kind of guy Maggie, Katie, or Lauren needed. And he meant to go on that way.

Just the other day, he'd been thinking about getting a dog. Some slobbery beast—like a mastiff or a Saint Bernard. Lauren hated dogs. Which probably should have been his first clue that the relationship was doomed.

Still, he scanned the dark bar to see whatever other unfortunate souls found themselves ripped from the warm embrace of their college sports or Netflix queues. No one looked quite as miserable as him, though. Not a single one of the long-bearded hipsters littering the red leather couches and old-timey booths looked like he'd flash a nun for a beer on tap.

Looking around, he thought maybe his next video could be *How to Not Ruin a Saturday Night Paying for $15 Drinks at a Douche-Magnet Bar.* Name needed work.

His gaze stopped right next to Chris and Joey on the ass of a woman in a tiny black dress that didn't match her gray moccasins. He didn't give a shit about her sartorial choices because there was so much velvet-soft-looking light-brown skin between the shoes, which looked as though they'd seen better days, and the bottom of that dress, which made Jack's lungs feel like they were going to combust. He hadn't even seen her face yet, but he knew that she was like whisky in woman form; he felt his judgment cloud and high-minded ideas about bachelorhood vacate the premises. In his head, she was already like the first puff of a cigar. Just her gorgeous legs made his throat itch and burn. Forty or so inches of skin had him choking on lust.

Thank freaking Christ the bartender showed up again with his drink. Jack knocked twice on the bar and, not taking his eyes off Legs, said, "Put it on Chris Dooley's tab." Jack was about to lose his wits to a woman, and it was all his friends' fault for making him leave the house. They were buying his drinks for the rest of the night.

He made his way back to Chris and Joey, still looking at their goddamned phones and not at the beauty next to them. No wonder they were constantly swiping and never actually meeting any of the bots populating most dating apps face-to-face. And no wonder Chris had been single since dumping Jack's sister, Bridget, a year and a half ago. They didn't pay attention.

Considering the sister dumping, maybe Jack should have drowned Chris in the kiddie pool when they were five.

But if they were aware of their surroundings, maybe Chris or Joey would be the guy getting to talk to Legs, and Jack would be left holding his dick. So, thank Christ his friends were idiots.

It wasn't until he was a few feet away that he noticed the other women with Legs. Both of the other women were knockouts, but they didn't rate for him. Jack had homed in on Legs, and he would not be deterred.

Maybe he could figure out how to keep things casual with Legs for the first three months or so. He doubted it. Once he'd tasted a little bit of a girl's magic, Jack didn't like to date around. He enjoyed flirting as much as the next guy, but he was—in essence—a commitment-phile. He liked having a girlfriend.

Maybe he and Legs could get a dog. He could compromise and live with a French bulldog. Small and cute, but still a real dog.

"Are you guys both swiping?"

"Yeah." Joey swiped left. "But I'm coming up empty."

"What the hell does that mean?" Because of his affinity for having one lady for years at a time, Jack had never been on a dating app. He didn't see the appeal. If he'd met Maggie on an app, he wouldn't have been able to figure out that the lotion she wore smelled like lilacs. He wouldn't have known that Katie's singing voice rivaled that of an angry tomcat, but that it was so charming he didn't care. He'd never have clocked Lauren's sassy walk across the stage in the production of *Hello, Dolly!* that he'd been reviewing for the *Michigan Daily* when he'd first seen her.

And he would have seen Legs's face first. To be honest, a picture of her face might be the only thing in the "pro" column for online dating. He needed to see if her face would captivate him as much as her rocking body did.

"It means he's not matching with any of the hot girls," Chris piped in as he swiped right multiple times. "I swipe right on everyone so that I get more matches."

"But he matches with mostly dogs," Joey said. "I'm not looking to get caught up with a girl so ugly I gotta put a bag over her head."

Yeah, he definitely should have drowned both Chris and Joey twenty years ago. Instead of clocking both of them, he pointed an angry finger in their faces. "Both of you are nothing to look at yourselves, so you get what you get."

He ran his finger under his collar, longing for his worn Michigan football T-shirt instead of a stupid button-down. It was damn sweaty in this goddamned hole of a bar that didn't have decent beer or a television.

"Yeah, you'll eat your words when you're forced to swim in the waters of Tinder, loser." Chris pointed back at him, finally looking up from his phone. "Then you'll realize that it's kill or be killed. The women on here are either bots or butt ugly."

That had to be the moment when Legs turned around. Jack could tell by the look on her—*beautiful, gorgeous, absolutely perfect*—face that she'd heard every word that his asshole, knuckle-dragging squad of buffoons had just said. Her eyes were so narrowly squinted that he couldn't tell what color they were. Her nose wrinkled up and her red-lacquered lips compressed with anger. Couldn't hide the fact that she was a knockout from all the angles. Not even with a raised middle finger partially obscuring her face.

She was like a sexy, rabid raccoon. And he was a goner.

Some dipshit with twinkling green eyes wasn't going to stop Hannah Mayfield from raining holy hell on the bros swiping left on the girls standing right next to them. *Two of whom happened to be her best friends.*

His tousled dirty-blond hair and the muscles straining his shirt's buttons didn't make her want to throw a drink in his face any less, and they weren't about to stop her from curb stomping his buddies. Didn't matter that the goofy fucking smile on his face said he couldn't read the room. She was about to de-ball all three of these assholes, and he was *smiling*. Maybe he was missing more brain cells than the average young professional man in Chicago— which is to say all of them.

"What the hell is your problem?"

Stupid-Sexy Green Eyes answered even though she'd turned her glare on his two bozo friends. "I didn't say anything."

No, his deep voice, which rolled over her with the subtlety of a Mack truck, wasn't one that had been calling all the women on Tinder, including her friends, dogs. But that didn't stop her from saying, "Well, then. Keep yourself busy sucking a bag of dicks while I disembowel your two friends here."

Although that was a harsh statement to lob at an innocent bystander, she couldn't risk showing any weakness in the face of the enemy. And all men were the enemy. Especially the pretty ones who looked at her like she was their favorite slice of cake. Those were the especially dangerous ones: the ones who could seep into her heart, which made it much harder when they left. And they always left—usually because they *just didn't want anything serious right now.*

"Why are you so angry?" He seemed genuinely perplexed, and honestly, she didn't know why she was so angry, either. It wasn't like she was on dating apps anymore. She'd given it the college try, but every petty humiliation suffered on those apps felt like a stab to the gut. And even when she'd met a few guys for drinks, she'd felt like she'd been at the worst audition for the worst reality show in the world. She didn't understand how people ever actually made it to sex with someone they'd never met before.

Probably drinks. Lots and lots of drinks.

"I'm pissed because they"—she pointed at Sasha and Kelly—"forced me to come to this hipster nightmare for drinks after I'd been working all damned day." She'd only been guilted into it because Kelly, a management consultant, was in town for the first time in months.

"The shoes." Green Eyes's gaze dipped to her feet.

"Not your business." She hated how warm his slow perusal of her made her feel, as though he'd already seen her naked. It was creepy, and she ought to have called him out. And the warmth melted some of her righteous indignation on behalf of her friends. *Not the plan here.*

"Working on a Saturday?"

"Event planner."

"Spent all day dealing with a bridezilla?" He took a sip of his drink, and she didn't roll her eyes at his stupid, sexist comment. The amber liquid rolling from the glass to his mouth was much more fascinating.

"That's a dumb, sexist thing to say when I'm already pissed." As if the only thing that event planners did was plan weddings. True, she wanted to plan weddings because that was where the money was, but she did so much more.

Then the stupid asshole smiled at her again. "Back to that."

She was surprised that at least half the panties in the room didn't incinerate under the force of his grin. *Good God.* He was so pretty that it hurt. Features cut from stone and stubble not quite artful enough to be on purpose. Drinking bourbon with his shirt-sleeves rolled up. He was citified masculinity that wasn't quite civilized. A contradiction, and the kind of thing Hannah went crazy for. The dimples that bisected the stubble had a feral quality that made her want to touch him.

He'd moved a little closer since she'd turned around ready to tear his buddies apart. They'd retreated, but he'd advanced. It was kind of sexy that he wasn't afraid of her, that he didn't buy her painstakingly cultivated bitchy exterior. His lack of fear was working on her in a major way, and that terrified her. After Noah, she'd sworn to herself that she wouldn't be foolish enough to believe that someone could want her for something other than a few rolls between the sheets, and a *Hey, babe, that was fun, but I'm just not looking for a girlfriend right now.*

Because they were never looking for a girlfriend, especially not *her* as a girlfriend.

That didn't hurt anymore. *It didn't.* She'd accepted that she was just not the kind of girl men romanced. With her ethnically ambiguous looks, bawdy sense of humor, and filthy mind, men wanted to have sex with her. And then—once they realized that she wasn't entirely domesticated—they wanted her to disappear.

She had to remind herself of this, make it her mantra whenever this man was near. Never forget that men were the enemy, regardless of how friggin' sexy his smile was.

He stepped even closer, leaving only half a foot of space between them. Hannah clocked Kelly and Sasha in her peripheral vision. They'd moved over to one of the stand-up tables.

Great. Neither of them believed her when she said that she was done with dating and romance and men for good. Their seeing her charmed by the prime cut of Chicago man-meat in front of her would not do at all. And yet, she couldn't seem to turn around and run away.

Maybe she should slap him. He hadn't done anything slapworthy, but he had her cornered. In the middle of a crowded bar, with multiple options for egress, she was pinned in place because he'd *smiled* at her.

"What's your name?" His voice softened, and she broke eye contact.

She looked around; his friends had made themselves scarce as well. "Hannah." She looked at his chest when she told him. Meeting his gaze was too intimate and it made her cheeks flush.

"I'm Jack."

That was a very good name. It made her think of hard liquor and sex.

"Of course you are." Damn, he smelled delicious. Like freshly showered man draped in freshly laundered shirt. With a little bit of citrus and bourbon on his breath. It was like a lethal dose of bro, but it appealed to her despite her struggle to maintain her antipathy along with her dignity.

His laugh surprised her. "Hannah, tell me something."

She didn't respond but made eye contact again. *Mistake.*

"Can I get you another drink?"

She looked down to the mostly melted ice and rye in her glass. It would be stupid to have a drink with him. If she spent any more time in his aura of good-natured all-American Chicago boy, she would think about him for months. She'd wonder if she'd been too harsh and why he didn't call. Because if she didn't leave right now, she was going to give him her number.

Green-eyed Jack was looking at her as though he was starved for her. He would ask for her number so he could try to sweet-talk her into no-strings-attached sex—if he didn't come right out and ask her if she wanted to bone that night. That was probably what he would do. If he did, he was so tempting to look at, and so not fooled into thinking that she was ready to hate him solely because he was a man, she would do it.

Then he still wouldn't call, and it would be even worse than if he was just some guy she'd talked to in a bar one night.

If she left now, she could be home in time and sober enough to pretend he was attached to her favorite vibrator. His tongue swept over his lower lip, and he must have taken her silence for assent. Large, blunt fingertips brushed her smaller ones as he took her glass.

He motioned to the bartender for another round without leaving her side. Probably sensing that she would leave if he gave her an iota of the space that she ought to crave.

"I don't date." It was only fair to warn him that she was done—so done.

He looked back at her. "Neither do I."

"I mean, seriously. I don't—um—" She just had to tell him that she didn't date, and she also didn't do the random hookup thing. Wouldn't be going home tonight and feeling his skin against hers. She hadn't clocked the light dusting of chest hair through the small opening at the collar of his shirt.

"We're just having a drink, Hannah." He smiled again when he passed her a fresh tumbler of rye. "Think of it as an apology from my friends."

"Why are you apologizing for them?"

"I don't talk like that about women."

But she was sure that he thought that way about women. He was young, handsome, and well built. His watch and the quality of his clothes said he wasn't obscenely wealthy, but he probably lived relatively well. His straight white teeth said that his parents had been able to afford braces. So while he was smart enough not to seem like an asshole whose interest in her would be limited to a one-night stand or a string of booty calls, there was no way that he saw someone who would bust his balls every day at the end of his dating tunnel. Too bad she would really enjoy busting his balls.

"But I'm sure you think that way."

"No." His face hardened, and he took a drink. "I don't. My friends are assholes, but I think those apps make it easy to be."

"They turn people into commodities."

"Exactly." One cheek muscle flexed, and the dimple was back. She wondered what he'd do if she put her fingertip in it. "You shouldn't shop for a partner like you shop for groceries."

Advice wasted on her. "I don't do that. I told you, I don't date."

"I don't do the apps, either."

That surprised her. But then again, he'd never be standing here with her if he did. With the face and the muscles and the nice-guy veneer, he could have been getting a half-decent blow job instead of shooting his shot with her. "Why not? You'd do well."

Although she'd hoped she'd kept her voice neutral enough that he wouldn't take her genuine desire to know why he wasn't on Tinder as a compliment, he totally did. "Are you saying I'm handsome, Hannah?"

She really liked the way her name sounded coming out of his mouth. Way too much for her own good. "You know what you look like, Jack."

The audacity of his wink had her fighting to keep from smiling at him. Even if he wasn't a total jerk, there wasn't room for both her and his easily stroked ego in this dank basement meat market. She drained her drink and put the glass on the bar. Reaching inside her purse, she pulled out a twenty and held it out to him.

"What's that?"

"For the drink."

"The drink was an apology."

"But that apology came with strings."

"No strings."

Then she did roll her eyes. "You're wasting your time."

"I don't see it as a waste."

She'd just bet he didn't. He liked that she was a challenge. "We're not going to"—she lowered her voice and leaned into him—"you know, do it."

He choked on his cocktail, and she barely fought the desire to bump his back until his windpipe cleared. Let him drown in his old-fashioned. If he died ignominiously, she wouldn't have to think about him tomorrow or next week and wonder if he wasn't a shithead of the same brand as every other man in this city.

Unfortunately for future Hannah, he caught his breath. "I never asked you for sex."

Her cheeks flushed. Maybe he really was just apologizing. "I'm sorry."

"For what?" His hand cupped her upper arm, good humor back on his face. "I'm flattered that you were thinking about getting naked with me."

"I wasn't." She shook her head and looked down at her shoes. The gray moccasins she'd thrown on after the last of the Lurie Children's Hospital people had left the event she'd thrown today for some local NFL players who had wanted to give a whole boatload of money to kids with cancer. They were terribly ugly, but her feet would have fallen off had she kept her heels on for ten more seconds. "I didn't think about that at all."

"I must be losing my touch, then." He wasn't. One smile and he'd melted part of her shell. A touch on her arm burned her skin through her dress. "I just wanted to apologize and share a drink with someone not staring at their phone."

"Oh." He couldn't seem to stop surprising her.

"But I was definitely thinking that I'd be lucky to get naked time with someone like you."

There it was. Jack was lethally sexy, dangerous to her equilibrium. The flutter in her lower belly just from being near him would lay waste to her inner peace, such as it was.

"I don't do that, either." Part of her hoped that he would argue with her. Try to convince her. She waited a beat for him to respond. When he didn't, she adjusted her over-the-shoulder bag and shifted away from him. "I've got to go."

He swigged back the rest of his drink and winced. It was kind of adorable on him—this totally gorgeous, seemingly self-contained man not used to the burn of bourbon in his throat. The contrast between his manly appearance and that slight show of weakness attracted her even more. Her hesitation at this point was pure self-preservation.

"I'll walk you out."

"There's really no need."

He took her arm again, and she was sorely tempted to shake him off and maybe stomp on his foot. She was just about to, she swore, when he said, "There's a taco truck outside, and my stomach will hate me tomorrow if I don't eat something."

"That many drinks?" No wonder he was flirting with her. In her experience, guys like him did not flirt with women like her unless they were drunk or trying to slake their curiosity about dating a biracial girl.

Like Joe Osborne, the insanely good-looking but profoundly lazy stoner she'd dated sophomore year. He'd been into new experiences in general—mostly drugs, loose women, and never finishing a paper on time—but she'd mistaken his curiosity about her for genuine interest. Too bad that curiosity had never extended to whether she'd enjoyed their hookups. A few dozen orgasms might have made the shocked look on his mother's face when he'd introduced them over parents' weekend a little bit worth it.

Since her father had evaporated as soon as the pregnancy test came back positive, and her mother had been busy working to pay for her education, she'd been on her own with Joe's family. For two days, she was subjected to the *I'm Trying to Prove I'm Not Racist* variety show. At multiple points, she'd wanted to stop Mr. and Mrs. Osborne from talking about all their Black friends and tell them she believed them. But that would have made them even more uncomfortable. Considering their son's lack of sexual prowess and the fact that he was probably going to flunk out once Hannah stopped pressing send on his papers, she spared them and broke up with Joe as they were driving away.

Which brought her to Jack. He was probably just drunk enough to step outside of his comfort zone to hit on her. Once he sobered up and/or figured out that she was pretty much just like the white girls he dated, only she would make his parents feel weird, she'd never hear from him again.

"Nope." He bent down close enough that his breath touched her ear when he said, "I just want to spend more time with you. Buy you a taco and see if you'll give me your number."

USA Today bestselling author **Andie J. Christopher** writes sharp, witty, and sexy contemporary romance about complex people finding their happily ever after. Her work has been featured in NPR, *Cosmopolitan*, *The Washington Post*, *Entertainment Weekly*, and the *New York Post*. Prickly heroines are her hallmark, and she is the originator of the Stern Brunch Daddy. Andie lives in the nation's capital with a French bulldog, a stockpile of Campari, and way too many books.

CONNECT ONLINE

AndieJChristopher.com

𝕏 AuthorAndieJ

📷 AuthorAndieJ

f AuthorAndieJ